THE ISAK WAS SPITTING MAD, ITS BLOODLUST FANNED TO A FRENZY . . .

Riker heard someone shriek—just before he fell. As he slid down the wall of the pit, he ducked and rolled.

A bolt of black lightning struck the dirt wall where he'd been, but by then he was on the other side of the pit, trying to get his balance. The isak didn't waste any time. It whirled and pounced, a slavering, roiling mass of coalblack fury—and this time, Riker couldn't scramble fast enough.

The thing was heavier than it looked—the impact knocked the breath out of him. He fell back against the pit wall, wrestling with the isak, trying to keep its nightmare of a muzzle away from the soft flesh of his throat . . .

Look for STAR TREK Fiction from Pocket Books

STAR TREK: The Original Series

STAR TREK: The Next Generation

#15

STAR TREK®
THE NEXT GENERATION

FORTUNE'S LIGHT

MICHAEL JAN FRIEDMAN

POCKET BOOKS

New York   London   Toronto   Sydney   Tokyo   Singapore

An *Original* Publication of POCKET BOOKS

POCKET BOOKS, a division of Simon & Schuster
1230 Avenue of the Americas, New York, NY 10020

ISBN: 0-671-70836-8

First Pocket Books printing January 1991

10 9 8 7 6 5 4 3 2 1

Printed in the U.S.A.

For Grandma,
who let us eat sugar and apple sandwiches
until the wee hours

FORTUNE'S LIGHT

Chapter One

As HE FED the holodeck computer all the information he had collected, First Officer William Riker found himself smiling—grinning, in fact, like a little kid.

And why not? He had been waiting a long time for this.

It had been nearly a full week since the idea popped into his head, and half his mind had been busy working out the details while the other half saw him through the routine functions of a starship second-in-command.

Of course, in a larger sense, it had been more than a week. He'd been waiting all his life for this moment.

Or at least since his seventh summer, when he'd taken that spill off Execution Rock and fractured his collarbone in three places. He still remembered all those summer days spent propped up among pillows, imprisoned in his parents' house while his friends swam in the river or hiked up into the highlands.

At first he'd been full of bitterness and resentment. After all, he was Kyle Riker's son. He had to be the best at everything, the leader—even at the tender age of six.

Thank God for his mother. She had taken advantage of that sedentary time to instill a love for the quieter pursuits in the son who was so quickly growing away from her.

First there was the music—all kinds, but mostly her beloved jazz, for her father had been a trombone player in a place called New Orleans. Will liked the happy music best, particularly during the endless rainy afternoons when it seemed there had never been and never would be any color in the world but gray.

Then there were the cooking lessons. What an absurdity—a six-year-old learning to cook! But the payoff was the privilege of eating whatever they had concocted, and his mother had a knack for making even the humblest dish taste wickedly delicious. Perhaps the most amazing moment in his life, even through the present day, was when he realized he could make ratatouille as good as hers.

Finally there were the books. At the beginning he had thought it kind of strange—who ever heard of reading books? There were tapes and such if you wanted to be entertained or—heaven forfend—*learn* something. The pictures came up on a monitor along with a voice that provided the narration. Simple. Easy.

In books there were no pictures. Most of the time, anyway. You had to come up with the images on your own, and that was a lot like work.

Still, he took to reading. It tickled his imagination, like the music. Like the cooking lessons, he had to put something into it to get something out.

And like both those things, the books gave him a window into his mother. He could see something incredible in her, something young and fresh and beautiful, every time she read out loud to him, and again when he read out loud to her.

Especially when they opened that certain book—the one that had given him the idea to do what he was doing now. It wasn't the kind of book he would have expected her to have, or the kind of subject he'd have expected her

2

to take an interest in. But then, his mother had not been easy to predict.

Now he was glad that he had broken his clavicle that summer. Immeasurably glad, because it gave him that much more to remember her by.

Not for the first time he wondered if in some way she had known that she would pass early from this life. Maybe that was why it had been so important to her to give him these gifts. These parting gifts.

Riker sighed, gently putting the memories away like the prized possessions they were. All but one.

Tapping in the final instructions, the first officer waited for confirmation that the holodeck computer had enough data to go on. A second or two later it indicated that it did.

Tingling with anticipation, he pressed the space on the keyboard marked Activate.

Beyond the closed composite-alloy doors, his fancy was working itself into a reality. Omnidirectional holo diodes were coming to life; electromagnetic fields were taking on form and substance and texture.

He felt the magic beckoning, took a step toward it. The doors to the holodeck parted, revealing the fruits of his attention to detail.

Perfect. It was *perfect*—just as he had imagined it, just as it had been described in the book.

And there they were, pulling on their uniforms. The men who had once captured the hearts of all Alaska, and then broken them again, in short order. The legendary figures who had stirred such passion in young Will Riker that he sometimes couldn't sleep at night.

He'd become obsessed with them. He'd learned everything he could about them. For a while he'd even pretended to be one of them.

Which, now that he thought about it, wasn't so very different from what he was doing now.

So what if they no longer seemed larger than life?

So what if their blemishes were there for all the world to see?

They were still his boyhood heroes, rousted from the pages of his mother's book. And they still fired his imagination as few things had done before or since.

He took another step into the holodeck. . . .

"Commander Riker."

It was Captain Picard's voice. The summons was clipped, compact, typical of the captain. But it had a little more weightiness than usual—a certain urgency to it.

The first officer looked longingly at the world he had created. Then he took a step back and watched the holodeck doors close.

He hit his communicator. "Riker here."

"There's a classified transmission for you, Number One. It is coming in from Starbase Eighty-nine."

Riker required a moment to absorb the information. "For me, sir?"

"Yes, for you. Specifically for you."

The first officer cleared his throat. "Really," he said. "Well, in that case, I'll take it in my quarters."

"As you wish, Number One. Mr. Worf is already making the necessary arrangements."

Riker nodded through force of habit, even though the intercom carried only audio communications. "Thank you, sir."

"You are quite welcome," said Picard.

As Riker started down the corridor toward the turbolift, he wondered what kind of message could require his attention rather than his superior's. Judging from the undertone of curiosity in the captain's voice, his superior was wondering the same thing.

As Picard got up, Wesley turned to watch.

"Mr. Data," he said, "you have the conn. I'll be in my ready room if anyone needs me."

The captain grasped the hem of his waist-length uniform jacket, pulled it taut with a crisp, compact motion, and headed for his ready room.

Wesley loved that gesture—the captain's tug on his jacket. If the bridge had been no more than a storage bay, if there had been no computers on which to feast his intellect and no controls to measure his skills against, he would still have aspired to it for the sake of gestures like that one.

Until recently he hadn't known exactly why, nor for that matter had he thought about it very much. Then he and his class had begun their course of study on Shakespeare.

"All the world's a stage . . . ." Well, maybe not *all* the world. But certainly the bridge of the *Enterprise*.

Wesley raised his eyes from his Ops panel long enough to scan the expansive two-tiered space. It *was* like a stage, wasn't it? Crew members entered through the forward turbolift and exited through the aft, crossed from Science One to the coffee dispenser and back again. There was always something going on, always something to watch. And somehow every movement—even a trip to the head—had a theatrical feel to it, a special quality that made it seem larger than life.

Of course it was more than just the place. It was the personnel as well. "And all the people on it merely players."

Wesley smiled to himself. Players, yes. But not "merely."

There was nothing "merely" about Worf, for instance, standing guard over the tactical console like . . . like the ancient Colossus standing guard over Rhodes. Nothing insignificant about Data as he gazed at the massive main viewscreen with a childlike innocence that sometimes seemed deeper than the deepest wisdom.

Boy—pretty poetic, Wes. Maybe that Shakespeare stuff is contagious.

But the players who really drew Wesley's interest were the ones at center stage, the ones who usually occupied the now-deserted command center.

Troi, with her . . . how would the Bard have put it? With her calm, Madonna-like beauty.

Riker, with that boundless energy that seemed to reach out octopuslike into every corner of the bridge.

And the captain—most of all, the captain. It always amazed Wesley how the man could rule with a glance, transform the mood on the bridge with the slightest change in posture. It was almost scary.

Even now, as the ready room doors closed behind him, Picard commanded. Even in his absence, he had a presence.

Like Julius Caesar, Wesley realized, in the play he'd just finished reading. Even after his assassination, Caesar had seemed to remain on stage, to be as much a participant in Rome's political maneuverings as any of his assassins.

But the captain did nothing without a reason. Why had he chosen this moment to repair to his sanctum? "There is a tide in the affairs of men . . ." Why had Caesar picked this juncture to withdraw to his tent?

No doubt it had something to do with the transmission from Starbase 89. The one that had come in for Commander Riker and not for the captain himself, as would normally have been the case with classified information.

Did the captain resent being bypassed? Did his indignation compel him to sit and brood in private?

No, that wasn't like him. Caesar . . . er, Captain Picard was not a petty man.

Then why? Was he waiting for something? For Commander Riker, maybe—to come to him and reveal the nature of Starfleet's message?

Of course Riker was under no obligation to do that. The message had been for him and him only.

However, the captain was giving him a chance to

discuss it. He was relieving his first officer of the need to ask for a one-on-one meeting.

Yes, that sounded right.

On the other hand, there was always the possibility that Riker would not want to talk about it, that it was so personal he would prefer to keep it to himself.

But when he came up onto the bridge and found Picard absent, wouldn't he have to inquire as to the captain's whereabouts? And then, after being told that Picard was in his ready room, wouldn't it be incumbent on Riker to at least check in with . . .

Suddenly Wesley could barely restrain himself from laughing out loud. It was brilliant—*brilliant!*

Whether the first officer wanted to share his information with the captain or not, Picard had maneuvered him into a position where it would be difficult for Riker to keep it to himself. Alone with his commanding officer, how could he not at least hint at the substance of Starfleet's communication?

And Picard had created this situation with a simple departure from the command center. He had removed himself from center stage, but not from the drama.

It was a move that would have prompted even Caesar to sit up and take notice.

Wesley was pleased with himself. Things like quantum mechanics and warp-drive engineering came easily to him. But human nature—human *drama*—was something for which he was just beginning to develop an appreciation.

He wondered how many others on the bridge had perceived Picard's intention the way he had. More than likely he was the only one.

Now all that was left to be determined was what Riker would do. Having digested his message, would he head straight for the bridge and Picard's counsel? Or would he wait until his next shift started and then come up to the bridge, only to find the trap that the captain had set for him?

Wesley didn't get his answer immediately—not that he'd expected to. Like any good play, he knew, this one would take time to unfold—hours, perhaps, if Riker decided not to cut short his rec period.

In the meantime Wesley busied himself with diagnostic checks of the various engineering functions. Normally his position and Data's were reversed, with the boy sitting at Conn and Data at Ops, but the captain had wanted Wesley to become more familiar with the other stations on the bridge.

All the engineering functions checked out fine. Next, he turned his attention to the communications system, which also came through with flying colors—and noticed that Riker's conversation with Starbase 89 had already terminated.

The minutes passed—dragged, even. But nothing happened. Picard remained in his ready room, updating files or polishing reports or whatever a starship captain did when he had some time to kill.

And then, maybe half an hour after Picard's retreat from the bridge, the doors of the forward turbolift parted to reveal the tall, straight form of the *Enterprise*'s first officer. Riker wasn't smiling.

He took the bridge in with a single glance, saw that the three seats constituting the command center were all vacant, and seemed to know immediately what that meant. He went to the ready room doors and stood before them to signal his presence.

A moment later they opened, and the first officer disappeared inside.

It was a quick ending but a satisfying one. And, Wesley told himself, he had been a privileged audience of one.

Then he heard the muted conversation in the aft stations: "I *told* you he'd come straight here. No way he wouldn't tell the captain about it." "All right, already. Dinner's on me, next shore leave."

Wesley chuckled to himself. Well, maybe not an audience of one, exactly. But a privileged audience nonetheless.

He regarded the ready room entrance, beyond which some new drama was undoubtedly taking place, if the expression on Riker's face had been any indication. Never a dull moment around here, Wesley told himself.

Captain Jean-Luc Picard considered his first officer across his ready room desk. "So, Number One? Care to tell me about it?"

Riker had been silent for some time, just staring into space. At the captain's invitation, his eyes focused.

"Yes, sir," he said. "Of course." He took a deep breath, let it out. "It's hard to know where to begin." And then, a moment later, it seemed that he had found a propitious place. "Have I ever mentioned someone named Conlon—Teller Conlon?"

Picard thought about it. "I believe you have," he decided. "A friend of yours at the Academy, wasn't he?"

"More than a friend, sir. My *best* friend. And not just at the Academy. We shipped out on the *Potemkin* together, and then on the *Yorktown*." Riker paused. "Five years ago, we were detached from active duty to serve on the team that forged the Impriman Trade Agreement."

"Ah, yes," said the captain. "Quite impressive, the job you did there. Stole a planetful of valuable resources out from under the noses of the Ferengi, as I recall. Or, more precisely, you recovered it, after trade with the Federation had been cut off for twenty years."

It had all been in Riker's service record, a file with which Picard had become quite familiar back when he was reviewing first officer candidates for the *Enterprise*. And the Impriman affair was one of the things that had set Riker apart from the others.

"The Imprimans wanted only one trading partner—the Ferengi, or the Federation." The first officer grunted.

"Truth be told, Teller deserved more credit for getting them to choose the Federation than I did. He really got into the Impriman psyche—came to understand them better than anyone had before him. Imprima seemed to hold this great . . . fascination for him. So much so, in fact, that when the Federation established a trade liaison office there, he volunteered to oversee it."

"And he got the post," said Picard.

"Hands down. Hell, *I* didn't want it. And Teller had the full support of the madraggi—the political-economic entities that make up what passes for government on Imprima."

"So your friend stayed," observed the captain. "And you left."

Riker shrugged, but it was less a shrug than an upheaval. It was as if his tunic had suddenly become two sizes too small for him. Did his discomfort have something to do with the transmission from Starbase 89? No doubt.

But Picard could wait to hear the rest of the story. For a change, he had no other pressing business. He could afford to let the younger man proceed at his own pace.

"I left," confirmed Riker. "Shortly after that, I was made first officer of the *Hood,* and our assignment was way the hell on the other side of Federation territory. I lost touch with Teller. A couple of times he sent messages to me via subspace packet or through some mutual friend I'd be bumping into, but I never got around to sending anything back."

The captain smiled as forgivingly as he could. He was aware that forgiveness was not the attitude that best suited his features. "These things happen, Number One, to all of us. It's difficult to keep up friendships in Starfleet."

But his first officer wasn't accepting absolution. Stubbornly he went on.

"Pretty soon the messages stopped on his end, too. But I knew he was doing well, because I'd see dolacite containers listing Imprima as their point of origin. Every indication was that Teller had become a big success there."

A "but" was coming. Obligingly Picard supplied it: "But?"

Riker accepted the prod. "But just now I got a transmission from Starfleet—telling me that my friend is a thief. Worse—a traitor."

The captain eased himself back in his chair. "Serious charges. What is the basis for them?"

Riker sighed. "Criathis and Terrin are about to merge."

"Criathis and Terrin?" Picard prompted.

"Sorry. Two of the madraggi. Criathis has been the Federation's staunchest ally over the years. Terrin has been a Federation proponent as well, though in a somewhat more cautious vein.

"As I understand it, Terrin has not benefited from the trade agreement as much as it had hoped. Criathis, on the other hand, has profited handsomely. Terrin still has tremendous resources, and political influence to match; Criathis has growth potential. From both points of view, it's a merger made in heaven.

"What's more, Madraga Terrin—as the larger of the two madraggi—would have the right to install its first official as head of the newly formed entity—in this case, a man named Larrak, disputably the best businessman on the planet. Armed with an even broader array of resources, who knows how far he can take Terrin-Criathis?

"Needless to say, not all the madraggi see this as a good thing. The merger stands to hurt the political enemies of both Criathis and Terrin—chief among them a madraga called Rhurig.

11

"But there is nothing Rhurig or anyone else can do to stop the merger—that is, as long as Criathis and Terrin follow the traditional protocols."

Picard nodded. "The Imprimans value tradition, do they?"

"Very much so. Before Criathis and Terrin can get together, there has to be an old-fashioned merger ceremony. And the merger must be made official by the use of special jewel-encrusted seals."

"Seals," repeated Picard. "Like those used to authorize documents on ancient Earth?"

"Precisely, sir. But these are priceless—even apart from any historical value they may have. Dismantled for its jewels, any one of the seals could buy a man an easy life in some obscure corner of the galaxy."

The captain was beginning to understand. "And it is believed that your friend Conlon lifted one of these seals so that he could buy himself this easy life?"

"That's what they're saying," agreed Riker. "Apparently one of the seals to be used in the upcoming ceremony has disappeared—and Teller along with it. Naturally they're putting two and two together. All the evidence points to Teller's having stolen the seal, and without Fortune's Light—"

"Fortune's Light?"

"The seal, sir—all of these seals have names. In any case, its disappearance is going to cause that merger to fall apart. Both madraggi will be scandalized, effectively crippling two of our biggest supporters on Imprima. And when the other madraggi get wind of Teller's guilt in the matter, the Federation will be booted off Imprima so fast our heads will swim."

"All unfortunate," said Picard. "*Quite* unfortunate. But what has this to do with you?"

Muscles rippled beneath the first officer's bearded jaw. He leaned forward. "They want me to go to Imprima. To find my friend and recover the seal—before the sched-uled date of the merger ceremony."

Picard absorbed the information. "I see," he said. "And of course it makes sense. You know Imprima as well as anyone in the Federation. What is more, you know your friend." He measured the younger man. "You have agreed to this assignment?"

"I had little choice, sir. It's Priority One."

The captain grunted. "Then I will be receiving a message myself, no doubt. And it will instruct me to remain in the vicinity of Imprima as your backup, should you need it." He grunted again. "Is your friend that dangerous, Commander?"

Riker straightened. "I don't think Teller's the culprit, sir."

"Really. You think the evidence is circumstantial?"

"I think it's no evidence at all. Teller was like a brother to me. I know him better than anyone, and I know he could never have done anything like this. Someone has framed him—set him up. And when I find out where the seal has been hidden, I bet I'll find Teller as well."

Picard did not discount his first officer's intuitive powers. He had proved himself a fine judge of character again and again. But the fact pattern *did* point to Conlon.

"Are you sure," asked the captain, "that you're not allowing your own regrets to cloud your assessment, Number One?"

Riker's face went taut. "What do you mean?"

"Simply this—that you feel guilty for having allowed your close friend to go astray. You feel as though you should have done something to prevent it."

"My brother's keeper?" suggested Riker.

"Something like that, yes."

The younger man shook his head. "No. Teller is innocent, and I'm going to prove it."

"All right," Picard said gently. "You do that. But first,

let's get you to Imprima." He looked up, as he always did when addressing someone via the ship's intercom computer. An unnecessary gesture, of course, but one that seemed to be endemic to Starfleet personnel.

"Mr. Data, set a course for the planet Imprima in the . . . Dante Maxima system?" He looked to his first officer for confirmation and got it in the form of a nod. Again, looking up: "Make it warp eight, Commander."

"Aye, sir," said the android. "Working . . . done. Course plotted and laid in."

"Engage," said the captain.

As the ship surged into warp drive, Riker got up to go. He mumbled something about having to prepare for his mission, though Picard privately wondered how much preparation could be required in this instance.

"Good luck, Number One. I hope the facts come to bear out your beliefs."

His first officer looked at him. "Yes, sir. I know you do."

When the ready room doors closed behind him, they barely made a sound.

Chapter Two

DATA HADN'T STARTED OUT with any intention of using the holodeck. He'd only been passing by when he noticed something that piqued his curiosity.

A combination of two somethings, really. Two bits of information displayed on the holodeck computer monitor. One indicated that the holodeck was in active use—that the program was proceeding in real time. The other told him that there was no one inside.

Of course this was explainable in any of several ways. Most likely someone had forgotten to terminate a program before leaving or for some reason had left before using all of it. It could also have been a sign of a holodeck malfunction—something that happened rarely, but happened nonetheless. Or someone could be inside, undetected by the computer.

Just to be on the safe side, Data called up the details of the programming. He scanned the identity of the user, the nature of the program, and the projected duration.

There did not appear to be anything potentially dangerous about the environment selected. In fact, it seemed quite benign. However, it was an environment with which Data had had no direct experience. The best course, it seemed to him, was to find the programmer— to make sure he wasn't trapped in the holodeck, a prisoner of his own creation.

The android tapped his communicator, waited less than a second before it beeped in token of its readiness. "Commander Riker," he said out loud.

"Riker here," came the near-immediate response. "What's the matter, Data?"

"You are safe?" confirmed the android.

A pause. "Assuming there are no poisonous lizards under my bed, yes. Why do you ask?"

Data told him.

"Oops," said the first officer. "Sorry about that."

"You need not apologize," said the android. "There has been no harm done."

Another pause. "Say, Data, I'm not going to get the chance to use that program—not for a while, at least. And I put quite a bit of work into it. Why don't you give it a try?"

Data reflected on the possibility. "Me, sir?"

"Why not? You might find it interesting. And anyway, it'll probably take a trial run or two to work out the bugs. You can test it out and let me know what you think."

Data glanced at the monitor and the information contained on the screen. "I do not know. I am not well acquainted with the environment you have synthesized."

"So what? Broaden your horizons."

"Indeed," said the android, unable to keep a note of skepticism out of his voice.

"Look," said Commander Riker, "it's up to you—I won't twist your arm. In any case, please don't erase it. As I mentioned, it took me quite a while to put it together."

"Of course," said Data. "I will be careful to preserve it."

"Thanks."

The android stood alone in the silent corridor, peering at the monitor—and then at the holodeck doors. At the monitor. At the doors.

It had been some time since he had used a holodeck, he mused. Neither pastoral settings nor comedy nightclubs nor Sherlock Holmes's London held much fascination for him lately.

Perhaps Commander Riker was right. Perhaps it *was* time for a new experience.

A beep told Riker that someone was in the corridor outside.

"Open," he said, swiveling around in his chair.

The door slid aside, revealing the stolid bulk of the ship's security chief. "May I come in?" Worf asked, in the same tone he might have used to propose the annihilation of a hostile vessel. Klingons always seemed to be engaged in a heated argument, even when they were uttering pleasantries.

The first officer nodded. "Sure. Have a seat."

Worf entered and headed for a chair. It was situated on the other side of a polished amber-colored wood table—one Riker had made himself out of wood from a thousand-year-old Alaskan pine after a landslide had toppled the tree and half buried it.

The Klingon sat eyeing him—but not before he'd darted a glance at the garments laid out on Riker's bed.

"What can I do for you?" asked the first officer.

Worf frowned. It was not necessarily a sign of displeasure—he frowned a *lot*.

"I have been notified that you will be beaming down to Dante Maxima Seven, also known as Imprima."

"Yes," said Riker. "That's correct."

"On a Priority One mission." Worf paused. "By yourself." Another pause. "Unarmed."

"Right on all counts."

The Klingon seemed to be at a loss for the right words.

Riker waited patiently, knowing that his visitor would in time find what he sought.

"Of course," Worf said at last, "it is a Priority One mission. You need not tell me anything about it—even though your safety is my responsibility."

The first officer found it difficult not to smile, but he restrained himself. So *that* was what Worf wanted. "In other words," said Riker, "you'd like to know what I'm going to be doing on Imprima. Even though it's supposed to be classified information."

Worf shrugged his massive shoulders. "If it will, in your estimation, enable me more efficiently to carry out my duties as security chief."

"Which, of course, extend to all members of the crew, even when they are not on the ship."

"Of course."

It was a rather liberal interpretation of Starfleet regulations. However, Riker wasn't disposed to argue with it. After all, he felt the same way on those rare occasions when the captain led an away team.

So he told Worf what he wanted to know. Not in the same detail he'd used with Picard, but nonetheless covering all the essentials.

The Klingon's frown gradually deepened. "Then this matter is of some personal importance to you?"

"Yes," conceded the human. "It is."

Worf digested that. Loyalty was something he could easily understand. "Naturally, you will remain in contact with the ship?"

"I'll report in occasionally. Besidia, the city where I'll beam down, is hosting something called a Trade Carnival. One of the rules of the carnival is that there are to be no high-tech devices, including communications equipment, and they've gone to the trouble of enumerating the items they don't want to see. Of course the list doesn't specifically mention our communicators . . ."

"But their use may be frowned upon."

"Yes."

"Still, you will carry one. Won't you?"

"Of course. Why?"

It was hard to tell what kinds of thoughts were taking shape behind those void-black Klingon eyes. Worf seemed to straighten a little in preparation for his next remark.

"There are few situations that do not have at least the potential to become dangerous. An ally—one who is immediately accessible—may prove quite valuable should trouble arise."

Riker was touched by the offer. But he didn't say so. It would only have embarrassed Worf, and to a Klingon, being embarrassed was worse than being flayed alive. The latter situation, at least, was something they were emotionally equipped for.

"I don't think the Federation had it in mind for anyone besides me to go. Besides, I'm in good hands. I've been assigned someone who works for Criathis, the madraga from which the seal was stolen."

"Someone who *works* there?" said Worf, his voice dripping with disdain.

"We're not talking about a bureaucrat," advised Riker. "He's a retainer—a lifelong employee of the madraga, specially trained to protect the house, its officers, and its interests in any way necessary. That includes hand-to-hand combat, the use of weapons, clandestine operations . . . Come to think of it, these retainers have a lot in common with security officers."

The Klingon grunted at the gibe. "But they are *not* security officers." Obviously he was unimpressed.

"No," agreed the first officer. "They're not. Nor do they operate by the same set of rules. But from what I saw during my last visit to Imprima, they are quite effective."

Worf did not belabor the point. He rose, considering Riker past the high bony ridge of his nose.

"If you find this retainer is insufficient . . ." He shrugged again. "I do not expect that I will be otherwise occupied."

The human stood, too. This time, he had to say *something.* "I appreciate that, Mr. Worf."

Without another word, the Klingon turned and walked out of the cabin. The door yielded at his approach and remained open for a second or two after he was gone. That's how brisk his exit was.

Riker marveled at his luck. What had he done to deserve a friendship like Worf's?

Or for that matter, like Teller Conlon's?

Perhaps, in Teller's case, not enough. He hoped it wasn't too late to make up for that deficit.

"We did it, Will. We actually did *it."*

"Looks that way, doesn't it?"

"I mean we honest-to-God did it!"

"I think you said that already."

Teller grinned that grin that drove women wild. He set his glass down, leaned back in his chair and ran freckled fingers through thick reddish blond hair. "I wish I could see the faces of the Ferengi when they get the news. Are they going to be fuming or what?"

"Fuming? You think so? Just because they lost one of their primary sources of hydranium and dolacite? You think that's going to bother a philosophical bunch like the Ferengi?"

They laughed. And laughed again.

Heads turned. A couple of women, one in the red of Terrin and another in the green of Ekariah, seemed to share in their amusement.

Riker lifted his glass to them. "Terrin and Ekariah on friendly terms. What does that *tell you?"*

"It tells me that now Terrin's got more influence than Rhurig has. At least with Ekariah."

A small space in time, filled with music and the sound of someone singing. Riker took it all in.

"You know, Teller, I've enjoyed this. I really have. But it'll be good to get back to the Yorktown.*"*

"Sure, real good. I'll bet you've missed the hell out of Captain Leadbelly."

"That's Ledbetter to you, Lieutenant. And maybe I haven't missed him, but I've missed a lot of other things. You know what I mean—being out there." Riker blushed. "You know what I mean."

Teller nodded. "Yes. You can spare me the John Masefield bit. I've been there, just as you have. I've whispered my share of secrets to the stars." He seemed to withdraw a little; his eyes sought the table between them. "Naturally that makes it a bit more difficult . . ."

Riker looked at him. "Makes what a bit more difficult?"

His friend met his gaze. "I'm staying, Will. I've signed on as permanent trade liaison to Imprima."

"What?"

"It's true. Everything's been approved, top to bottom." A pause. "You knew they were looking for somebody; I just threw my name in the hat." Another pause. "Who'd have believed they'd actually give it to me?"

Riker felt empty inside, as if he'd been betrayed somehow.

"I don't get it, Teller. Aren't you the one who said to throttle you if you even thought of becoming a diplomat? What happened to all that?"

For once his friend was at a loss for words. He shook his head. "I don't know, Will. It's just that . . . damn, I feel as if I belong here. Like these people are my people." He shook his head again. "And maybe I can do the Federation some good as a liaison. Lord knows, I won't do that serving on a starship—not the way you will."

"Come on, Teller. They didn't make you a lieutenant for the hell of it."

"We both know why they made me a lieutenant, my friend. So let's not use that as an argument."

"I'm not talking about Gamma Tobin. I'm talking about your whole career. You've shown as much promise as anyone."

Teller smiled ruefully. "No, I haven't. But that's not even the point. I'm not running away from Starfleet by taking this post. Dammit, I was happy in Starfleet. But now I've found something that makes me happier. A lot happier."

Silence.

"Give me a break, Will. Can't a man want a change? Can't he love something that doesn't move at the speed of light?"

Not this man, Riker told himself. But then, he and Teller weren't Siamese twins. They were two different people—more different, perhaps, than he'd allowed himself to admit.

"All right," he said finally. "If that's what you really want . . . hell, do it."

More silence.

"Hey, don't give me the cold shoulder, all right? I wanted to tell you about this sooner. But I was . . . well, I was scared. I thought you might talk me out of it." A pause. "Don't hold that against me, for God's sake."

Riker grunted. He looked into his friend's eyes, and the anger left him. "I've got enough to hold against you, you slimy bastard. You think I need something else to add to the list?"

"Then you're not mad?"

"I'm not mad."

Teller blinked. His eyes seemed bluer than ever. "Good. Damn good. But I want you to prove it. Drink a toast to the new trade liaison to the planetary government of Imprima."

They raised their glasses and drank.

"Not as good as that stuff you brought up from Dibdina."

Teller smiled. "Nope. Nothing was as good as that stuff."

"What was that toast you made, then? To the art of the . . . something. I forget."

"Me, too. But what the hell, it was just a toast. There's plenty more where that came from." Teller looked at him. *"Keep in touch, Will. Don't be a stranger."*

"I promise."

"I'll hold you to it."

"Listen—give these Impriman ladies a break, all right? Without me to chaperon you, you might get into all kinds of trouble."

"I'm looking forward to it, son. Looking forward to it indeed."

As the holodeck doors slid away, the android stepped inside. He found himself in a roomful of lockers.

At one end of the room a man sat watching two other men converse on a primitive video monitor. The watcher had his feet up on a chair.

"Sure," he said. "A beautiful day for baseball. And if it stays that way, I'll eat my shorts. Hell, I'll eat *your* shorts."

Data approached, took up a position to one side of the fellow. It wasn't long before his presence was noted.

The man turned a pinched face to him, looked at the android through squinty eyes. "You the new kid?" he asked. "What's his name—Bogdonovich?"

Was that a persona that Commander Riker had picked out for himself? There was only one way to be certain.

"Stop program," he said. Suddenly the man with the pinched face came to a dead stop—not that he had been moving that much to begin with. "Query," said Data. "An individual named Bogdonovich—is this the role Commander Riker had intended to play?"

"Affirmative," responded the computer in its pleasant female voice. "Bobo Bogdonovich. No other information included in program. Shall I access main data banks?"

"No," said the android. "That will not be necessary."

For the time being he knew all he needed to know. "Resume program."

The man came to life again. He had asked a question; he was expecting an answer.

"Yes," said Data. "I am Bogdonovich. But you may call me Bobo."

The man pointed past the android to one of the lockers along the wall. "There ya go, Bogdonovich. Nice fresh uniform—Tonelli's old number. Hope it's as lucky for you as it was for him." He glanced up beyond a flight of stairs at a rectangle of pale blue sky framed in a doorway. "We're gonna need all the luck we can get."

Data walked over to the indicated locker. The uniform hanging inside it was red and blue; the word "Icebreakers" was emblazoned on the shirt in flowing letters.

The android gathered that he was supposed to exchange his own clothes for these. Of course. One often wore specialized attire when participating in sports.

"You'd better get a move on," said the man in front of the video monitor. "They're already halfway through batting practice, and Terwilliger doesn't take kindly to rookies who waltz in late. Even if they *did* just get off the red-eye."

Data frowned. Rookie? Red-eye? He was unfamiliar with the terminology. But he sensed that it was not essential for him to understand these terms—not yet, at any rate.

On the other hand, he had a feeling that he should learn more about Terwilliger, who seemed to be in a position of some authority here. As he pulled off his Starfleet garb, Data decided that it might be more challenging to glean the information from his companion than to query the computer again.

The android tried to effect a casual manner. "Is this Terwilliger the kind of man they say he is?"

The videoscreen watcher grunted loudly. "You bet he

is. Tough as nails. Mean as they come." He shrugged. "'Course, I'm no player. I'm just the clubhouse man. I never get chewed out by Terwilliger. But I've seen plenty of those who have been."

Data didn't understand all the colloquialisms, but he got the gist of it. Apparently Terwilliger's management style was a bit different from that of Captain Picard.

"It's really too bad," added the self-professed clubhouse man. "After all he's been through, all those seasons of finishing in the cellar, he finally had a shot this year. Prob'ly his only shot. Put together a damned fine team—Sakahara, Kilkenney, Gilderbaum. Built up an eight-game lead. But he had too many veterans; I could see that from the start. Came August, they started to drop like flies—a hamstring here, a busted wrist there. Before you know it, that lead starts to dwindle and . . ." He stopped himself, grinned a little sheepishly. "Hell, I don't have to tell *you*. You know the rest."

For a moment, Data thought he would have to ask another question to learn any more. But it turned out not to be necessary. The man resumed of his own accord.

"So now the whole season—all hundred sixty-two games—comes down to one measly playoff. And with the walking wounded Terwilliger's got out there today, it'll be a wonder if we even finish the thing—much less win it."

The android had just slipped on the shirt with "Icebreakers" scrawled across the front of it. He reached into the locker for his shoes and socks, all the while piecing the scenario together.

"Then again, Bogdonovich, maybe you'll make a difference. Maybe you'll live up to those Triple A clippings of yours and put a jolt in this team—and give Terwilliger a championship before he retires." The man made a dry, cackling sound. "Yeah. Maybe."

"You do not seem hopeful," observed Data.

His source of information turned to look at him. "You could say that."

"But in any game, there is always an element of unpredictability. If there were not, there would be no point in playing it."

A smile crept slowly over the clubhouse man's face. "I didn't know you were a philosopher, kid. I kind of like philosophers—all flakes, in fact. They liven things up a little." Abruptly the smile vanished. "Just don't go spouting any philosophy in front of Terwilliger. He hates that stuff."

The android finished dressing and considered himself in the mirror. Actually, the uniform fit quite well. But that was no surprise—the computer would have automatically tailored it to his physique.

"If I were you," said the man, "I wouldn't stand there admiring myself. You-know-who could come down here any moment. And if he catches you preening like that, you'll be riding the pines today, no matter how bad he needs a third baseman."

"Yes," said Data. "Of course." Observing the clubhouse man's urgency, he headed for the wedge of blue sky, which he gathered was in the direction of the playing field. As he got closer, he could hear what sounded like surf on an ocean beach. It took him a moment to realize that it was an amalgamation of human voices—a great *many* human voices.

"Bogdonovich! Hey, Bobo!"

The android stopped just shy of the threshold and turned around. "Is something wrong?" he asked.

Grumbling, the clubhouse man got to his feet. He walked over to Data's locker, took out something brown and leathery-looking, and with a quick flip of his wrist sent it whirling in the android's direction.

Data snatched it in midair. It was some sort of glove, though it looked far too big for him. He looked at the clubhouse man.

"And that's the last time I'm gonna fetch yer damned leather for ya. I don't care who you are."

"My apologies," said the android. "It will not happen again."

Then he turned around and followed the voices to their source.

Chapter Three

RIKER MATERIALIZED in a large but seedy-looking hotel room. Long, open shutters on his right let in shafts of ruddy sunlight and the sounds of a street clown show—not to mention a good cold breeze, which turned his first planetside breath into a shivering wisp of frost vapor. The fireplace on his left was stocked with wood, but unused—and had been for some months, judging by the rakannad webs that had proliferated inside it.

He had forgotten how cold-blooded these Imprimans were.

Riker went to the window. Outside, there was snow on the ground, churned into mud around the clown show. A couple of ascetics sat against a wall, apart from the festivity and the laughter, dressed in their brown robes. Brightly colored balls rose into the iron gray sky and fell again. Everyone cheered except the ascetics.

Nothing had changed.

Just as he thought that, he heard the scrape of footsteps in the next room. His partner, of course. The retainer who would be working with him.

A figure emerged. He glanced at it over his shoulder.

28

And did a double take.

The newcomer was female.

That was evident from her smooth, pale skin, her sea green eyes and exotic cheekbones. It was evident in her blue-black hair, pulled back to reveal ears like delicate little half-crowns.

She was not only female, but beautiful—in a way that transcended Impriman standards.

Had O'Brien screwed up the transport somehow? Was he in the wrong suite—or even the wrong hotel?

That was possible, but not probable. They'd gotten the coordinates directly from Starfleet. And O'Brien's performance had been impeccable up until now.

Was this female his partner, then? Perhaps things *had* changed around here.

She looked at him, placing her hands on her hips. She was dressed in rather unremarkable Besidian street garb, just as he was—low boots, a belted tunic, a hooded cloak with the hood pulled down for now. Her bare legs, he couldn't help but notice, were slender and shapely at the same time.

"You're staring," she said.

He felt his cheeks grow hot. "Sorry," he said.

"You didn't expect to see a woman, did you?"

Riker's first inclination was to deny his surprise. But that would only have made things worse.

"No," he said. "I didn't."

"That's all right," she told him, but there was a stiffness in her voice that belied the assurance. "No one expects a female retainer. That's what makes me so effective. I can go places where Criathis's other retainers can't. Or, as in this case, work on an investigation without drawing attention to the fact."

"Makes sense." He nodded. "I'm—"

"I know who you are. Let's just get started, shall we?" She indicated a low-slung couch to one side of the fireplace. Riker sat and tried not to stare again as she began to pace.

"All right," said the woman, rubbing her hands together. "Here's where we stand. As you already know, if you've spent any time at all on this planet, a high-tech ban is imposed on Besidia during the Trade Carnival. That means no weapons or other devices of the sort introduced into Imprima over the last seven hundred years—in deference to the age of wisdom that spawned the madraggi in the first place.

"Another rule is that people can come in whenever they want—but no one can leave. That's not just a custom—it's enforced through the use of energy shields. Though of course they are dropped momentarily to permit arrivals like yours."

"You're right," he said evenly. "I'm already aware of all this." Probably he should have just shut up and listened. But he had the distinct feeling that he was being talked down to. Worse, it seemed to him that she knew she was doing it—had, in fact, assumed this condescending attitude to mock him.

But why? Not over the issue of her sex, he hoped. He had apologized for that mistake already.

The Impriman went on as if he'd never interrupted. "Since Teller Conlon was entrusted with the seal *after* the beginning of the carnival, he couldn't have left Besidia with it. Therefore, it is somewhere within the city limits. When we find *him,* we find *it*—and I've already discovered a trail that may lead us to him."

"You sound certain that it was Conlon who took the seal," said Riker.

She regarded him. "Aren't you?"

"Far from it. If he's missing, it's because he was kidnapped to make it *look* as though he took the seal."

She grunted. "I see. And his history of petty smuggling does nothing to make you doubt that?"

He stared back at her. *"What* history of petty smuggling?"

The Impriman frowned slightly. "My apologies. I thought you had been better informed by your Starfleet." Pulling a leather wallet out of her tunic, she tossed it to him.

He caught it, opened it, and drew out its contents. "What's this?" he asked her.

"The details," she said, "of Teller Conlon's illegal activities, in which he used the power of his office to amass personal wealth."

Riker pored over the information, aware that she was watching him the whole time, waiting to see his reaction. Finally he replaced the material in the wallet and tossed it back to her. "I don't believe this—any of it. All it shows is that someone's gone to great lengths to set up my friend—created an elaborate trail that would eventually lead to him." He shook his head. "I just don't buy it."

The Impriman nodded. "I was warned you might feel this way."

"Whoever warned you was right. I'm here to get Teller out of this mess safe and sound. Not to participate in his incrimination."

The woman eyed him. "Rest assured," she said, "that I'm a professional. I'm not here to incriminate your friend, just to conduct my investigation. Criathis will decide the question of guilt. And I think you'll agree— whether he's guilty or not, the discovery of Teller Conlon's whereabouts may be of some importance in recovering the seal."

Riker spread his hands. "No argument there. You said you had a lead?"

"Yes. We can pursue it now, if you like. Or if you have some ideas of your own, I can pursue it by myself."

Her tone was brisk, businesslike. But there was something very *un*businesslike beneath it. Something decidedly hostile.

"No," said Riker. "I think we can work on your idea. Together." He paused, seeking the right words. "You know, I think we may have gotten off on the wrong foot here. It's just that Teller Conlon is my friend and—"

"Yes," she interjected. "You said that."

He looked at her, trying to remain calm and reasonable. "So I did," he said. Clearing his throat, he took another stab at it. "Listen—there's obviously something about me that bothers you. If it's not my belief in my friend's innocence, then what is it? The fact that you caught me staring at your legs?"

Her eyes narrowed. "Are you sure you want to know?"

"I'm sure."

"Then know this," she said, the edge in her voice becoming even sharper. "The theft of Fortune's Light is an Impriman affair. It should be dealt with by Imprimans, not by offworlders who have passed through on their way from one place to another. We are your allies, not your puppets." The muscles in her temples rippled. "The mere suggestion that we need the help of the Federation in this instance is . . . irksome to me. More than that—it's hateful." Her delicate nostrils flared. "However," she said, and her voice was calm again suddenly, "as I told you, I'm a professional, a retainer of Madraga Criathis. I will carry out my assignment to the letter, no matter whom I must ally myself with."

Her declaration caught him a little off-balance. "I see" was all he could get out.

"No doubt you're glad you asked."

Riker shrugged. "Actually, I am. It's important for us to know each other, at least a little bit." He managed a smile. "What our names are, for instance."

Her features seemed to soften a bit.

He held out his hand. She took it, and her grip was stronger than he'd anticipated. No shortage of surprises in this retainer, no matter what her name was.

"I'm Riker," he said. "Will Riker."

"Yes," she told him. "I know that. It was in my briefing. I'm Lyneea Tal."

"Pleased to meet you."

She took back her hand. "Are you? I wouldn't have thought so, under the circumstances."

"The circumstances—meaning our apparent inability to agree on anything substantial?"

She nodded. "More or less, yes."

He grunted. "So it's not the most congenial of partnerships. We don't have to get along—we just have to do our jobs."

Lyneea eyed him. "You make sense—for an offworlder."

Riker didn't take offense. He'd been called a lot worse.

"Thank you," he told her.

Troi sat in Beverly Crusher's office going over her patient logs on the chief medical officer's desk monitor. Not, of course, that she needed to remind herself of anything—she'd reviewed her notes as recently as a few hours before. However, since the alternative was to sit and watch the med techs continue their routine maintenance checks on the biobeds . . .

"Deanna?"

Troi looked up and saw her friend breeze into the room. Plunking herself down behind her desk, Crusher took a deep breath and smiled.

"Sorry," she said.

Troi smiled back. "That's all right. I had a lovely time gazing at the naked mechanisms of your biobeds. Who would have thought that they'd be as fascinating inside as out?"

Crusher's hand shot to her chest, as if she'd been stabbed. "I stand accused," she said.

Troi looked forward to these periodic meetings with Crusher—these note-comparing sessions based on the long-ago-accepted belief that maladies of the body and those of the mind were inextricably entwined. Nor did she really mind that she'd been kept waiting.

But the doctor would have been disappointed if she hadn't given her at least one friendly jab. After all, what were friends for?

"You weren't delayed by anything serious, I trust?"

Crusher sighed. "That all depends. Is an obsessed teenager something serious?"

The Betazoid pretended to ponder the question. "Could be," she decided. Then: "What is Wesley obsessed with now?"

"Well," said her colleague, "it all started when he was sitting on the bridge, watching Captain Picard subtly maneuver Will Riker into telling him about his Priority One mission."

"Oh, yes," said the counselor. "The one Will didn't even confide in *me* about."

Crusher chuckled. "As if he's going to make a Priority One mission common knowledge! Of course, it's that very secrecy that piqued Wesley's interest."

"Ah," said Troi. "So *that* is his obsession."

Crusher nodded. "He was so wrapped up in the human interactions on the bridge, he overlooked the substance of Will's summons—but not for long. And when my son sinks his teeth into a mystery . . ."

"I understand," said the counselor. "So it was difficult to tear yourself away."

"Quite. Before I left the ship for Starfleet Medical, I might've had an easier time of it. But he's so independent now that when he does want to share something with me, I find it hard to say no."

"Don't say another word," Troi told her. "At least not by way of apology." Her smile broadened. "If the ship's counselor can't be forgiving, who can?"

"Right," said Crusher, assuming a somewhat more professional demeanor. "Then let's get down to business." She activated another monitor, which resided on the bulkhead nearest her. "Why don't we start with Mukhurjee in engineering? She gave birth to twins recently. I think there's a little postpartum depression setting in."

"Yes," said Troi. "I think you're right."

"What do you think?" asked Lyneea.

The dark tavern was packed full of simply dressed laborers, men and women puffing on nohnik pipes or tossing back mugs of korsch. Imprima's working class, whether native or offworld-born, favored nothing but the gloomiest of colors in their garb, so only their faces threw back the lurid light of the hanging i'ekra lamps. Loud, wild music reverberated from wall to wall, punctuated by the cries of some rowdy patrons seated deeper inside the low-ceilinged chamber.

But the sense that took the greatest beating was that of smell. The odors of nohnik and perspiration made a potent combination, to say the least.

Back in the days when they were negotiating the trade agreement, Teller would have looked down his nose at a place like this. His taste was for amber-toned parlors where everyone dressed in the gaudy hue of his or her madraga and where power wafted on the air even thicker than the perfume.

Riker had always been a little uncomfortable in those establishments. Not that he hadn't enjoyed the soft music and the rich light and the velvety skin of the madraga-dzins' daughters—because he had.

But the power part hadn't intrigued him as it had his

friend. Which was probably why Teller had been so much better at negotiation with the leaders of Imprima—he was more in tune with their way of looking at the world. . . .

The reception hall was Impriman through and through, right down to the thread of gold in the furnishings. The tall open windows on the east wall let in the cold, crisp air and provided a glimpse of the stars.

But even an offworlder could find warmth here. In the subtle potency of the drinks. In the gentle intimacy of the music. And in the company.

Teller stared at a trio of young ladies as they made their way across the room. They wore yellow, signifying their kinship with Madraga Alionis; the color seemed all the more vibrant against the paleness of their perfect skin.

"I'm in heaven," he said.

"No way," said Riker. "Not unless they've lowered the entry standards considerably."

"Well, then, a reasonable facsimile thereof. I mean, if these aren't angels, I'll eat my communicator."

"Which is back on the ship, thanks to the high-tech ban. Try again."

Teller shrugged. "You get the idea."

Riker nodded. "Don't forget, though—these are the daughters of the people we're trying to impress. Let's not offend anyone, shall we?"

His friend looked hurt—but he wasn't very good at it. The twinkle in his blue eyes gave him away.

"Will, old sod, if I'm not the picture of propriety, who is?"

Riker never got a chance to answer that, because Norayan answered it for him. It was as if she'd appeared from out of nowhere, tempting in the dusky blue of Criathis.

"I'd sooner trust an isak with a newborn muzza," she said, "than turn you loose in a place like this." She took Teller's arm. "How did you get them to let you in? Either *of you? Obviously they haven't heard about your exploits as I have."*

Teller blushed. *"Come on,"* he said. *"That was just a line of malarkey. We were trying to impress you back then."*

"And now?" asked Norayan.

"Now you're on to us. You know how harmless we are." Riker grinned sheepishly in support of his friend's claim.

Norayan shook her head, smiling too. *"Whatever will I do with you?"*

Teller tilted his head in the direction of the bar. *"You could introduce us to those young ladies."*

"Which?" asked Norayan. *"The ones in yellow?"*

Teller looked at her ruefully.

"Oh," she said. *"That's right—sorry. I forgot you were . . . what did you call it? Color-blind?"*

Riker nodded. *"A small flaw in an otherwise perfect human being."*

Teller laid a hand on his friend's shoulder. *"You said it, not me. Now, are we going to get acquainted with those lovelies or what?"*

"You go ahead," said Riker. *"I want to talk with Norayan."*

Teller eyed them with mock suspicion. *"Something going on that I don't know about?"*

"Impossible. You know everything."

His friend sighed. *"Well,"* said Teller, *"if I can't get any moral support, I'll have to handle this mission on my own."*

And smoothing his uniform, he headed toward the ladies in yellow.

"He's one of a kind," Norayan said affectionately.

Riker grunted.

She turned to him. *"Now, do you really want to talk? Or do you plan to whisk me away to someplace romantic?"*

"Perhaps later. Right now I want to know if you've heard anything."

"From my father? About the trade agreement?" She shook her head. "You would probably hear before I would. I'm just a madraga-dzin's daughter—for now. Nobody tells me anything." She paused. "Why? Have matters taken a turn for the worse?"

He used his eyes to point across the room at a large Impriman dressed in the black of Madraga Rhurig. The man was loud and arrogant, but he was holding a group of green-robed Ekarians in thrall.

Norayan followed his gaze. "Kelnae?"

Riker nodded. "Looks as if Rhurig's first official is gaining a following in Ekariah. Rumor has it he won them over today. Convinced them that the Federation isn't interested in the industries they control."

"But the Federation is interested," said Norayan. "Ekariah owns a bunch of dolacite mines."

"I know that. You know that. But Kelnae has told them that the Federation has other sources of dolacite—cheaper sources—and that the Ekarians can't compete. Judging by that crowd, I'd say they bought it."

"Spiteful old man. Just because his madraga doesn't have anything to interest offworld traders—"

"Doesn't mean he should deprive other madraggi of the opportunity. I agree. But that, apparently, is just what he has in mind. And Kelnae can be persuasive, especially when he goes into his 'Imprima for Imprimans' speech." He bit his lip. "In the end, it may not be a choice between us and the Ferengi. There may be no offworld trading at all."

Norayan shook her head. "I wouldn't worry about Kelnae if I were you. Madraggi like Rhurig are in the minority. Almost everybody makes a profit from offworld trading, and profit is their main concern. They may remain with the Ferengi, but there will be a trade agreement with someone."

Riker looked at her.

"Sorry to have to put it that way," she said. "Did you have any luck with Larrak?"

"I don't know. Terrin could do better with the Federation, but it could also do worse. And he's got a pretty sweet deal right now. Why should he take a chance?"

Norayan smiled. "You don't understand us, Will. Not as your friend Teller does. We're a greedy bunch. If there's a possibility of amassing greater wealth, we'll always take a chance."

She entwined her arm in his. "Come on. Wipe that frown off your face and get me a drink. Then we can watch Teller make a fool of himself with those girls from Alionis."

Riker chuckled as he let her guide him to the bar.

"Riker? I asked you a question."

Will looked at Lyneea. "I think Teller would have avoided this place like the worst variety of plague."

She accepted the assessment with equanimity. "Nonetheless, this is a known meeting place for smugglers. In fact, my information—which you dispute—is that Conlon himself used to come here when he had something to sell." She tilted her head to indicate the crowd. "You'd be surprised at how many of these seemingly innocent workers are actually agents of offplanet interests—one of the hazards of opening your world to galactic trade, I suppose."

Riker ignored the bait. It was becoming plainer and plainer that Lyneea wasn't Imprima's biggest xenophile.

"So no matter what Teller's involvement is, someone here may know where to find him. And if we come up empty regarding him, we may still dig up some information about Fortune's Light."

"That's the hope, yes. And remember," she added, as they made their way to the bar, "let me do the talking."

"The floor," he assured her, "is all yours."

Satisfied, she slung herself into a short-backed stool. Riker took the one beside it, eliciting a shrill creak as he sat down. Imprimans tended to be long and wiry, and the stool obviously wasn't built to accommodate someone of his bulk, even though there were plenty of non-Imprimans in the crowd.

He'd half expected to see Ferengi here as well. But of course there weren't any. The madraggi had long ago decided that if they had an agreement with the Federation, they didn't want Ferengi around to undermine it. The same had been true for Federation personnel during the years the Ferengi held exclusive trade rights.

What's more, this rule was backed up by some pretty severe penalties, not only for offworlders in violation but for any madraga found to be involved as well. Occasionally there were exceptions, but the last one had been made five years ago, and he and Teller had been the beneficiaries of it.

The bartender came over when he saw them sitting there. His eyes sought out Riker's beneath the hood. "What can I get you?" he asked.

Riker looked at Lyneea.

"Korsch," she said crisply. "Two."

The bartender moved down the bar, found a ruby-colored bottle and poured. The liquid caught a light from somewhere and reveled in it.

Clunk. And again, *clunk,* as the second of two ceramic mugs met the bar in front of them. The bartender raised his eyebrows, a reminder that the drinks weren't free.

Riker reached into his tunic and took out a couple of the plastic chits that served as money on Imprima. They were yellow, and stamped with the crest of Madraga Alionis, half a world away; there was no point in giving away their association with Criathis by paying with Criathan money.

Without a word the Impriman swept up the chits and placed them in an open stoneware trough suspended from the wall in back of him. In the places Riker had visited during his first sojourn on this planet, the troughs had been elaborately decorated, sometimes rendered in the shape of a fanciful bird or beast. Here it was simply a trough, and not a very clean one at that.

Lyneea picked up her korsch and tossed her head back, downing half the mug's contents at a swallow. The human flinched inwardly at the quantity of warm red liquid in his own mug, sniffed at the pungent scent of it.

He had never been very fond of the stuff, even in delicate little snifters. To him it tasted like vinegar straight up.

Oh, well, he told himself. When in Rome . . .

The korsch was just as strong as he remembered. Taken half a mug at a shot, it was comparable to a small landslide.

Eyes smarting, throat closing so that he could barely breathe, Riker replaced the mug on the bar. His head swam dangerously, but he weathered the storm until his senses reestablished themselves.

Whew. Synthehol, it was not.

His ears having relented in their ringing, the human was able to detect the beginnings of a conversation that Lyneea had apparently managed to strike up with the bartender.

"Too bad," she said.

"What is?" asked the one behind the bar.

"We were looking for a friend, but I don't see him."

"You were supposed to meet him here?"

Lyneea shook her head. "Not exactly. He didn't know we were coming. But I'm sure he'd have been glad to see us."

The cries in the back of the room rose in a sudden crescendo and died just as quickly. The bartender glanced in that direction, and a slow smile took charge of his mouth.

"Why's that?" he asked absently.

Lyneea shrugged—a small, economical gesture. "Business," she said.

That seemed to get the bartender's attention again. His eyes—as green as Lyneea's—were now riveted to her, though his sideways-leaning stance remained casual.

"This friend," he said. "How well do you know him?"

Another shrug—a little broader. "Not well at all, actually."

The bartender regarded her. "Know his name?"

"Teller Conlon."

"That's what I thought. He'll be here later."

Lyneea nodded. "Any idea how much later?"

The bartender seemed to pull back a little at that. Had she pushed too hard? Riker wondered.

"No idea," said the man. With a nod of his head, he indicated the small crowd at the back of the tavern. "Why don't you partake of the entertainment? It'll help pass the time."

And with that slow, small smile reemerging, the bartender glided over to take care of another pair of customers.

Riker peered at Lyneea from under his cowl. "Good? Bad?"

"Somewhere in between," she told him. "We're to face a test."

"Oh? What kind of test?"

"You'll see in a moment." Lifting her mug, she quaffed the remainder of her drink, then looked expectantly at Riker. "Well?" she said, a little louder now. "Don't you like korsch anymore?"

On the one hand, the comment was directed toward anyone who might have been listening—a likely reaction on Lyneea's part to his lack of eagerness in consuming his drink. Human or not, a working-class Joe in Besidia would have been expected to have developed a taste for korsch—and in fairly large quantities. It came with the territory.

On the other hand, Lyneea's comment was a gibe at his offworldliness and, by extension, at the absurdity of asking an outsider to do an Impriman's job.

No question—he *was* out of his element here. But then, their search for his friend had only just begun.

Again resisting a return comment, Riker picked up his mug and drained it. This time, expecting the maelstrom, he was able to tolerate it a little better.

In fact, he slid out of his seat before his partner did, albeit on legs that were not quite steady. "After you," he said, gesturing to the group in the back.

She glanced at him—perhaps with a touch more respect, it was hard to tell—and led the way. Riker followed.

About halfway to their destination, she slowed down, allowing him to catch up. He gathered that this was a better time for an explanation, away from the bartender as well as the barflies. Away, also, from the greatest concentration of tables.

"So?" he said.

Lyneea spoke in a low voice so that only he could hear—and even then, only barely. "The bartender has never seen us in here before, and he knows we're asking questions that could get someone in trouble. So he has opted not to take sole responsibility for giving us the answers; he wants to run us past his board of review." And by looking straight ahead, she showed Riker what constituted the board of review: the knot of patrons in the back of the room.

As before, their voices rose, cutting through the overall din, and subsided after a moment or two. Riker could tell now that they were gathered around something, but he couldn't tell what.

As he and Lyneea approached, he got a better idea.

There was a pit in the back of the tavern, cut somewhat haphazardly into the floor. Inside it, leaping and snarling, was a black and sinewy isak.

Unlike the big ones Riker had seen used as watchdogs and zoo exhibits, this isak was barely an adult. But still, it must have stood a good three feet high at its powerful shoulder, and it sported a collection of teeth already too prodigious to fit easily into its cruel, blunted snout.

What's more, the isak was spitting mad, its blood lust fanned to a frenzy, and for good reason. An Impriman had been lowered into the pit and was being passed around its perimeter, from one pair of hands to the next, his heels dangling just inches above the swiping paws of the enraged beast.

Will took Lyneea's arm, and she looked up at him. "This," he asked, "is what we're supposed to take part in? This is our test?"

She nodded. "We'll put our lives in the hands of these people. If none of them have a reason to distrust us—and they should have no such reason—we will come through unscathed. However, if one of them believes that we are dangerous or that we are something other than what we seem . . ." She regarded Riker meaningfully. "Someone's hands may slip. It will be officially considered an accident."

He looked at the pit and the isak, then back at Lyneea. "How often does one of these *accidents* take place?"

"Not often. But then, one does not generally offer oneself up if there is a possibility of slippery hands."

Riker winced a little as the animal's claws raked the boot of the Impriman suspended over the pit. The man pulled his feet up instinctively, and the crowd lifted him another hand's breadth.

"And in our case?" he asked. "What are the chances of someone here knowing what we're about?"

She shook her head. "It's highly unlikely. We've taken

44

every precaution to keep our mission a secret. Of course, if you are concerned about your safety, I can go first."

Will felt the heat of his machismo rising into his face. "No," he told her. "It will be my pleasure."

A couple of moments later the Impriman in the pit was raised up—sweat dripping off him, a rictus of a grin on his face.

"Who's next?" called a tall, broad-shouldered Pandrilite. He looked around the group that circled the pit. "Who's got the guts?"

As if echoing the question, the isak snarled. It was a sound like ripping metal.

"I do," said Riker, turning sideways to cut a path through the tightly clustered bodies.

Suddenly all eyes were on him, sizing him up, trying to figure out why a man who wasn't even drunk yet would want to take his chances in the pit.

But at least some of them had figured it out, because they were looking in the bartender's direction. Looking and understanding.

"All right," said the Pandrilite. "Step right up and have your heels cleaned."

With a last glance at Lyneea—whose grin might not have been all for show—he took hold of the Pandrilite's hand and then that of someone else—a Maratekkan, but thankfully a big one.

If he thought they were going to lower him slowly, he had another think coming. For a fraction of a second he felt as if they had simply thrown him to the beast.

Instinctively he brought his knees up, tried to grab for the edge of the pit. But they hadn't let go of him after all.

The isak leapt and snapped, and he could feel its muzzle brush the soles of his boots, just barely feel it, as if a feather had touched him, instead of the business end of a flesh-and-blood killing machine.

Then the passing began, the hand-off from one sweaty

grip to the next. Up top, the faces quickly became indistinguishable from one another. Pandrilite blurred into Andorian, Andorian into Rhadamanthan, Rhadamanthan into Impriman. Down below, the beast in the pit was death on a spring—leaping up for a meal one moment, falling to earth the next.

The music and the laughter and the cries of encouragement made a din in his ears, amplified by the korsch, punctuated by the isak's blood-stopping screams. A stench came up to him, of rotting meat and animal droppings and Impriman parasites.

But underneath it all, underneath the madness, judgments were being made. Judgments that would determine how close he came to those gnashing teeth and razor-sharp claws.

His arms and shoulders were growing sore from the strain; his lower back was aching. He felt a sharp pain as a claw raked his ankle—nothing crippling, but bad enough to draw blood.

Damn, Riker. How could you let yourself be talked into this?

And then it happened. One hand let go of him. Another took its place, but it never got a good enough grip. Whether the hand was too slick with perspiration or the slip was purposeful he would never know.

He swung sideways, held only by a single hand now, and glanced off the hard dirt wall of the pit, his stretched-out rib muscles bellowing in agony. Felt the grip that was his only hope start to yield, unable to bear his entire weight.

Riker heard someone shriek—just before he fell.

If it had all happened at once, he would have been isak meat—period. But in the couple of seconds he spent dangling by one hand, he'd had time to prepare himself. To gather his wits.

So as he slid down the side of the pit, he was ready for

the beast's frantic charge. As soon as he saw the first hint of those hell-coal eyes, those flashing teeth, he ducked and rolled.

A bolt of black lightning struck the dirt wall where he'd been, but by then he was on the other side of the pit, trying to get his balance. The isak didn't waste any time. It whirled and pounced—this time, before he could quite set himself.

Somehow he managed to elude it again. His tunic was torn away where the beast had gotten its jaws into it, but the body beneath seemed to be intact.

Riker hadn't expected to survive one charge, much less two. By the time the isak collected itself a third time, he knew he'd run out of luck.

Panting, trembling with his exertions, he couldn't scramble to his feet fast enough. He saw the beast spring—a slavering, roiling mass of coal-black fury—and braced himself as best he could.

The animal was heavier than it looked—the impact of its charge knocked the breath out of him. He fell back against the pit wall, wrestling with the isak, trying to keep its nightmare of a muzzle away from the soft flesh of his throat.

Strangely it wasn't all that difficult. In fact, it was laughably easy. The isak wasn't struggling at all.

The damned thing was unconscious! Something had stunned it as it went for him.

Thrusting the beast off him, Riker looked up. And saw confusion among the revelers—the turning of heads to determine who had ruined their fun.

But Riker knew who it had been. The same slender Impriman who now leaned out from the brink of the pit and offered him her hand.

In her other hand, he saw, was a crude-looking pistol, which she was just now restoring to its place of conceal- ment. The weapon was primitive enough, no doubt, to get around the Besidian prohibition against high technology at carnival time. If he searched the pit, he'd probably find the projectile that had knocked out the isak.

"Nice shot," he told her as he accepted the offer of help. "Though it might have come a few seconds sooner."

"Stop talking," she said, "and start climbing. If we hurry, we can turn this fiasco into something productive."

Lyneea proved stronger than she looked. Bracing herself, she gave him all the leverage he needed to scramble up the wall and out of the pit.

"Productive?" he asked, brushing himself off, feeling the pain in his ankle now where the beast had clawed him. He returned a couple of the stares he was getting from disgruntled patrons as they complained about the unfair use of a gun against a poor defenseless isak.

"Yes," she said, grabbing his wrist and dragging him after her through the crowd. "Productive. Nobody here is going to talk to us, not after you failed their sincerity test." She shoved aside a fellow Impriman who'd made the mistake of getting in her way. "But just as you fell into the pit, I saw someone bolt out of here. And if I'm not mistaken, it was the muzza who dropped you."

Riker caught her drift. Anyone might have let him slip—all it meant was that they didn't like the smell of him. But to drop him and then run—that suggested something more. That suggested a measure of guilt—if they were lucky—in the matter of Teller Conlon and Fortune's Light.

Suddenly he and Lyneea were out of the tavern and into the frigid white vault of Besidia. She let go of his wrist, scanned the snow-covered ground for a moment, and pointed.

There were lots of footprints there, but most of them had been filled in with drift. Only one set stood out clear and distinct, fresh as baby's breath and twice as sweet.

Without another word, Lyneea took off along the path described by the tracks. They led across a small plaza into a benighted alleyway, but that didn't seem to daunt her one bit.

Riker couldn't stand there while his reluctant companion was giving chase. Tugging his tunic closed where the isak had ripped it open, he plunged after her into the shadows.

Chapter Four

BASEBALL WAS one of the topics for which Data had no references in his positronic memory. But in the short time since he'd left the locker room, he had managed to learn a great deal about it. First, during batting practice, he had observed and familiarized himself with its component acts—pitching, hitting, running, throwing, and catching, all of which had been in progress on one part of the field or another.

Then came the more difficult part—identifying the game's objectives and rules. He could deduce some of that from the physical characteristics of the playing field and even more from offhand references made around the batting cage. The android had been able to clear up much of his confusion through casual conversations with the other players. He also found out that, due to the injuries the clubhouse man had referred to, Terwilliger had no choice but to start him in this game.

However, even after the game began, there were gaps in Data's comprehension. So during the first half of the first inning, while he stood beside third base with his glove on his hand, he observed as carefully as he could—not only the occurrences at home plate but also those on the pitcher's mound, in the field, on the scoreboard, and even in the stands.

Before he knew it, however, his teammates were trotting off, abandoning their positions. Taking the hint, he trotted off with them.

But no sooner was he in the dugout than Terwilliger grabbed him by his shirtfront. The man was half a head shorter than Data, with a rounded physique that one did not associate with physical presence. But there was something about Terwilliger's eyes that the android found compelling.

"Listen," he said, "you cocky son of a bitch, I don't know where you think you are, but I want that empty, echoing head of yours in the game!"

"In the game?" the android repeated, groping for comprehension. Here, as elsewhere, much of the vernacular still eluded him.

"That's right, you worthless heap of Triple A garbage! Here you are, a rookie, privileged to play in a game like this one, and you're staring at the sky, the stands—everywhere but where you *should* be staring! Those guys know you're a green apple. You think they're not going to test you? Maybe lay down a little ol' bunt and see how badly you trip over your feet trying to come up with it?"

It took Data a moment to glean some sense out of Terwilliger's tirade. "Are you suggesting," he asked, "that my attention should have been more focused? Actually I would welcome any recommendations in that regard."

The man's face seemed to change colors then. Yes, decided the android. It was noticeably redder, noticeably darker.

"Is that *back talk?*" he asked, in a hushed voice.

Data shrugged. "I do not know what back talk is. I was merely attempting to improve my understanding of baseball."

Terwilliger's eyes narrowed. He seemed to hesitate—

as confused, in a way, as Data himself. When he spoke—not to the android, but to one of his coaches—his voice was still hushed, but it had a cutting edge to it.

"Is this guy for real?" he asked.

"They say he is," came the response. "And, Willie, we need a guy with some punch in the lineup."

Terwilliger spat. He turned to Data again. "Tell you what, Bogdonovich. I got a game to manage here. But we'll discuss this later—you can be sure of that."

"Thank you," said the android. Naturally he understood that the man was preoccupied with the situation at hand. His questions could wait. He was grateful that Terwilliger was offering to answer them at all.

As Data watched the manager stalk off, he reflected that he was already profiting from this holodeck experience. Terwilliger's management style *was* different from Captain Picard's—*vastly* different. His approach seemed to hinge more on emotion and physical confrontation than on confidence and clear thinking. It was most intriguing.

Suddenly there was a hand on Data's shoulder. He turned and traced it to its owner—Denyabe, the second baseman.

"Pay no attention," said the black man, grinning. "You just play your game."

Recognizing it for the encouragement it was, the android smiled back and watched Denyabe stride out onto the field, bat in hand.

Removing his glove, Data chose a spot on the bench and sat down. As the Icebreaker second baseman approached the plate, the crowd responded with a huge roar. It could be felt in the vibration of the stadium structure as well as heard.

Cordoban, the left fielder, had explained to Data during batting practice that this was the Icebreakers' home field. Therefore the spectators were expected to cheer for them more than for the visitors, though after the Icebreakers' spate of defeats in recent weeks, the fans were as likely to jeer as to provide positive reinforcement.

Apparently, in Denyabe's case, the crowd had decided to be charitable. The android heard nothing but accolades.

Nor did their optimism go unrewarded. On the very first pitch Denyabe drove a ball between the shortstop and the third baseman. It bounced twice before it reached the outfielder, and by that time Denyabe had reached first base.

It was, as Data had learned earlier, a single—a promising development, though one that did not necessarily result in a score. That would depend on the success of the batters who followed.

The next man in the lineup was Sakahara, the Icebreaker catcher. He walked with a slight limp, and his left wrist was taped—reflecting injuries that had hampered his performance of late and contributed to the team's decline. Or so the android gathered from his conversations with the clubhouse man and others.

"If Sakahara gets some hits, we win." That had been Cordoban's opinion, expressed as they watched the catcher take batting practice. "He goes hitless, we lose. It's that simple."

With that in mind, the android was intent on Sakahara's performance. Apparently, so was the opposing team; as the first pitch was delivered, the infielders participated in a complicated maneuver that had the first and third basemen approaching the batter rather precipitously—with little regard, it appeared, for their safety.

A second later Data saw the reason for the move—as Sakahara squared around to bunt. However, after the ball hit his bat, it plunked down in foul territory.

"Stee-rike!" called the umpire.

On the next pitch, the fielders shifted again, and again

Sakahara failed to bunt effectively. This time, in fact, he missed the ball entirely.

"Stee-rike two!"

The crowd responded by hooting volubly. It was an unpleasant sound. For Sakahara it must have been even more so.

On the third pitch he was not expected to bunt. As Data had learned, one did not bunt with two strikes. If the ball went foul, it would mean the end of the batter's opportunity to score runs for his team—at least until it was his turn again to bat.

This time the infielders remained at their positions. No one charged toward home plate.

Then, to everyone's surprise, Sakahara bunted down the third base line—a fair ball. Limp and all, he raced toward first base while Denyabe headed for second.

Caught unaware, the opposing team's third baseman started in for the ball. However, by the time he picked it up, he was too late to make a play. Both Sakahara and Denyabe had secured safe positions on their respective bases.

The hit was a source of great satisfaction to all in the Icebreaker dugout as well as to the crowd.

Only Terwilliger seemed unencouraged by it. He just glared at Data.

"You see?" he said, pointing to the field of play as he approached the android. "The third baseman was in dreamland—just like you, Bogdonovich. If he'd known anything about Sakahara, he'd have charged that ball and nailed him at first. Take a lesson, rookie. And get your rear end out to the on-deck circle—or do I have to get someone to show you where it is?"

Data held up his hand. "That will not be necessary. I know where it is."

Terwilliger looked at him. That was all—he just looked at him. His eyes seemed rounder than usual, and they were red around the edges.

"Come on," one of the coaches said to Data. "Get out of here before Terwilliger has a heart attack."

Like much he had encountered in this program, Data didn't understand the implied causality of the remark. But it was his turn to be on deck, so he chose a bat from the rack and headed for the appropriate spot.

In the meantime, the Icebreakers' first baseman, a big fellow named Galanti, had come up to bat. The first pitch thrown to him was a ball—a term that Data had thought a bit obvious until he learned its specialized meaning. The second pitch, too, was a ball.

"Awright!" came a cry from the dugout. "You got 'im where you want 'im!"

"Your pitch!" came another cry. "Wait for your pitch!"

On the next offering, Galanti swung. It was a prodigious stroke that turned him almost completely around.

It did not propel the ball very far or very fast, however. The pitcher fielded it on one hop. He threw to second and the shortstop relayed to first.

Double play.

The crowd made clear its dissatisfaction. It was a loud and infelicitous sound.

Data understood that the play had expended two of the three outs they were allowed in this inning. However, it hadn't been completely counterproductive. Wasn't Denyabe standing on third base?

Nor did it take a computer to calculate what the score would be if Data stepped up to the plate now and hit a home run—something of which he felt fully capable. Certainly he had had no trouble hitting them in batting practice.

Nonetheless, the android had hardly left the on-deck circle when his teammates began shouting advice to him from the dugout.

"Okay, Bobo, a little single!"

"Just a single, baby! Bring that run in!"

Data was a bit surprised. But of course there were

undoubtedly nuances of the game that he did not yet comprehend. If a single was preferable to a home run in this instance, he would do his best to hit a single.

Taking his cue from Denyabe, the android resolved to hit the first pitch that came his way. The ball was hardly out of the pitcher's hand before he had gauged its velocity—ninety-seven miles an hour—as well as its mass, its trajectory, and the point at which it would cross home plate.

Reaching out, he stroked the ball into center field and started off for first base. Out of the corner of his eye, he could see Denyabe jogging home with the first score of the contest.

The crowd exploded with approval. However, as Data rounded first base, he saw that the opposing team's center fielder had misplayed the ball. It had glanced off his glove and dribbled a few feet away from him.

The android knew he had to keep going. One could not remain on any given base when there was an opportunity to advance to the next one.

Yet his teammates had *specifically* called for a single. If he went on, it would become a double—and he had no idea what effect that might have on the fate of the Icebreakers.

It was an agonizing moment. Surely it *seemed* that going to second base would be a good thing. But then, it had *seemed* that a home run would be preferable to a single, and yet his teammates had indicated otherwise.

Torn, Data hesitated—and finally decided to follow his instincts. As the center fielder pursued the rolling ball, he took off for second base. Halfway there, he saw that the ball had been recovered.

He took a few more steps, then dove. The throw was made; the ball came in low and true, beating Data's hand to the base by the merest fraction of a second.

Both Data and the shortstop looked up at the umpire. The man didn't do anything right away. The respective arrivals of Data and the ball would have appeared simultaneous to the human eye.

Despite that, the umpire came to a decision—and, as it happened, the correct one. Pumping his thumb in the air, he cried, "Yerrout!"

The crowd uttered unkind comments at the upper limits of their vocal range. But the opposing team was quite happy as it left the field.

Data was happy, too. He had done his best to reach the next base safely, as the rules seemed to dictate. And yet, he had complied with his teammates' exhortations by limiting his hit to a single.

In light of all this, he expected that there would be some back-patting in store for him in the Icebreaker dugout. However, as he approached it, Galanti came loping out with his glove.

"Here," he said, tossing it to the android. "You don't want to go in there—*believe* me, you don't."

Before he turned and headed for his position at third base, Data got a glimpse of what his teammate was talking about. Terwilliger, it appeared, was livid. But for the two coaches restraining him, he looked as if he might have leapt out of the dugout and come after Data with a bat.

The android frowned. Obviously he still had a lot to learn.

"Save program," he said, and exited the holodeck.

The air was cold; it rasped in Riker's throat as he ran down the long, winding alley, just a couple of strides behind Lyneea. Nor could he have easily caught up if he'd wanted to—Lyneea was a lot more surefooted than he was in the soft snow that had accumulated here.

As a youngster, he would undoubtedly have done better. But it had been a long time since he'd had a chance to skid and slosh through the kind of half-frozen soup one used to find in the streets of Valdez.

His senses alert, Riker found himself noticing minutiae that were irrelevant to the task at hand. Like the way Lyneea trailed white wisps of breath that dissipated before he could reach them. Or the way her heels threw up little white rooster tails, her footprints mingling with those of the one they sought—though there was no confusing them. Hers were slender and shallow, his deep and extremely wide.

Up ahead, Riker saw an opening off to one side. Another alleyway? He wondered if she'd spotted it, too—then was certain she had, for she slowed down, angled closer to the wall, and stopped running.

Sure enough, the bigger set of footprints ran around that corner. Lyneea took out her projectile gun again, shot a glance at him.

He had no trouble deciphering her message: *Be careful. We're getting closer.*

Riker was glad she'd suddenly become concerned about his welfare. Maybe she thought that a single close call a night was all one should have to put up with—even if one *was* an offworlder.

Hugging the stones that made up the wall, Lyneea stuck her head around the corner. She took a moment to peer into the shadows.

Then, apparently satisfied that the coast was clear, she swung herself into the alley.

It was almost the last thing she ever did. Only sheer luck kept her from being cut to ribbons by the bright-blue blaster beams that fried the air all around her.

Riker reached out and caught Lyneea's tunic. As he reeled her in, a beam caught the corner they'd been waiting behind and shattered some of the stones, sending splinters flying in every direction.

Lyneea pushed herself away from Will and cursed.

"Problem?" he asked, unable to resist.

"So it would seem."

Silence. The fugitive with the blaster was biding his time, knowing he had the superior firepower or they would have struck back without hesitation.

"I guess not everybody takes the high-tech ban seriously," he observed.

She grunted.

"So what now?"

She thought for a moment. "He's not going anywhere, not on a bellyful of korsch, anyway. If he could have gone on, he wouldn't have bothered to stop in the first place." She chewed her lip, then abruptly thrust her projectile weapon into Riker's hand.

"You know how to use this?" she asked.

He turned it over. "Doesn't look too complicated. Eight chambers, seven projectiles left." He wasn't exactly an expert in antique arms, but he'd seen a few in his day.

"Good," she said. "Then use it to keep our fugitive distracted."

"Does that mean you're leaving me? Just when we were starting to work so well together?"

Glowering at him, the Impriman seemed about to say something, then thought better of it. Without warning, she bolted across the mouth of the perpendicular alleyway, drawing a barrage of sizzling blaster fire from their prey, and kept on going. In a few seconds she reached the opening at the far end and disappeared.

Riker appreciated the simplicity of Lyneea's plan: circle around behind their blaster-happy friend and catch him unaware. But her strategy was dangerous as all hell.

Which was why it was so important to do as Lyneea had instructed—keep their fugitive busy, so he wouldn't realize that one of his pursuers might be plying the alleys to outmaneuver him. And waste her, perhaps, as she came creeping up on him.

However, at this range, Lyneea's pop pistol was fairly

useless. One or two shots and their friend in the alley would know that and take off again, confident that they couldn't stop him. And if Riker didn't shoot at all, the fellow would come to the same conclusion—maybe even faster.

He needed to get closer to his target, but not so close he would scare him off and ruin Lyneea's approach.

Quickly Riker peered around the half-destroyed corner—and almost paid the price for it. But just before the cornerstones erupted again in an explosion of blue light, he caught a glimpse of something helpful.

A row of large metal containers, mantled in shadow, stood against one wall of the alley. Overflowing with discarded clothes and ruined furniture and all sorts of less easily identifiable things that might or might not have been Impriman foodstuffs at one time. In a warmer climate, he thought, the stench would have been unbearable.

But that wasn't significant right now. What *was* significant was that those containers looked solid enough to withstand a blaster barrage, at least for a while.

Oh, what the hell, he thought. *What's a poker game without a bluff or two?*

As he darted out from cover, the one with the blaster seemed to go berserk. There were beams all around him, carving up the alley walls and the ground beneath his feet and eliciting a scream from the very atoms in the air as they were torn one from the other.

Riker rolled—once, twice—scrambled to his feet and lunged for the nearest container. He miscalculated and came up against it harder than he'd intended, rattling his teeth with the impact. But after a quick inventory, he found that he was still in one piece, unscathed by the blue light beams. Better than that—with all the adrenaline pumping through him, his ankle had stopped smarting.

The blasterman's weapon fell silent again. Was he waiting for Riker to come out from behind the container? Probably. Was he wondering where his Impriman companion was? Maybe that, too.

Riker couldn't allow him time to wonder. Leaning out past the container, he peered into the shadows and got off a shot—not that he had any hope of actually hitting anything. To do that, one generally had to see one's target.

Nothing. No response.

Could it be that the fugitive had already fled?

Riker knew he couldn't take that for granted, but he couldn't just sit there, either—so he left the protection of the container, took a couple of steps, and launched himself in the direction of the next one.

This time he didn't hit the container so hard. He was getting better with practice. Brushing some of the larger clumps of slush from his tunic, he lay on his belly and listened.

Still nothing. But for the sound of Riker's own breathing, the alley was preternaturally quiet.

Damn. Could I have spooked him so easily?

But he wasn't going to jump to any conclusions. Maybe something had gone wrong with the blaster. Maybe it needed a new battery—and was getting one right now.

He took a deep draft of the frigid air, expelled it, and scuttled out from behind the second container. The hairs at the nape of his neck prickled with a sudden premonition of disaster; if the blasterman was still there, Riker was getting devilishly close—probably too close for the fugitive to miss.

Spurred by the eerie feeling that he'd bluffed his way into a trap, he wasted no time flinging himself behind the third container.

But the reaction was the same: nonexistent. The impression of imminent peril faded rather quickly.

In fact, he was starting to feel silly. To feel certain that their prey had departed, leaving him here to play hide-and-seek with refuse containers.

Then the real fireworks started.

In the next fraction of a second Riker realized that it *had* been a trap—just not the kind he'd expected. The force generated by the blaster at this range was enough to topple the massive container and send it crashing down on him, garbage and all. He tried to get out of its way, but it fell too quickly and before he knew it, he was pinned under the container, fighting to keep it from crushing him altogether.

That was the moment in which the fugitive chose to reveal himself. He walked out from the shadows, blaster at the ready, seeming to take his time.

Riker tried to free himself, to roll the weight of the container off him, but it was hard work. Slow work. He couldn't seem to get enough air into his lungs; his chest seemed to be caught in a vise. And the fellow with the blaster was getting closer all the time.

He had no idea what had happened to his projectile gun, nor would it have helped him much now—he needed both hands to keep the container from caving his ribs in.

The fugitive came out of the shadows far enough for Riker to get a good look at him. A Pandrilite. Big, heavyset—Lyneea had been right. He never could have outrun them.

And where in blazes *was* Lyneea? He peered down the alley, saw no sign of her.

The Pandrilite smiled and aimed his weapon at Riker's face. He was standing no more than four meters away now. There was no way he could miss.

"Stop struggling," said the broad, bony face behind the blaster. "It won't do you any good." Suddenly the smile fell away. "Where's your friend?"

"Damned if I know," said Riker.

But just as he said it, there was a soft, scraping sound above them—and something fell on the Pandrilite, knocking the blaster out of his hand and bringing him to his knees. Something long-limbed and, at a second glance, very Lyneea-like.

The two of them fell in a heap, the Impriman on top. Both went for the blaster; Lyneea got to it first.

"All right," she told him. "On your feet—and over to that container." She indicated the one that was still doing its best to compress Riker's anatomy.

The Pandrilite did as he was told.

"Now help him remove it."

The Pandrilite stooped and, bringing his considerable strength to bear, gave Riker the leverage he needed to roll the container off him. That was only fair, thought Will, since he had put it there in the first place.

With an effort, Riker got to his feet and belted the Pandrilite, sending him staggering into a wall.

"That," he said, "was for dropping me into the isak pit."

The Pandrilite wiped his mouth and glared at him, but refrained from retaliating. After all, Lyneea still had the blaster pointed at him.

"Now," she said, smiling approvingly at Riker's outburst, "I want to know what made you nervous enough to drop my companion and flee the tavern."

The Pandrilite's lip curled. He barked out one word: "Raat."

Riker looked at Lyneea. The word didn't seem to mean anything to her, either.

"What's *raat?*" she asked.

The Pandrilite's eyes narrowed. "You don't work for Drohner?" he asked.

"Ah," said Lyneea. "Drohner. Sure, I've heard of him." She turned to Riker. "Big labor broker. Corrupt as they come." Then she turned back to the Pandrilite. "What's he got to do with you?"

The Pandrilite shrugged. "I . . . crossed him. Organized a little labor crew of my own—an independent called Raat. It's a Pandril word. Means 'freedom.'" He spat. "Drohner didn't like it. I heard he was trying to find out more about me, maybe teach me a lesson." He stared at the Impriman. "You *sure* you don't work for Drohner?"

"Positive," she said. "If I did, would I have come after you with a projectile gun?"

Realization dawned. "You're a retainer," he said.

Lyneea nodded. "And I couldn't care less about Drohner's difficulties in maintaining his monopoly. But I do need information, and I think you can give it to me."

The Pandrilite straightened. "What kind of information?"

"We're looking for someone named Teller Conlon," Riker cut in. "Heard of him?"

The Pandrilite was expressionless. "Maybe. What do you want with him?"

Riker shook his head. "I asked you first."

"The way I see it," Lyneea told her captive, "you have a choice. You can be incarcerated for a little while, for possession of a high-tech weapon during carnival time. Or we can contact Drohner and see if we can do some business with him."

The Pandrilite measured her. "You wouldn't."

"Try me," she said.

A pause. "All right. But I don't know very much about Conlon. Only that he did a little smuggling on the side."

Riker felt the heat as it flooded his face. "You know that for a fact?" he asked.

The Pandrilite shrugged a second time. "That's what I heard. Nothing big—just a few artifacts here and there. Things the madraggi would have preferred to keep on Imprima."

"Have you seen him lately?" asked Lyneea.

The Pandrilite shook his head. "No, I haven't. The last time was probably a couple of weeks ago, now that I think about it. And that's a little strange, because he's around here all the time."

"Around where?" Lyneea pressed.

"You know," said the Pandrilite. "The tavern."

Riker didn't believe it. He didn't *want* to believe it.

"You're lying," he told the Pandrilite. "You're in league with whoever's framing him."

"No. I'm telling the truth—I swear it." He paused. "What do you mean, *framing* him? Is he wanted for something?"

Riker frowned. He'd already gone too far. "Never mind."

"Conlon must have had agents," said Lyneea, dragging the conversation back on course. "People he met at the tavern. Who were they?"

The Pandrilite didn't seem eager to provide the answer. But he must have been less eager to face Drohner. "As far as I can tell, he worked with only one outside player. An Impriman by the name of Bosch. Reggidor Bosch."

"You know," said Lyneea, "if my companion is right and you're lying to us—"

"I know, I know." The Pandrilite held up his hands. "I heard you the first time. But I'm giving it to you straight. Bosch. You can find him in the Gelden Muzza. That's where he stays."

Lyneea nodded. "Thanks."

It took a little while to find the projectile gun; it was mixed in with some of the garbage that had fallen out of the container. Riker had to clean it with a rag before he could shove it into his tunic for safekeeping.

When he was done, Lyneea gestured with the blaster. "Let's get a move on," she told the Pandrilite. "I think my companion is getting cold."

It was untrue. Riker was all but oblivious to the weather. If anything, he was hot—seething, in fact—as he tried to reconcile the Pandrilite's information with his faith in his friend.

Damn it, Teller. What the hell have you gotten yourself into?

Chapter Five

THE FIRST TIME Wesley's door beeped, he thought he'd imagined it. That's how deep he was in his research.

The second time, however, he was listening for it, and therefore it was unmistakable. The boy sighed, the slightest bit annoyed at the interruption.

"Come in," he said.

The doors parted to reveal Data. Suddenly Wesley forgot that he was annoyed.

Data was probably the only one on the ship—his mother included—who would listen to him expound indefinitely on whatever subject had most recently caught his fancy and never, but *never*, invent an excuse to leave before Wesley was finished. The boy still hadn't figured out if the android was really interested or just too polite to leave him hanging, but it almost didn't matter, as long as he listened.

Data greeted him. "I hope I am not disturbing you," he said.

"Heck no." Wesley motioned the android to a seat. "In fact, I'm glad to see you."

"It is nice of you to say so," said Data, folding himself into the chair. "Actually, I—"

"You see," the boy plunged on, caught up in his excitement, "I've been curious about Commander Riker's mission. But I haven't been able to get the captain to drop a hint about it—Priority One and all that." He frowned. "I think Mr. Worf knows something about it, too, but he's just as closemouthed as the captain. So I decided to check out Impriman culture on the library computer and see what I could dig up."

Data's features seemed to recast themselves as Wesley spoke—a subtle change, but one the boy couldn't help noticing. Was he boring Data now, too?

"Is everything all right?" he asked.

"Certainly," said the android. "Please proceed."

"You're not just saying that so you won't hurt my feelings? I mean, you really want to hear this?"

"Yes, Wesley. I really do."

Thank God. "Okay—so where was I? Oh, yeah. Impriman culture. It's pretty interesting—for instance, the institution of the madraga. In one respect, it's like some sort of monarchy, with control passing from parent to child. But in all other respects, it's more like one of Earth's old business entities—the corporation. The madraga isn't limited by geographical boundaries, as a nation-state would be. Instead, it's defined by the extent of its involvements in various Impriman industries."

"Interesting," said the android.

"Anyway, these madraggi all get together once a year, during the time of the winter solstice, in the ancient mountain city of Besidia. They hold trade meetings during which the course of Impriman economics is charted for the foreseeable future." He couldn't suppress a smile. "And when do you suppose the winter solstice *is?*"

Data's eyes moved abruptly, as they sometimes did when he was computing something. "Now," he answered.

"Absolutely right."

"So," said the android, "you believe that Commander Riker is involved somehow with the trade meetings?"

"Right again. And—ready for this?—Commander Riker has been to Imprima before. As a trade liaison." Wesley outlined the details of that mission, including its successful conclusion.

"I see. And have you a theory as to Commander Riker's role in the current meetings?"

The boy leaned back and shook his head. "No. Unfortunately, that's as far as I've gotten."

"Still, you seem to know a good deal more about Commander Riker's mission than I do, and I am third in command of this vessel."

Wesley looked at him in a new light. "Say, Data . . . if you asked the captain—"

The android thrust his chin out, as he always did when remonstrating with someone. "I am sorry, Wes. If the captain had wanted Commander Riker's mission known, I am sure he would have made it so by now. Since he has not . . ."

The boy held his hands up and smiled. "Okay, okay. No harm in asking, is there?"

"No," agreed Data. "There is never any harm in that. And speaking of questions, would you answer some for me?"

That was when Wesley realized the significance of Data's change in expression a few minutes earlier. "Oh," he said, pounding his fist on his desk. "That's why you came here in the first place, isn't it? To ask me some questions. And here I go spouting off like the egghead everybody thinks I am." He shook his head as he regarded the android. *What was I thinking? That Data came to visit just so I could have a sounding board?* "I'm sorry, Data. I really am." He leaned forward. "Now, what do you want to know? I'm all ears."

Data cocked his head slightly. He had that quizzical look in his eyes.

"It's an expression," explained Wesley. "It means I'm listening."

"Ah," said the android. "In that case, have you ever played baseball?"

"Baseball?" echoed Wesley. He'd expected Data's inquiry to be something in the area of human nature—the type of thing he usually discussed with Geordi. "Sure. I've played it, mostly when I was smaller. Why?"

The android told him about the goings-on in the holodeck. About the dilemma he'd faced between first base and second, how it had been resolved, and the manager's reaction to the resolution.

Wesley found it pretty funny, but he didn't let Data know that. "The problem," he said, "is that you took the players' encouragement too literally."

"I see." Data looked a little disappointed—in himself, no doubt. "And I thought I was making strides in that regard."

"You *are*," the boy assured him. "At least from what I can see. But in this case you should have taken as many bases as possible. In fact, you should have hit a home run in the first place. That would have taken the guesswork out of baserunning."

The android nodded. "Actually I was *thinking* of hitting a home run. But when my teammates recommended I hit a single—"

Wesley shook his head.

"Too literal again?" Data asked.

"That's right. A single would have brought the runner home from third base, and that would have been good. But it would have been better to bring *two* runs home."

The android seemed to absorb the information. But he still looked puzzled. Wesley said so.

"What I do not understand," said Data, "is

70

Terwilliger's reaction. Even if I *did* make a mistake, why should he have become so incensed over it? Is baseball not a game? Or am I missing something else?"

"To tell you the truth," remarked the boy, "I'm a little puzzled myself. I guess everybody takes something a little too seriously. Lord knows, *I* fall into that category from time to time." He shrugged. "It would probably help if we knew more about the environment Terwilliger was operating in—or the pressures he may have been under. I mean, this was his job, wasn't it? From what I understand, baseball was an industry as well as a sport."

Data looked at him as if he was expecting more.

"Unfortunately," said Wesley, "I don't have all the facts. I'm not exactly an expert on twenty-first-century social history." An idea came to him. "But wouldn't that sort of information be stored in the ship's computer archives?"

The android's eyes seemed to brighten a little. "I believe you are correct," he said. He rose. "Thank you, Wes. You have been most helpful."

"Don't mention it," said the boy. "It was my pleasure."

Data started for the exit, then stopped, as if he'd forgotten something. He wheeled around to face Wesley. "Incidentally," he said, "I really *am* interested in your research on Imprima. Please let me know how it goes."

Wesley grinned. "You've got a deal," he told him.

And with that, the android departed.

As the doors to his quarters came together again, the boy sat there for a second or two in appreciation of the marvel that was Data. *He wants so badly to be more like us,* Wesley mused. *But it wouldn't hurt us to be more like him.*

Then he remembered Imprima and turned back to the array of information on his desktop monitor, downloaded from the library computer. "Let's see," he said out loud. "What's so important about these trade meetings that Commander Riker had to be called back for them?"

The first official of Madraga Terrin stood before the picture window in his library. The grounds outside were a snow-covered expanse broken only by a few stately trees.

"I have given your proposal much thought," said Larrak, his hands locked behind his back, his narrow features unreadable. "But it bears more thought still."

"Then you've yet to make your decision," said Riker.

"That is correct."

"Is there some additional information we could provide?" asked Teller.

The isak sitting by the door growled softly. Riker tried his best to ignore it.

Larrak eyed Teller, giving away nothing. "I do not believe so. But if anything occurs to you, you may send it on."

"I appreciate that," Teller said, without the slightest hint of irony in his voice. "And if anything occurs to you, First Official, please let us know."

"I will. I assure you."

It was the shortest interview they'd had yet. Riker felt Larrak's vote slipping away. And Terrin was one of the most powerful madraggi on the planet—it was a vote they needed. He started to drag out his speech again—the by-now standard oration about the virtues of trading with the Federation—figuring that it couldn't hurt.

But Teller had subtly placed his hand on Riker's. He was standing up.

"Thank you," he told Larrak, "for your time and your attention."

The first official inclined his head ever so slightly. The movement emphasized the waspishness of his appearance.

Following Teller's lead, Riker stood too. His friend knew these people better than he did; he'd figured that out days

72

ago. With a smile, Riker turned and fell into line behind Teller.

The isak looked up at them hungrily. Saliva dripped from its massive jaws, leaving little pools on the floor.

To Riker's surprise, Teller didn't go through the open doorway. Instead, he knelt beside the isak.

The thing's eyes went wild. It made an ugly sound deep in its throat, but it held its ground.

"Beautiful animal," observed Teller, showing no sign of fear. "Did you train him yourself?"

"I did." Larrak eyed Teller curiously. "I have seldom seen anyone get so close to him. Even trained isakki are unpredictable sometimes—or didn't you know that?"

Teller rose. "I knew," he said. "Good day, First Official."

"Good day, Lieutenant Conlon."

As they made their way down the hall to the front door, Teller elbowed Riker in the ribs. "Impressive, huh?"

"Crazy, if you ask me. You could've lost half your face. Or worse."

A retainer was waiting in the foyer to show them out. He opened the door for them; they turned up the collars on their Impriman tunics, which weren't nearly warm enough to stave off the frigid weather.

The gate was about twenty paces away. There was a retainer there, too.

"I took a chance," Teller went on. "I showed Larrak I trusted his training of the isak—that I trusted him. And that should show him the extent of our commitment, how much we want this trade agreement, and that we're operating on the level."

Riker shook his head. "I would never have thought of all that. And even if I had, I don't think I'd have had the nerve to pull it off."

"Sure you would," his friend assured him. "Thought of it and done it. Or maybe you'd have found something even better."

"I doubt it."

The retainer at the gate swung it aside at their approach. As they made their exit, Riker had a funny feeling. Turning, he saw Larrak out of the corner of his eye. The first official was standing at the front door, watching them go.

"Don't look now, but our host is seeing us off."

"Guess it worked, then. Though that's no guarantee that he will vote us in. He's still risking an awful lot if he breaks his ties with the Ferengi—and the promise of greater profits with the Federation could just be pie in the sky."

"On the other hand, he seems to have no great love for Rhurig. And Kelnae would just hate it if Larrak sided with the Federation."

"Good point," said Teller.

An ascetic was sitting just outside the gate. A female, Riker thought, though the shapeless brown robes didn't give him too many clues.

Before he knew it, Teller had dug into his tunic and produced a chit. He went over to the ascetic and held it out. A moment later a slender hand emerged and accepted the offering.

Riker looked back. Larrak was still watching them.

They began walking again, away from the estate of Madraga Terrin and back toward more familiar precincts.

"Another gesture?" asked Riker.

"Huh?"

"That bit of charity. To impress Larrak?"

His friend grinned as he began to understand. "Hell, no. A reflex." He paused. "But if it impressed Larrak, so much the better."

"Daydreaming again, Riker?"

"Thinking."

"About what? Your friend?"

Riker looked at her as they approached the doors of the Golden Muzza. "As a matter of fact, yes. Is it that obvious?"

She shrugged, opening one of the doors. "After you," she said.

He went inside, and she came after him.

All the way here, Riker had been at odds with himself, alternately hurrying and dragging his feet. He wanted to hear what Bosch had to say—but at the same time, he dreaded it.

Because if what the Pandrilite had told them was true, it opened up some pretty dismal possibilities. First, that Teller *had* been involved, in some way, with the theft of Fortune's Light. Second, that Riker had perhaps not known his friend as well as he thought.

And Reggidor Bosch would tip the scales one way or the other. Either he would confirm the fact that Teller was a smuggler or he would reinforce Riker's belief in the man.

The desk clerk was of mixed blood—part Impriman, part Tetracite, part something else as well. It was an uncomplimentary combination.

And they soon found out that, at least in this case, it was possible to judge a book by its cover.

"Maybe he lives here and maybe he doesn't," the clerk told them in a whiny, high-pitched voice. "Who wants to know?"

"That's none of your business," said Lyneea. She reached inside her tunic and plunked down a half-dozen variously colored chits on the counter—chits from various madraggi so, as in the tavern, no one would link them with Criathis in particular.

The clerk looked down at the chits, a little surprised. Apparently they didn't get too many big tippers at the Golden Muzza. Gathering up the pieces of plastic, he put them away below the counter.

"He's in three-oh-three. Two flights up. But . . ." He paused, the skin around his eyes crinkling. "What do you want with him?"

Lyneea produced two more chits.

The desk clerk grunted. "Have a nice day."

The lift was in need of repair. It jerked as it came to a halt at the third floor, and the doors opened on completely different sequence schedules.

Bosch's suite was to the left and all the way down the hall, which gave them a chance to sample the threadbare imitation Andorian-weave carpet. At one time, Riker knew from his last stay on Imprima, the Golden Muzza had tried to affect an offworldly kind of splendor. It had long since faded.

He knocked on the door, an elaborately embellished version of the sort found on ancient Earth. It sounded hollow.

For a moment or two, nothing. Then, "Who is it?"

"Room service," said Lyneea.

The door swung open a crack, and a slice of Impriman features appeared in the opening. "I didn't order any—"

By the time the Impriman realized that it wasn't room service, Riker had inserted his boot between the door and the jamb. Lyneea pushed it open the rest of the way.

The occupant retreated a couple of steps and stared at them, fear etched on his narrow face. Riker felt sorry for him. Obviously this kind of thing didn't happen to him very often, despite his line of work.

Lyneea closed the door behind them gently, so as not to scare the fellow any more than he was already scared.

"What . . . what do you want?" asked Bosch.

"Not what you may think," said Lyneea. "We're not here to rob you." She smiled—a rare expression for her, but one she was quite good at.

"We're friends," said Riker. "Friends of Teller Conlon." He glanced sideways at his partner. Well, it was half true. "We haven't seen him in a while, and we're

76

worried. He mentioned your name a couple of times; we thought you might be able to put our minds at ease."

Bosch shook his head. "I don't know who Teller Conlon is. I've never heard of him."

Lyneea chuckled. "Of course not. You're not his outside player, right?" Her tone was mild but assured. "You've never taken a commission from him—is that correct?"

Bosch looked from one to the other, then gave a nervous half smile. "All right," he said. "I admit that I've done some business with him."

Riker cursed silently. "When was the last time you saw him?"

The smuggler's agent shrugged. "A month ago. Maybe more." He put his hand to his head, shivered a little. "Listen," he said, "give me a moment, will you? I need to take my medication."

"Medication?" echoed Riker.

The smuggler's agent lifted his chin and pointed to his jawline, where he bore the scars of korrus fever. They were faint, but they were there.

The first time Riker visited Imprima, korrus had still been fatal. When he'd heard about the cure a couple of years ago, he rejoiced—with a toast in Ten Forward to the researchers who'd made it possible, some of whom were Federation personnel.

Of course there were still some lasting symptoms of the disease—like the involuntary muscle tremors Bosch was experiencing now—and, if left unmedicated, some rather grisly seizures.

"Sure," said Lyneea. "Go ahead. Don't mind us."

Bosch crossed the room to a chest of drawers. But the closer he got, it seemed to Riker, the less he trembled.

Covering the room in three strides, Will arrived just in time to grab Bosch's wrist as he started to open the top drawer.

The Impriman looked at him. "I thought you said you were friends."

"We are," said Riker. "But we've got to be careful. You know how it is."

Lyneea was giving him a look of disapproval: *We're trying to gain his confidence, Riker, and you're not exactly furthering the effort.*

Maybe he had jumped to a conclusion. He released Bosch's wrist.

As the Impriman opened the drawer, Riker saw the vial of tablets inside.

See? You're getting paranoid.

He started to turn away, to return to where Lyneea was standing, so Bosch could have some privacy.

But out of the corner of his eye, he saw the flash of something that was definitely not medicine. He whirled and kicked—and sent a blaster flying out of Bosch's hand.

Lyneea was quick to recover it. She held it up, looked reproachfully at her fellow Impriman.

"What did you expect?" he asked, massaging his hand. "You say you're Conlon's friends, but I never heard him talk about you, not once. And you come barging in here—how do I know what you're really after?"

"Just what we said," Lyneea told him. "We're looking for Conlon."

"To help him," added Riker.

The smuggler's agent looked at them again. Finally he seemed to accept that there was no more to it than that—or very little more, anyway.

"Conlon's in some kind of trouble," he concluded. "Isn't he?"

"We think he might be, yes," said Lyneea.

Bosch cursed. "Look—I don't know anything about Conlon disappearing, truly. But if there's something I can do, just tell me." He swallowed. "You've got to understand that Conlon's my livelihood. Not part of it—all of it. And it's not easy to pick up new clients these days. Too much competition, too many aliens out there crowding the field."

Suddenly Riker found he had a bad taste in his mouth. But he believed that Bosch knew nothing of Teller's whereabouts. Lyneea was of the same mind. Her expression confirmed that.

"When I find our friend," he told Bosch, "I'll inform him of your concern."

In the meantime, Lyneea was removing the battery from the blaster. She tossed both components to Riker, one at a time.

Riker replaced them in Bosch's drawer. Disconnecting the battery had rendered the weapon useless, and it would need a minute or so to recharge after it was connected again.

Just in case.

"Watch where you take that thing," Lyneea said as she opened the door. "There's a carnival on, you know. High-tech ban and all that."

Bosch nodded. "Thanks for reminding me." He turned back to Riker. "You going now?"

The human nodded. "Yes." Crossing the room, he followed Lyneea out the door.

"Don't forget," said the smuggler's agent, his words trailing them down the hall. "I really do want to help. Honest."

"Subject?" queried the computer voice, silken and female as ever.

"Baseball," said Data, confronting the monitor in his quarters. "Specifically, the state of the professional game in the year 2026 Old Earth Time."

It took less than a second for the computer to call up the requisite information. "On screen?" it asked.

"No," said the android. Though some of his colleagues liked to interact silently with the ship's electronic brain, Data preferred to converse with it out loud and did so whenever circumstances allowed, as they did now. "Voice mode, please. Narrative format."

"Very well." There was a pause, which no one else on the *Enterprise* would have noticed. Then the computer began. "By the year 2026, the game of baseball had entered a period of decline. A series of bitter and protracted labor disputes, starting in 1981 and escalating shortly after the turn of the century, gradually eroded the popularity of the sport. What is more, sharp increases in ticket prices denied large segments of the population access to the games. As time went on, younger fans in particular became—"

"Stop," said Data. "I am unfamiliar with the term 'fan.'"

"Fan," repeated the computer. "An abbreviated version of the word 'fanatic.' In this context, used to denote devotees of the game, those who have an enthusiastic admiration for players, their efforts, and the results of those efforts."

"I see," said the android. "Please proceed."

"Younger fans in particular became alienated, and the market for the game dwindled. Fewer and fewer people watched baseball on television and purchased related paraphernalia. Surveys in the year 2019 indicated that the body of baseball enthusiasts was less than half the size it had been two decades earlier. While all franchises were financially damaged by this trend, those that catered to smaller populations were damaged the most. In the period from 2018 to 2023, four teams went bankrupt and another eight changed hands a total of nineteen times.

"Dismayed by the decreasing opportunities and increasing uncertainties associated with a career in baseball, talented athletes and managers opted for other sports or avenues of endeavor. Those who took their place were generally less gifted and willing to play for lower salaries. Ironically, the professional baseball player

in 2026 had less in common with his immediate prede-
cessors than he did with the players of one hundred years
earlier."

The computer stopped there, its summary complete.
But having been supplied with a perspective on the
matter, Data now had other questions.

"Tell me about the game played on October 7, 2026,
between the Phoenix Sunsets and the Fairbanks Icebreakers."

"The game was a playoff," said the computer,
"to determine the champion team of the American
League, which would go on to face the National
League's San Diego Padres in the World Series. The
contest was decided in the seventh inning when Sunset center fielder Rob Clemmons hit a home run
with the bases empty. The final score was four to
three."

It took a moment for the information to sink in. "The
Icebreakers lost?" asked Data.

"That is correct."

He digested that. Terwilliger had failed—again. "Interesting," he said out loud.

But it was more than interesting. It was disconcerting,
somehow.

Data had just assumed the Fairbanks team had won.
After all, it was Commander Riker's program, and he
had placed himself in the role of an Icebreaker. It stood
to reason that he would have preferred to experience a
positive result.

"Do you require additional information?" asked the
computer.

"Yes," said the android, straightening in his seat.
"Describe the role played in the game by Bobo
Bogdonovich."

"Miroslav 'Bobo' Bogdonovich was a minor league
player called up to replace George Kilkenny, the Ice-

breakers' regular third baseman. Bogdonovich hit safely once in three official times at bat, with one run batted in. His fly ball to deep center field was the final out of the game."

Data experienced a pang of disappointment. The knowledge of the Icebreakers' loss—of Terwilliger's loss—bothered him even more.

But why? *He* wasn't Bobo Bogdonovich, any more than he was Sherlock Holmes or Henry IV or any of the other guises he had assumed in the holodecks. He bore no responsibility for Bogdonovich's performance on October 7, 2026.

The Icebreakers had played that game more than three hundred years ago. It was a matter of historical record.

Terwilliger and Denyabe and the clubhouse man were long gone. He had never become acquainted with any of them, only with their holographic replicas.

It seemed that the outcome of the contest was still in the future, still to be determined, but that was an illusion, of course. Only the outcome of the *program* might be malleable, depending on how Riker had structured it; the reality certainly was not.

And yet Data still felt troubled, as if he had left something incomplete.

Some*thing*—or some*one*?

Did that make sense? The android wasn't entirely sure. But he knew one thing: he was obliged to finish the program. And to try to succeed, if he could, where the historical Bogdonovich had fallen short.

One last question occurred to him, and he posed it to the computer. The answer was appallingly concise.

"Professional baseball finally succumbed to mounting losses in the year 2059. At that point only eight franchises remained of the thirty-two that had populated the American and National Leagues at the peak of their prosperity.

"In the twenty-second century, entrepreneurs attempted to resurrect the sport with a ten-team intraplanetary league. However, their enterprise folded after less than two seasons."

"Thank you," said Data, though a part of him was sorry he'd asked.

Chapter Six

THE FIRE FELT GOOD. Riker nudged his chair a little closer to it.

Lyneea stood on the other side of the room, disdaining the warmth of the hearth. After all, as she had reminded him, it wasn't even the coldest part of the winter yet.

For the last half-hour or so they had been examining their options. There were precious few.

No one at the tavern would talk to them now—that was for sure. The Pandrilite was in the custody of the Besidian authorities, but he'd probably told them all he knew. Likewise for Bosch.

"We could tail him," suggested Riker. "Maybe we were wrong. Maybe he was lying."

Lyneea shook her head. Brittle light slanted in through the window behind her; as she moved, it played along the soft lines of her hair and shoulders. "I don't think so. And even if he *was,* he's too smart to lead us anywhere. If he's got something to hide, he'll expect to be followed."

"So where does that leave us?"

"Nowhere we want to be."

"I don't suppose you've got any other leads?" asked Riker.

There was a knock on the door.

Lyneea frowned, half at the interruption, half at his implication that she was somehow remiss in doing her job. "Come in," she said.

The door opened.

Riker wasn't sure what he'd expected to see. A chambermaid, perhaps, or someone else from the hotel staff.

He had not expected the figure that stood hunched in the doorway, wrapped in long brown robes complete with a veil of the same color. It was an ascetic—one of the beggars who flooded Besidia at carnival time preaching an end to materialism and the ways of the madraggi.

Ironically, it was the madraggi who maintained places for the ascetics to sleep and eat for the duration of the carnival. And that was more than a gesture of tolerance; it was a nod to tradition. The ascetics had been protesting the principles of the madraggi for so long that the carnival wouldn't have been the same without them.

But they normally carried on their begging in the street, not door-to-door. Riker approached the robed figure, delved into his pocket for a chit, and held it out.

The robed one held up a slender hand. "No." Her voice was muffled, but the eyes that peered over the veil looked into his with an unflinching audacity.

Strange, he told himself. Ascetics never looked directly at offworlders.

"I need only to talk. To you, William Riker."

That caught him off guard. "To me?" he repeated.

"Yes," said the robed one.

By then Lyneea had joined him at the threshold. "Excuse me, sister," she said. "Who are you? And how do you know this human's name?"

The ascetic averted her eyes. "I speak only to Riker," she insisted. "No one else."

Lyneea looked at him. He shrugged. "I'm just popular, I guess."

His partner stifled a curse. "Popular indeed."

"Perhaps I should go," said the robed one.

"No," said Lyneea. Her voice took on a softer tone: "Stay, sister. I'll go. At least, for a little while."

Riker didn't protest. Whatever this ascetic had to say, he wanted to hear it. If she knew his name, there was a good chance she knew about his mission as well. If so, he had to know where the security leak was before the whole business became common knowledge.

Lyneea, of course, had the same concerns. And if that meant swallowing her pride a little, it was a small price to pay.

But she wouldn't stray too far from the room. Will was certain of that. This robed one had already proved herself to be more than she seemed. Who knew what other surprises she might have up her sleeve?

"I'll be back in half an hour," said Lyneea, slipping on her cloak. She addressed the ascetic: "Time enough?"

The robed one nodded. She stood back as Lyneea made her exit, slipping Riker one last warning glance.

As his partner strode down the hallway, bound for the lift, Riker turned to the ascetic. "Come in," he said.

She nodded, made her way into the room. He closed the door behind her.

"Can I get you anything?" he asked. "Something to eat? To drink?"

"No," she said. "Thank you."

She sat on the couch. Riker took the chair he'd been sitting on and pulled it away from the fire. Straddling it, he leaned on the backrest.

"You said you needed to talk," he opened. "I'm listening."

For a small space in time there was only the crackling of the logs in the fire. Her eyes seemed to hold him. Then to see right through him. Finally she spoke again.

"You've grown a beard," said the robed one.

Her voice was still muffled by the thick brown veil. But something about it was familiar. *Very* familiar.

"And you," he told his guest, "have taken to wearing an ascetic's robes." He felt a grin coming on. "What's the matter? Have the colors of Madraga Criathis become tedious for its second official?"

She removed the veil and pulled back her brown cowl, revealing the perfect features of an Impriman aristocrat.

"Norayan," he said, rising and putting his chair aside.

"Will." She rose, too, took the hands he extended in greeting. The warmth of her smile was genuine and only too welcome after the events of the last couple of days.

"It's good to see you," he told her.

"Yes. Too bad the circumstances couldn't have been happier." She sighed, let go of his hands, and sat again. "Then I might not have had to come to you in disguise."

He placed himself beside her on the couch. "Why *did* you come? To see what kind of progress we've made? And why couldn't you talk to your own retainer?"

She bowed her head. "I came to tell you something—something that will help your investigation."

"You've heard something," he concluded. "About Teller? Or the seal?"

"No," she said. "You don't understand. I've . . . I've come to make a confession, Will."

Riker looked into her eyes. How could he not have recognized her, even with that veil? No one had eyes like Norayan's. So wise. So regal.

"What the devil are you talking about?" he asked.

Her composure seemed to falter a little. In the average Impriman, that wouldn't have meant anything. In a madraga official, it was the equivalent of going to pieces. But a moment later she caught herself and straightened.

"This isn't easy for me to talk about," she said, underscoring the obvious. "You and Teller and I were wonderful friends—do you remember?"

He nodded. "I still have fond memories. Lots of them."

"As I do. It was a special time. I had not yet been

named second official of Criathis. I was still free to pursue adventures I cannot pursue now. And I had two gallant Earthmen with whom to pursue them."

"Yes," said Riker. "We were quite a threesome." Where was she going with this?

"Then you left," said Norayan. "And it was just Teller and myself. And the nature of the adventures changed." She paused. "We fell in love, Will."

He hadn't been prepared for that. Or had he? Had he seen it in her eyes even before she said the words?

And how did he feel about Norayan and Teller being lovers? A little jealous? Hell, it had always been the three of them. How could they have fallen in love without him?

"Really," he said.

"I've shocked you," observed Norayan.

"No," he told her. "It's all right. Go on."

She frowned. "Of course we had to keep our love a secret. I was next in line for a position on Criathis's council, and you know the rules. A council member must be chaste, lest he or she succumb to undue influences that might in turn affect the fate of the madraga."

"Sexual blackmail," Riker interpreted.

"Exactly. If my relationship with Teller had been made public, it would have cost me the opportunity to serve Criathis. And that is what I had been trained for all my life."

"It must have been difficult."

"It was. Every time we met, we risked everything—his future as well as mine. For what would the Federation have thought of a trade liaison who offended one of Imprima's more powerful madraggi by bringing scandal to its doorstep?" A moment of remembering. "But in time Teller made it much less difficult: he made it impossible for us to go on."

Riker looked at her. "How so?" he asked, though he had an inkling of what the answer might be. After all, the evidence had been piling up.

"He began smuggling," said Norayan.

There—the final nail in the coffin.

"You see, Will, he started to change after you left—perhaps even *before* you left, though neither of us saw it. We Imprimans . . . we have a great love of wealth. By the standards of some races, I know, it would be called an obsession. But we have learned to live with it, to place limitations on it, so that our basic social fabric remains intact.

"Teller was exposed to our culture all at once. It was too much for him. He was surrounded constantly by riches and by individuals whose daily pleasure was to acquire more wealth. He finally became more Impriman than any of us, and he got into the game in the only way he could."

"By taking advantage of his position as trade liaison—to spirit out historical artifacts to collectors all over the sector. On Federation ships, no doubt."

And who was he holding accountable for that? He could hear Picard's words as clearly as if he were still sitting in his ready room: "You feel guilty for having allowed your close friend to go astray. You feel as though you should have done something to prevent it."

Riker had seen Teller's pronounced affinity for things Impriman, but he hadn't seen where it might lead. *Should* he have? Could he have stopped his friend from destroying himself and his career?

Or was the captain right? *I am not my brother's keeper.*

"You sound bitter," said Norayan.

He shrugged. "Maybe I am. It seems to me that I could have prevented this. I don't know . . . somehow."

"I was here," she reminded him. "And I couldn't stop it. By the time I found out, it was too late for me to change him. Teller was in too deep. The day came when I realized I could no longer trust him. He still loved me, but he had found a greater love."

"I understand," said Riker. She had been right to call

this a confession; he offered her whatever absolution he could. "The risk had become too great."

"And the stakes too high. It was no longer just a question of fidelity to Criathis or to the Federation. Now there were crimes against the Impriman world government, crimes I knew about and, by rights, should have reported to the authorities. Association with Teller's activities could have brought sanctions against my madraga—crippling sanctions—from the other madraggi. So . . . I ended our affair. Just like that, I'm afraid."

"How did he take it?"

"He was stunned," said Norayan. "He claimed he had done it all for me, that he only wanted to become my peer in wealth and power, to put us on an equal footing. But I knew better. He said that if I'd leave things as they were, he'd stop smuggling then and there, but it was plain that he wouldn't. That he couldn't. I told him to leave this world, to remove himself from temptation, to find another post somewhere else. Or to rejoin Starfleet, as you had done.

"He promised me that he would do this. It gave him hope, he said, that perhaps he could return to Imprima someday, reformed, and on the morning my tenure as administrator was over, claim me for his bride." She drew a long breath, exhaled it softly. There was only the slightest hint of a ragged edge to it, but Riker noticed. "I couldn't destroy his hopes entirely. I said that was a possibility."

"When was this?" he asked.

"A few months ago, just before I was named to the council of Criathis. But that wasn't the last time I saw him. About a week after my ascension, he came to see me at my father's estate here in Besidia—openly, as one would visit a friend. But at his first opportunity Teller took me aside and told me he couldn't abide by his decision. He wanted things to be the way they were before. I stood firm, for his sake and mine, and for the sake of the Federation and Criathis as well. When he left, he was terribly disappointed.

"I didn't know what to do, Will. I didn't know what Teller would do in his desperation. Every day that passed was an agony of uncertainty, but I could not turn him in, not while there was a chance he would eventually come to his senses.

"Then he disappeared—and Fortune's Light along with him." She regarded Riker. "You know the rest."

"Do you believe that Teller took the seal?" he asked Norayan.

She frowned. "Yes, I do. He had easy access to it. After all, he was trusted by everyone in Criathis, not only because he was a delegate of an honorable entity like the Federation but also because of his long-standing friendship with me."

Riker grunted. "His big haul?" He'd said it out loud, but the question was really directed to himself.

Thinking a response was required, Norayan nodded.

"But once he had it," he asked, "what could he have planned to do with it? During the carnival there would be no opportunity for agents to contact prospective buyers, not with the high-tech ban limiting offworld communications. And afterward, with the merger destroyed and the disappearance of Fortune's Light made public, no sane outside dealer would touch it. There would be too much scrutiny—from the authorities as well as from Criathis's retainers—to make even the grandest commission seem tempting."

"You're right," said Norayan. "That's why I believe Teller chose to find a buyer on his own. Not among offworld collectors but among the madraggi themselves."

"The madraggi?" echoed Riker.

"Just one, really. Madraga Rhurig."

It was starting to make sense. Rhurig, a powerful rival of Criathis, had never taken kindly to the trade agreement with the Federation, possibly because the Federation wasn't interested in any of the resources Rhurig controlled.

"By making a shambles of the merger," Norayan explained, "Rhurig stood to prevent its two most influential political adversaries—Criathis and Terrin—from joining forces. What's more, after they had arranged safe passage for Teller off Imprima, and after his involvement in the theft became known, Rhurig would have been rid of the Federation as well."

"A neat package," said the human.

And his friend was even more of a traitor than he'd thought—that is, if Norayan's speculations jibed with reality.

"And of course," she continued, "Teller would reap the additional benefit of seeing me suffer. He would make me regret my rejection of him."

That didn't sound like the Teller Conlon that Riker knew. He said so.

"Does *any* of this sound like Teller?" asked Norayan. "I tell you, he has changed." She looked at Riker. "We must find him."

"We've been trying," he told her. "Though it seems we've hit a dead end. My partner had one lead, and it didn't pan out."

"I think I know where he might be hiding," Norayan said. "In the Maze of Zondrolla."

"The maze?" Riker asked. "What would he be doing there?"

"Well . . ." Norayan began. Was that a faint blush in her cheeks? "It was the place where Teller and I used to . . . to meet."

"Of course," said Riker, sparing her the indignity of further explanation. He didn't have to be bludgeoned with a blaster butt to figure out why they met there.

"My story," she said, "was that I liked to go there to

contemplate the affairs of my madraga. To seek wisdom from the ancient stones."

He nodded. If Teller knew the maze, he might have chosen it as his hiding place, or at least hidden the seal there. "Say no more. We'll search the maze."

She put her hand on his. "But you mustn't tell anyone how you came to look there. Not even Lyneea. If it becomes known that it was I who pointed you to the maze, people will start to ask questions. How did I know Teller would be there? How often did I visit Zondrolla to meditate? And I will be ousted from my office as surely as if I'd been discovered in Teller's arms."

He smiled as reassuringly as he could. "Put your mind at ease," he told her.

"Thank you, Will." She got up, put the veil in place, and drew the cowl back over her head. "I will see you again. Sooner rather than later, I hope."

He escorted her to the door. "That depends on what I find in the maze, I guess."

She looked at him. "Yes. Of course." Then she departed.

Riker watched her go. Then he went back inside, shut the door, and sat down on the couch. He stared into the tiny molten caverns created by the burning logs.

The memories started to come again—one in particular. It ate away at him as the fire ate at the logs.

Nor did he do anything to distract himself, to stop it. If it hurt to remember, maybe that was just the price he had to pay. . . .

"Teller?"

"Um? Oh—Will. About time you showed up."

"They wouldn't let me in until the surgery was over. Can you imagine that?"

"Hard to figure out these medical types."

Teller didn't look as bad as Riker had expected. Then

again, the lighting here in sickbay was designed to make people look a little better than they felt—at least, that had always been his personal theory.

"How do you feel?"

"Not bad, considering. I guess the ceiling caved in, huh?"

"The whole damned *power station* caved in. If you hadn't found me by that time, Ito would have been forced to beam you up alone. And I would have been a historical footnote—the only casualty in the Gamma Tobin colony earthquake."

Teller grunted. "You could have been famous."

"I'm not complaining, though I wish that last tremor hadn't come when it did. Then I wouldn't have fallen, and I wouldn't have lost consciousness—or my communicator."

Another grunt. "I would have preferred that, too. What made you climb that catwalk in the first place?"

Riker smiled sheepishly. "A cat—what else? He must have scampered up there when the quakes started getting bad, and he wasn't about to come down on his own." *A pause.* "It was stupid, I know. But my mother always had a soft spot for cats, and . . . hell. Anyway, we found him later on—reunited him with his owners and all that."

"Terrific," *said his friend.* "I love happy endings."

"Teller . . . I heard you volunteered to go in and get me."

"Somebody had to. Why waste real officer material?"

"Somebody *didn't* have to. The captain wanted to conduct a sensor search. He said it was too dangerous for anyone to beam down. The understructure was too delicately balanced."

"All the more reason to go. The sensors would never have found you in time."

"You know that now, but you didn't know it then. By rights, you should've stayed put."

Teller chuckled, his blue eyes dancing. He brushed back

some of that unruly reddish blond hair. "Lucky for you I was stupid and irrational, huh?"

"Yes. Lucky for me."

"Say, Will . . . while you're here, why don't you make yourself useful? Hand me that glass of water, will you?"

"Sure. Here."

"Thanks. I owe you one."

"I think it's the other way around."

"Uh-oh. I had a feeling this was coming."

"You saved my life, not only by finding me but by covering me when the place started coming apart. I can't just let that slide."

"If I'd known you were going to get all teary-eyed on me, I'd have left you there."

"Bull." *A hard swallow.* "I appreciate what you did, Teller."

His friend looked at him. "You'd have done the same thing for me, right?"

"Sure. But that's different—you owe me half a month's salary after the last card game."

Teller smiled. "Right."

"Not to mention the card game before that."

"You're a real bloodsucker, Riker. No wonder they made you a lieutenant."

"Um . . ."

"What?"

"Don't look now, but I'm not the only lieutenant around here."

"You're kidding."

"I wish I were. But the captain insisted. Something about bravery and a job well done. I forget the exact words."

"You sure you're not kidding?"

"I never kid a kidder, Teller. It's bad form."

"Boy, Will." *Teller whistled softly.* "Can you imagine if you were somebody *important*? They'd probably have made me an admiral."

* * *

Riker sighed. Teller had saved his bacon without even a thought for his own life. If he hadn't taken the brunt of that ceiling collapse, at least until their transporter chief could beam them up . . .

He had to return the favor. No matter what his friend had done, Will had to get him out of this mess. Put him on his feet again.

Certainly he owed him that much.

Suddenly the door opened. Before Riker had a chance to react, he saw Lyneea slip inside and close the door behind her.

"So?" she asked.

"So what?" he responded.

"What was so important that only you could hear it?"

"I think I've got a lead."

"Oh?" She took a seat on the couch. "Tell me more."

"There we were," said Geordi. "One mangled shuttle and three apple green rookies, lucky to be alive. The damned photon storm made communications impossible, so our ship had no idea which Beta Bilatus satellite we were on—and Beta Bilatus happened to have twenty-two legitimate planets, not to mention a whole mess of oversize moons. Our food dispenser was squashed in the crash, we had one working phaser among us, and the local fauna had decided we looked tastier than lemon meringue pie."

"Sounds rough," observed Guinan, seeming to absorb the story with every pore in her body. *Nobody* listened the way she did. "What did you do?"

"Glad you asked," said the chief engineer, plunking his glass down on the bar. "The first thing I did was calm my buddies down. The two of them were as fidgety as guinea pigs at a python convention. Then I phasered us out a hole underneath the shuttle. The wildlife couldn't move the twisted hulk to get at us, and it was easy enough to defend a little hole from unwanted intrusions."

"What did you do about food?" asked Guinan.

Geordi shivered a little, remembering. "Sometimes you eat the lemon meringue pie," he said, "and sometimes the lemon meringue pie eats you."

Surprisingly Guinan didn't seem put off by the idea. She just smiled that knowing smile of hers.

"Fortunately," said Geordi, "we weren't there long enough to get bored with the menu. As it turned out, our planet was the third one on the search agenda. Our phaser was still three-quarters charged when the cavalry arrived."

"I see," said Guinan. She paused. "You know, it's funny."

Geordi looked at her. "What is?"

"This story of yours. I could swear I've heard it somewhere before." She gave it some thought, then nodded. "I have. On Starbase Eighty, while I was waiting to be picked up by the *Enterprise.*" Her brow wrinkled ever so slightly. "If I'm not mistaken, it was told to me by someone named Stutzman. Jake Stutzman, I think it was."

Geordi felt an unwelcome heat creep into his face. "Oh?"

"Yes. You don't know him, by any chance, do you?"

Geordi was starting to feel like a kid caught with his hand in the cookie jar. "Actually," he said, "he was one of the other two rookies."

Guinan made a sound of mild surprise. "Small galaxy," she remarked. "But you know, the *really* funny thing is that this Stutzman fellow told the story differently, as if it was *he* who'd had to calm down his companions." She shook her head. "And now that I think about it, he also took credit for making that hole." A sigh. "Can you imagine? I guess some people just let their egos run away with them."

"Right," said Geordi. The jig was up. He could see it in her eyes. "Uh, Guinan . . . ?"

"Mm?"

"Maybe I mixed up a few of the facts."

She regarded him. "You? Of all people?"

"You're laughing at me," he said.

"I never laugh *at* people," she corrected. "Only *with* them."

"It's all right," he said. "I suppose I deserve it." He leaned closer. "But do me a favor, will you? Don't let it out that I . . . um, embellished the story a little." With a tilt of his head, he indicated the young medical officer to whom he'd related his tale the night before. "I kind of impressed her, I think—and with the shape my love life's in, I need all the help I can get."

Guinan clucked softly. "Geordi, Geordi, Geordi. All you need to do is be yourself. When will you learn that?"

He grunted. "When *myself* starts seeing some romance. So—will you keep this in confidence? Or do I have to admit to that nice young lady that I'm not the hero of Beta Bilatus Seven?"

"I'm your bartender," said Guinan. "Whatever you tell me is strictly confidential." However, something about her expression told him she wasn't going to let the subject drop.

Guilt, he mused. *Just what I needed.* "Fine," he said flatly. "I'll tell her the truth. But *you're* the one who's going to have to listen to me after I ask her out and she laughs in my face."

"If it comes to that," said Guinan, "I'll be here."

Geordi was so wrapped up in his own life's drama that he hardly noticed Wesley's approach. It was almost as if the boy had materialized at his side—a stunt he wouldn't quite put past Transporter Chief O'Brien.

"Hi," said Wesley, acknowledging both Geordi and Guinan. He claimed an empty stool, but not with his usual alacrity.

"Hi, yourself," said the Mistress of Libations—a

sobriquet Will Riker had bestowed on her in one of his more jocular moments.

"Looks like you've got something on your mind," remarked Geordi.

"Actually," said Wesley, "I do. I've been researching Imprima. You know—to see if I can figure out what Commander Riker's up to."

"And?" prompted Geordi. He'd been a little curious about the first officer's mission himself, though he'd known better than to press Captain Picard for details.

Wes filled them in as best he could. And, no surprise to Geordi, he'd done a pretty thorough job of researching the matter.

"Interesting," observed the chief engineer.

"That's what Data said."

"Data?" echoed Geordi.

"So much for Priority One secrecy," said Guinan.

Wesley shook his head ruefully. "No need for concern. The mission's still a secret." He sighed. "I still can't figure out what Commander Riker's doing down there. I mean, I was doing pretty good until I spoke with Data, but since then I haven't made any headway at all."

"Is that the reason for the long face?" Guinan asked.

The boy looked at her. "Not exactly." He paused, then turned to Geordi again. "I guess I'm a little worried."

"Worried?" said the chief engineer. "About Commander Riker?" He dismissed the notion with a wave of his hand. "Listen, Wes, if there's one thing I've learned since shipping out on the *Enterprise,* it's that Will Riker can take care of himself."

Wesley frowned. "Normally, I'd agree with you. But studying their history . . . under that veneer of civilization, the Imprimans can be a pretty tough bunch. Especially during carnival time."

Guinan leaned forward across the bar. *Her* bar, Geordi couldn't help but think. "Is there something in particular that's got you worried, Wes?"

The boy's expression suggested he was reciting from something he'd memorized. "During the carnival," he said, "the influx of foreign elements into normally placid Besidia drives the mortality rate up more than two hundred percent. Street violence—including certain forms of dueling permitted by law—is the most common cause of death."

"Statistics," said Geordi. "Never yet met one I liked."

Wesley looked at him and shrugged. "I don't know. Maybe I am taking it too seriously. It's just that I've got this feeling . . ."

Geordi clasped his shoulder and gave it a reassuring shake. "Take it from me, Ensign. Whatever's going on down there, it's nothing Commander Riker can't handle."

Wesley regarded him and nodded. "You're probably right," he conceded.

"I'm *definitely* right," said the chief engineer. "Trust me on this one."

Chapter Seven

RIKER HAD HEARD ABOUT the Maze of Zondrolla on his first visit to Imprima—as in "You really should see the maze while you're here. Just make sure to go in with a guide; otherwise, we may never see you again."

The maze had been built on the heights overlooking Besidia by the first official of Madraga Porfathas, to please a wife some twenty years his junior. The young woman, whose name was Zondrolla, was inordinately fond of puzzles—especially children's puzzles—and it was her husband's greatest delight to present her with one she had never seen before. Toward this end, he sent his retainers ranging across the face of Imprima, searching every last pawnshop and gallery, every warehouse and museum.

As time passed, of course, it became harder and harder to find a gimcrack or doodad that would make Zondrolla's eyes light up. After all, how many puzzles could there *be* in the world? So the first official got smart—or so he thought. He stopped looking and started building. And by the time the dust cleared, he had built Zondrolla a prodigious maze—a puzzle she could actually set foot in herself, and one it would take her a lifetime to tire of.

Zondrolla, the story goes, was delighted. As a result, so was her husband—until the bills for the maze started coming in. Not too much later, Porfathas—hardly one of the more stable madraggi to begin with—went belly up bankrupt, and its holdings were eagerly divided among its rivals.

Worse—for the first official—Zondrolla wasn't cut out for poverty. When the madraga lost its wealth, she ran away with one of the builders who'd grown wealthy constructing the maze.

The structure itself was allowed to stand, as a reminder of what might happen when one put one's personal interests before those of the madraga. Some four hundred years later, it remained a monument to their foolishness.

And the warnings about getting lost in it? Actually, Riker had found them a bit exaggerated. The walls were marked at intervals with indelible color coding so that one could find one's way in and out. Patterns in red and yellow took one closer to the heart of the maze; green and purple guided one to an exit. Quite a dependable system, once one got used to it.

The lower level was a little trickier. One needed a portable light source to see the colors on the walls. What was more, the corridors—tunnels, really—were narrower and more confusing than those above. The air was cold and dank, and there seemed to be too little of it, and every now and then something not entirely wholesome skittered by. So if one was prone to fits of nervousness, one was better off staying on the upper level and not venturing below ground at all.

In any case, the worst parts of both levels were inaccessible—blocked off by stone-support collapses during an earthquake a century or so ago. When Riker's acquaintances suggested he visit the maze, those weren't the sections they'd had in mind.

"Damn," said Lyneea, her eyes hard and glittery in the bright sunlight. "This place is even bigger than I remembered."

They stood before the maze's south entrance—or exit, depending on how one looked at it—the closest one to the slope they'd ascended to get here.

Actually, there were two entrances in front of them, as there would have been wherever they tried to get in. That was just the way the maze had been designed.

"Are you sure about this, Riker?" Lyneea's breath froze and billowed on the air. "Are you *certain* you want to spend the time required to search this thing—on the word of some nameless, faceless ascetic?"

He nodded. "I'm sure."

Lyneea didn't think much of the idea of searching the maze. If she'd had another lead, even a tenuous one, she would have refused to trudge up here. Riker was certain of that.

But of course, she *didn't* have another lead, so she came along, grumbling at each and every opportunity. Apparently she saw this moment as her last chance to make her feelings known, and she wasn't about to pass it up.

"You're not going to listen to reason, are you?"

"Nope."

Lyneea sighed. She considered the dual-entrance set-up. "All right. Which one?"

"This one," said Riker. He indicated the one on the right.

They entered. Immediately the temperature seemed to drop ten degrees. With the gray walls of the maze rising five to six meters from the ground, the sun's rays couldn't quite reach them, and Riker shivered. He could feel his mustache crusting up with ice.

And this was only the upper level.

He looked around. Ahead, on the right, he spotted a dash of color. Approaching it, he saw how little of the horizontal bar was purple and how much of it was green. It was just as it should have been—exactly the kind of symbol he'd expected to see near an entrance.

It was reassuring to know his memory was working so well. Wrapping his cloak more tightly about him, Riker followed the curve of the stone passageway.

There wasn't room for them to walk side by side, but Lyneea was only a step or two behind him. He noted that she'd stopped grumbling, at least.

It was unlikely that Teller Conlon would have hidden the seal—or himself, for that matter—in one of the unobstructed passages. Hardly anyone ever visited the maze during carnival time, but why would he take a chance of being found by a casual stroller, especially when the collapsed sections offered so much more in the way of seclusion?

So they concentrated their efforts on the areas ruined by the earthquake. They scraped and clawed their way past fallen rocks and rubble, lowered themselves into wells of darkness with only their beamlights for illumination, dug like moles into hard ground that looked as if it might have been disturbed with a shovel or something similar.

And came up empty.

It was frustrating as hell, and Lyneea finally said so. "This is ridiculous, Riker. We would need every retainer in Madraga Criathis to comb this place effectively."

Her words echoed slightly. Or was that some crawling thing making its exit, disturbed by the sound?

He thought about Norayan and shook his head. "We've got to keep this under wraps." The sunlight was receding steadily up the stones. Outside, it had to be approaching sunset. "Look, let's get as far as we can. If we don't find anything, we can come back tomorrow and search again."

"*You* come back," said Lyneea. "I've had it with this burrowing. Somewhere in Besidia, there's a real lead, and we're not getting any closer to it by playing with rocks."

Riker felt a gobbet of anger rise into his throat. "All right," he said, surprising himself with the calm in his voice. "I'll pursue this by myself." And he walked on ahead.

"You've been duped," called his partner, standing her ground. "*We've* been duped. The robed one deceived us, Riker—can't you see that? She sent us up here to throw us off. Who knows? Maybe Conlon hired her."

He kept walking. The passage turned abruptly to the left, and he followed it. Lyneea's voice followed him.

"Damn it, Riker! What makes you so sure that beggar knew anything? Just tell me that, will you?"

He couldn't—he'd already said so. Up ahead there was some debris. Evidence of another collapse—a small one?

The sound of Lyneea's boots scraping on the floor. "Don't walk away while I'm talking to you, Riker. Who in the name of ten thousand credits do you think you are?"

Arriving at the brink of the cave-in, he knelt and peered into the blackness, then took out his beamlight and activated it.

"I thought we were partners," rasped Lyneea. She was coming up behind him—and fast. "That implies some kind of trust, don't you think? Some duty to let the other partner know what in blazes is going on?"

The beam sliced open the hole's black belly. At first glance, there was nothing—the same nothing they'd found in all the other holes they'd slithered through. He moved the light around.

"Chits and whispers, Riker. At least have the decency to *look* at me. I mean, I—"

He must have gasped then. Or shouted. That's what he told himself later. At the time, however, he wasn't aware of having done either. The blood was pounding too hard in his ears, like a heavy surf thundering on a rocky beach.

Ice blue eyes, staring unflinchingly at the light. High cheekbones, a cleft chin. The reddish blond hair that had become its owner's trademark.

Teller. No . . .

He played the beam over his friend's features again and again. Hoping that what he saw was only an illusion, a trick of the way the rocks had come to rest on one another, and if he looked at them long enough, he'd find a way out of the nightmare. . . .

Finally it was Lyneea's voice, coming from over his shoulder, that made the reality of it congeal and hold fast: "Damn it, Riker, it's him."

Even then his impulse was to deny it—if not Teller's presence here, then the fact that he was dead. Clamping the beamlight between his teeth, he began to descend into the pit.

"Careful, Riker. *Careful,* I said. Blazes, there's no need to hurry like that. He's beyond your help."

But Riker wasn't buying it. He lowered himself by hanging on to a flat rock that had fallen across the opening until he was suspended directly above a short slope of gravel and detritus. Then he dropped, landed on all fours, and slid and crab-walked his way down to the bottom to where Teller lay—open-mouthed as if in surprise, eyes like jewels in the flickering, unsteady light. Unsteady, Riker realized, because he was trembling, and the beamlight was trembling along with him.

Teller was pale, terribly pale. There should have been at least a wisp of breath twisting up from between his lips; there wasn't. Riker took off a glove and felt his friend's neck: there was no pulse.

Somewhere in the back of his mind, where he could still think clearly, where the thing he confronted had not spread its pollution, Riker heard the stones grind on the debris-covered escarpment. Lyneea had followed him into the pit.

"Are you all right?" she asked him.

"Fine," he told her. The word came out of him, anyway. He wasn't sure how or from where, but it came out.

He touched the pallid brow, cold as the stones. Shut the obscenely gawking eyes.

Teller, Teller, Teller.

He had to accept it now; the evidence was only inches from his face. He had to embrace the truth.

"Are you sure you're all right?"

He forced himself to turn around, to look at her. He saw her eyes screw up a little as she looked back.

"I'm sure," he said.

And he was. He could feel the horror leaching out of him into the clammy cold of the pit. He wiped the sweat from his face with the back of his bare hand.

Lyneea's expression changed, mirroring his recovery. "Yes, I guess you are."

Reluctantly he relinquished his friend to the darkness for a moment and beam-searched the rest of the hole. After all, their work wasn't finished. They had found Teller, but not the seal.

Never mind what you're feeling, he told himself. *You've got a job to do.*

Meanwhile, Lyneea crept past him. She knelt down next to the body to get a better look—to determine, as best she could, a cause of death. They needed clues; she would do whatever was necessary to find them.

The pit wasn't big, but it was the most confusing space he'd seen yet. There were lots of little niches where something the size of Fortune's Light could have been tucked away. Lots of places that might be the beginnings of tunnels leading, perhaps, to other pits—places that would have to be scoured out with light before they could be dismissed as dead ends.

It took a while before he could be certain that the seal wasn't there. By that time Lyneea had completed her search as well.

He looked at her. "Well?"

"A knife," she told him. "Once—in the heart. Clean and quick."

It was small consolation, but it was something. He clung to it.

"Unfortunately," Lyneea went on, "his pockets are empty. Not even so much as a chit." She shook her head. "Your luck was no better, I take it."

"No sign of the seal," he confirmed. "Either the killer took it out with him or it wasn't here in the first place."

"Probably the latter," she said. "My guess is that Conlon never saw this hole. He was probably murdered up above somewhere and then dumped here to conceal the fact."

Riker grunted. "But the murderer didn't just stumble on him here in the maze, recognize the seal, and decide to kill him for it."

Lyneea agreed. "The murderer had to know Conlon's whereabouts in advance. Odds are, they were partners in this, one way or the other."

"Maybe the bastard planned it this way from the start. To let Teller steal Fortune's Light and then to lift it from him afterward. Less risk that way."

"And no one to split the profits with," Lyneea concluded.

Riker no longer argued the question of his friend's guilt, not even within himself. Innocent people didn't get stabbed and left in places like this one.

"So we're back where we started," he said. "No—even farther back than that. Before, we at least knew whom we were looking for. Now it could be anyone."

His partner's face twisted in a scowl. "And the seal could be anywhere. Still in the maze—assuming it ever *was* in the maze—or wherever Conlon's killer decided to stash it." She glanced meaningfully at the opening above them. "Come on. Let's get out of here."

He looked at her. "What about Teller?"

Lyneea didn't look entirely unsympathetic. "We leave him here," she said, in a softer tone than the one she usually used. "It's not as if we have much of a choice. Even if we could get him out without attracting attention, where would we take him?" She got up, stretched. "And there's the killer to think about as well. If he comes back and the body's gone, he'll know there's someone on his trail—and he'll be twice as careful to hide his tracks."

It made sense. Riker had to admit that. And yet, the thought of leaving Teller here in this godforsaken hole. . . .

"Just give me a minute," he told Lyneea. "Alone—all right?"

She regarded him. "Sure." And with an effort, she scrambled up the little slope. Riker didn't see her leave; he just heard the scrape of her boots on some rocks as she kicked herself up through the opening.

He sighed, played the light on Teller's face again, and forced himself to study each feature individually, as if that might make the totality somehow more palatable. Memories came, lots of them—all maudlin, all the stuff of melodrama. He pushed them aside, did his best to dredge up clear thoughts.

Had he failed Teller Conlon? And if he had, did it really matter any longer?

What was the proper course of action now? What did a man *do* when a friend died, anyway? See this investigation through, as a sort of memorial to the man Teller used to be, as opposed to the man he'd become? See his killer brought to justice?

Of course. All of that.

Would it be enough? When it was over, would he feel that he had set Teller's soul to rest?

There was only one way to find out. Getting up, he took one last look at the dead man. Then, slipping his glove back on, he turned and started back up the escarpment.

He was peering at the rocks above him, trying to determine how Lyneea had hauled herself out, when he heard a sharp, distinct yelp.

Damn. He scampered up the rest of the slope, saw a rocky projection that might give him the access he needed, and used it to boost himself toward the exit. His fingers caught the cross piece; he swung a leg up, lodged his heel against the lip of the pit, then pulled and twisted his body up after it.

Riker was sprawled on the ground above the hole, one leg still dangling within, when he caught sight of Lyneea.

Contrary to his expectations, she didn't seem to be in any trouble. True, she was kneeling as if doubled over, but there was no sign of pain on her face. In fact, she looked as if she'd just remembered something funny.

"What's going on?" he asked, getting to his feet. "When I heard you yell, I thought the killer had come back."

Lyneea glanced at him. "No such luck." Picking something up off the ground, she held it out so he could see it.

It was an emblem of some sort, with torn cloth and threads around it, as if it had been removed by force from whatever garment it was meant to adorn.

"May I?" he asked, holding his hand out. She gave it to him.

A black field cut into two parts by a large yellow lightning bolt. In the upper right-hand corner, two yellow sheaves of grain. In the lower left, two yellow aircraft.

All along the bottom edge, something had made the

material stiff and maroon-colored. Riker recognized it as blood.

"The emblem of Madraga Rhurig," explained Lyneea. "Agriculture, hydroelectric power, air transport—the industries they control in various parts of Imprima." She paused. "The stuff on the bottom wasn't part of the original design."

"Rhurig," Will repeated, recalling Norayan's suspicions but unable to identify them as hers. He turned the emblem over in his hand. "You think they would stoop this low? Would they steal Fortune's Light or arrange to have it stolen?"

"I wouldn't put it past them. They've never seen eye to eye with Criathis."

"And the merger would only have made Criathis more powerful. So they moved to prevent it the only way they could."

"Yes," Lyneea said. "And then—who knows? Maybe it was their intention to kill Conlon from the start, so that he couldn't tell anyone what had happened to the seal. Or maybe he tried to hold them up for more money than was originally agreed upon. To blackmail them."

"Either way," said Riker, "they killed him." He could feel the excitement of discovery giving way to the heat of anger. "And whoever belongs to this patch must have been in on the deed—and lost it in the course of a struggle."

His partner nodded. "This is *big*, Riker. It's no longer a matter of an individual, or even two. We're talking about a madraga that has helped shape Impriman history for nearly eight hundred years. If Rhurig is involved with this, and it can be proven . . ."

"Then Rhurig will be ruined," he said. "Shunned by the other madraggi until it collapses of its own weight."

"Or worse." She shook her head. "It's hard to say what would be done. Nothing like this has ever happened before. But I can tell you this—the economic repercussions would be massive. Global."

For the first time since they'd known each other, Riker thought Lyneea seemed uncertain, almost overwhelmed.

"This is big," she repeated. *"Very* big."

He looked at her. "You're not suggesting that we shouldn't pursue it, are you? Just because of the implications?"

"No," she said. "Of course not. It's just that we can't keep it to ourselves any longer. We've got to contact Criathis—tell the first official what we know. Let him decide what we should do next."

"We can't," said Riker. *Not if we're to keep Norayan's secret, as I promised.*

"We *can't?"*

"No."

Lyneea's brow wrinkled. "Why not?"

"Trust me," he told her. "We just can't."

Her eyes narrowed. "There you go again, Riker. Keeping things from your partner." A little muscle in her jaw began to twitch. "If you've really got a good reason to keep this kind of information from the first official of Madraga Criathis—the man to whom I've sworn my loyalty—then I want to hear it." She pointed a gloved finger at him. "But I'm telling you in advance—I don't think there's a reason in the world that's even *halfway* good enough to make me do that."

Riker started to object and then realized it was no use. There was only one thing he could say at this juncture that would keep Lyneea from going to her superior.

The truth.

Forgive me, Norayan.

He didn't hold anything back. He related the whole story, just as Norayan had related it to him. And by the time he was done, Lyneea's expression had lost some of its hardness.

"Well," she said at last, "that does put a different face

on matters. Norayan is a great asset to Criathis. Mind you, I don't approve of what she did. But her exposure could only hurt the madraga."

Riker breathed a sigh of relief. "Then you'll keep Norayan's secret?"

Lyneea frowned. "Yes."

"Good," he said. "I'd hoped you'd see it that way."

"But if we are to handle this ourselves, Riker, we must be careful. *Very* careful. We can't afford to let Rhurig know of our investigation, or we could find ourselves sharing a pit with your friend."

"I agree," he said, shutting out her image. He held out the emblem. "Is there something we can do with this?"

She thought for a moment. "Yes," she decided. "There is. Every madraga member's emblem is just a little different from any other—a vanity that seems to pervade Impriman society. You or I might be hard-pressed to tell whose tunic that came from, even if we had another of his tunics lying right beside it. But there is one man in Besidia who can identify it at a glance."

"And that is?" he asked.

"His tailor," she told him.

Chapter Eight

PLUNK.

There was something immensely soothing about repetition, Picard noted. *Automation has relieved us of the need for it, but perhaps that is not all good.* For at least the hundredth time in the last half hour, he lunged.

It was an easy, graceful motion—one he had been taught long ago at Salle Guillaume, on the Rive Gauche in Paris. In fact, his old fencing den had provided the inspiration for this dark, hardwood environment he'd created here in the holodeck.

He could almost hear the gibes of his fencing master: "Like a cat, not like your plodding old grandmother. Watch me now, Jean-Luc!"

First the point, as if it had a will of its own, an energy independent of the fencer himself. Then the arm, pulled by that headstrong point, and finally the rest of him, until his right leg had no choice but to fly out and catch his weight.

Head held high, left shoulder back. Trapezius muscles relaxed to permit maximum extension. Balance, always balance.

Of course, none of this really mattered unless the

ultimate goal was reached, the ultimate test met and passed. Everything depended on that hard black rubber ball hanging by its meter-long cord just a few feet in front of him.

Plunk.

If it swung straight back, he had succeeded. If it bounced or shot off in an oblique direction, he would know that his mechanics had been off, that perhaps he had not been as graceful as he'd thought.

It swung straight back.

For good measure, he held his lunge until the ball returned. Just as he would have in a match, in anticipation of a counterattack.

Plunk.

Once again he caught it on his point, but it didn't swing out nearly as far this time. Then, shifting his weight back onto his left leg, he withdrew and retreated to an *en garde* position to wait for the ball to become still again.

"Captain Picard?"

The voice sounded eerie here, out of place. It broke Picard's concentration; he frowned.

"Yes, Mr. Aquino?"

"It's Commander Riker. He'd like to speak with you."

Picard took off his mask. He planted his point on the deck, which he'd programmed to simulate the hard cork floor of Salle Guillaume.

"Put him through, Lieutenant."

"Aye, sir."

The ball's arcs were getting smaller and smaller, thanks to the ship's artificial gravity. His programming, he told himself once again, had been impeccable; the place even smelled right—like wood soap and well-earned perspiration.

"Captain?"

"Good to hear from you, Number One. How are things progressing down there?"

Riker's grunt was audible. "They could be progressing better."

"How so?"

"For one thing, we've found my friend."

That piqued the captain's interest. "Have you?"

"Yes. But if he's guilty of the theft, he has more than paid the price."

"More than . . . What are you saying, Number One? Not that he's *dead?*"

"That's exactly what I'm saying, sir."

Had they been face to face, Picard might have found a way to adequately express the sympathy he felt for his first officer. The grief he shared.

As it was, he had only words. "I'm sorry, Will. Damned sorry."

"So am I."

"How did it happen?"

Riker told him. It seemed that this affair was a good deal more complicated than anyone had expected. More complicated *and* more dangerous.

"So now," Picard extrapolated, "you're trying to identify the one whose emblem you found in the maze?"

"That's right. Lyneea has gone to the tailor Madraga Rhurig retains in Besidia. She's posing as a servant for Rhurig, hoping that she can get the tailor to mention the name of the emblem's owner."

"Very clever. And if she's successful?"

"We'll trail the party in question. See if he'll lead us to the seal—or at least give us some clue to its whereabouts."

"I see," said the captain. "You know, Number One, time is running out."

A pause. "No one knows that better than I do, sir." Was that a hint of resentment in Riker's tone?

"Of course not," said Picard. "Forgive me."

"I think I'd better go now," said his first officer. "But I'll contact you again next chance I get."

Silence.

Picard took a deep breath, exhaled. He knew what Riker was going through. After all, he'd lost his share of friends over the years. And in at least one case he'd felt responsible for the loss, though a court-martial had concluded that there was nothing he could have done to prevent it.

Suddenly he didn't feel like hitting the little black ball anymore. Or looking at Salle Guillaume.

At times like this he was more comfortable on the bridge, ensconced in the present rather than the past.

"Terminate program," he called out.

And in the wink of an eye his old fencing den vanished —in its place, the stark, gridlike pattern of a naked holodeck.

He had been testy with the captain—Riker knew that. A less understanding superior would have given him hell for it. What was the matter with him, letting his emotions get in the way of his job? They'd better not. Not now, when things were starting to heat up.

His thoughts were interrupted by the sound of footsteps in the hallway outside his room. Opening his tunic, he slipped the communicator back inside.

Not that using it to contact the ship was wrong. As he'd explained to Worf, Federation-issue communicators weren't specifically listed among the high-tech items prohibited during the carnival. Technically he should be allowed to use it.

It was a fine point, however, and one he didn't care to argue with Lyneea. At some point, a link with the *Enterprise* might come in handy.

A key rattled in the lock. The door opened and Lyneea came in. She looked at him.

She smiled.

"You've got a name," he said, rising to his feet.

"Indeed I have," she told him. "Kobar. Third official of Madraga Rhurig—the first official's son."

"Doesn't ring a bell."

"I'm surprised. He's a real firebrand. And he's got designs on Norayan, if half the stories are true. If he suspected that she was having an affair with the trade liaison, that would have given him an additional reason for wanting to see Conlon dead."

Riker nodded, not bothering to hide his admiration. "Good work," he told her.

"I don't do any other kind."

"The tailor didn't give you any trouble?"

"Far from it. He was so proud of being associated with a madraga like Rhurig, he would have recited Kobar's genealogy if I'd let him." She indicated the street outside with a jerk of her thumb. "Come on. Let's see if we can find this Rhurig whelp."

He got up. "I'm with you. Sitting in hotel rooms gives me too much time to think." In a couple of strides, Riker joined her in the corridor, then closed the door and made sure it was locked. "Where do we start? At Rhurig's estate in Besidia?"

Lyneea shook her head. "According to the tailor, Kobar prefers to stay in town during the carnival, with a friend or two."

"That makes it more difficult," Riker noted.

"Not necessarily. Our informant also told me that the third official is a collector. Ancient weapons. Knives, mostly."

Something hardened in the pit of Riker's stomach. "Knives," he echoed.

"Yes. And if I'm not mistaken, there's a rather well known antique-weapons merchant in the marketplace."

Data could have entered the holodeck back in the first inning and tried to hit a home run this time instead of a single or, at the very least, used his speed to beat the throw to second base.

But somehow, it wouldn't have seemed right. If he was going to thwart history, it would have to be on history's terms. And history proceeded one step at a time, in a linear fashion.

As a result, he came in exactly where he'd left off, joining his teammates as they stood in the field, defending against the Sunsets' second turn at bat. There were runners on first and second and no one out.

As the next batter stepped up to home plate, Data saw him glance in the direction of third base. Did that mean he would try to hit the ball to Bobo? It seemed a fair assumption.

Meanwhile, in the Icebreaker dugout across the field, Terwilliger was behaving strangely—touching the top of his head, his belt, his shoulder, elbow and wrist in a rapid, apparently random series of gestures. The android wondered if it was some sort of nervous condition brought on by the stress of the moment. After all, having put their first two batters on base, the Sunsets had an opportunity to tie the score and perhaps even go ahead.

Then Data saw Terwilliger ascend to the top of the dugout, stare at him, and repeat the gestures—this time more slowly and deliberately. The android had no idea what it meant, but he resolved to remain alert. If both the batter and his own manager were directing their attention to him, there was obviously a good chance that he would be involved in the next play.

Data crouched as he'd seen the other players crouch. He picked up some loose dirt and pounded it into his mitt, again in imitation of the others.

"Hey, Bobo!"

Data looked up and found the source of the greeting. It was Jackson, the rangy fellow at shortstop. He was calling to the android from behind his glove.

"You look a little confused," observed Jackson. "You know what's going on, man? You know the score?"

Data nodded. Was this one of the rituals of the game? "One to nothing," he called back.

The shortstop stared at him from beneath the bill of his cap. Then he laughed.

"Right, Bobo. One to nothing. Funny guy."

Then there was no more time for banter. The pitcher eyed the runners, breathed in and out, and went into his windup.

That was when the first baseman charged toward home plate, Denyabe took off for first, and Jackson shuffled toward third—all at the same time, as if by prearranged design.

Data realized he'd seen this maneuver before. And a moment later he remembered the circumstances. It was when Sakahara had laid down his bunt.

There was the sound of ball meeting bat—but gently. And as Data turned back toward home plate, he saw the ball dribbling slowly up the third base line—while all of the Sunset runners advanced.

Suddenly the android knew what he had to do. Making good use of his superhuman physique, he pounded toward the ball. Caught it in his bare right hand, whirled, and threw to first, just in time to beat the batter to the spot.

There was a roar of approval from the crowd. But not from Terwilliger, who came stalking out of the Icebreaker dugout with his head down—though not so far down that Data couldn't note his discontent and hear some of the phrases he was muttering.

Terwilliger headed straight for the pitcher's mound. So did the catcher. So did the first baseman and Denyabe and Jackson.

Data gathered that a conference of some sort was taking place. He decided to use the time to brush the dirt from his shoes.

"Hey, Bobo! Cretin!"

Terwilliger was yelling at the top of his lungs.

The android pointed to himself. "Are you calling me?" he asked.

The manager's eyes seemed on the verge of leaping from his head. He balled up his fists and took a swing at the empty air.

"Yes, goddammit!" he cried, taking a step toward Data, his complexion assuming that dark and dangerous cast again. "Yes, I'm calling you. You wanna join us or you got something better to do?"

The android thought for a second. "No," he said. "I have no other duties at the moment."

And he trotted to the center of the diamond, where the others awaited him.

Terwilliger watched him every step of the way. By degrees, he calmed down, and the darkness left his face.

Everyone huddled close together. Data huddled with them.

"All right," said the manager, "listen up. Thanks to twinkle-toes here at third base, we got ourselves one out." He glared at the android. "Though it seemed to me he could've taken off a little sooner, and then maybe we'd have gotten the lead runner instead of the guy at first." He cleared his throat. "In any case, I got a decision to make. Do we put the next guy on and set up the force or do we pitch to him?"

Data understood. This was a matter of strategy. He felt fortunate to have been made privy to such a deliberation.

Nor would he fail to make a contribution—not after Terwilliger had gone to the trouble of soliciting his opinion. He made some quick calculations.

"It is preferable to avoid intentional walks," he said.

Terwilliger glanced at him. "What?"

"Intentional walks have the desired effect only forty-eight-point-two percent of the time," expanded the android. "Situations are more often resolved successfully when the temptation to fill an open base is resisted."

The manager said something under his breath. This time it was too low for Data to make out.

"I beg your pardon?" said the android.

"I said to shut up," explained Terwilliger.

"I only offered the—"

"Shut up," the manager repeated. "Shut up, shut up, *shut up*. Do you understand what I'm saying? *Shut up!*"

And with that he turned his attention back to the pitcher. Data looked at Denyabe. The second baseman winked at him.

"I feel good," said the Icebreaker pitcher, answering Terwilliger's question. He plucked the ball out of his glove and popped it back in. "I think I can blow this guy away."

Terwilliger looked to Sakahara. "What do you think?"

Sakahara shrugged. "He's got good stuff. They're just finding the holes."

Terwilliger frowned and chewed his lip. Then he chewed his lip some more.

By that time the home plate umpire had joined them on the mound. "All right, ladies," he told them. "The sewing circle's over. What's it gonna be?"

Terwilliger made his decision. "We pitch to him."

Abruptly the group broke up. Data found himself standing alone on the mound with the pitcher.

The man looked surprised to see him still standing there, and Data gathered that he was supposed to have left with everyone else. With a quick inclination of his head, he took his leave of the pitcher and jogged back to third base.

The next batter approached home plate. He watched the first pitch miss for a ball. Then the pitcher reared back and threw again, and again the ball missed the strike zone.

Statistically, the android knew, batters were more

likely to swing on two-and-oh pitches than on any other kind. This instance proved no exception to that rule.

The Sunset player hit the ball about as sharply as Data imagined a baseball could be hit. However, his android reflexes stood him in good stead. Launching himself toward the third base line, his body horizontal to the ground, the android caught the ball as it went by him— and landed directly on third base, abdicated by the Sunsets' lead runner only half a second earlier.

It was a double play. The Sunsets' half of the inning was over.

The stadium vibrated with the thunderous applause and cheers that followed. The sound cascaded from the stands to the playing field in waves.

Getting to his feet, Data tossed the ball in the direction of the pitcher's mound and made his way toward the dugout. Before he got there, a couple of his teammates had swatted him on the rump with their gloves.

It was a good feeling. A feeling of belonging, of being appreciated. Data savored it.

Down in the dugout, Terwilliger was standing with his arms folded. He seemed to be intent on something in the outfield, though Data couldn't imagine what.

As the android took a seat on the bench, Denyabe plunked himself down next to him. The second baseman grinned as he regarded Data.

"You didn't tell me you were *that* good," he said.

Data shrugged. "You didn't ask."

"And you showed it at a good time, too," added Denyabe. "I think Terwilliger was getting ready to yank you."

Data looked at him. "To yank me? As in remove me from the game?"

The second baseman nodded. "Hey, don't look so surprised. It's not like you're not giving him good reason."

"I don't understand," the android confessed.

123

"Sure," said Denyabe. "You're not razzing him, right? You're not pulling his chain?"

"Razzing? Pulling . . . his chain?" More unfamiliar terminology. One day, Data hoped, he would comprehend every colloquialism that was thrown in his path. But for each one he came to grasp, it seemed two more waited just around the corner.

Denyabe shook his head, smiling lazily. "I guess some guys just like to live on the edge."

As Data pondered the remark, the Icebreakers' half of the inning seemed to fly by. It seemed he'd only been in the dugout for a couple of minutes when it was time to take the field again.

In the top of the next inning, the Sunsets sent up only four batters. But the third hit a home run, tying the score at one all.

Then it was the Icebreakers' turn again—and the chance Data had been waiting for. Denyabe was to lead off. If either he or Sakahara or Galanti reached base safely, the android—or rather, Bobo—would come up to bat again. And this time, Data resolved, Bobo would not stop at a single.

As if to pave the way, the Sunset pitcher suddenly became wild. Denyabe drew a walk, and so did Sakahara. Then Galanti hit a ball to deep shortstop that resulted in an infield hit.

The bases were loaded, and Data was the next scheduled batter. Apparently the historical Bobo had failed to drive in any of the three runners—but that would not happen *here,* the android vowed as he stepped up to the plate.

The spectators cheered and stamped their feet, no doubt remembering Data's play at third base. For the moment he put them out of his mind.

Sixty feet away, the pitcher focused on his target, his eyes slitted with concentration. Slowly he brought his hands together, coiled his long arms and legs—and unleashed them. Somehow the ball shot out of that flurry of motion.

The android clocked it at one hundred miles an hour—even faster than the first time he came up. But it was too far out of the strike zone for Data even to consider swinging at it. In fact, the catcher had to scramble to keep the ball from getting past him.

Again the pitcher set his sights on home plate. Again he rocked back on one leg, gathered himself, and let fly.

Data had already started his stride when he noticed something different about this pitch. It was approaching more slowly than the one before it. This throw had fooled him, and he would have to make an adjustment in order to connect with it.

That hardly seemed like an insurmountable task. And even though he was a little off-balance, Data decided, he should be able to propel the ball over the outfield wall.

Applying a level of strength and coordination no human player ever enjoyed, the android swung. *For the fences,* he thought, recalling a phrase he had heard in batting practice.

But even before the ball left the bat, he could tell that it would not reach the fence. It would not even *approach* the fence.

The first clue was the sound: a flat *plonk* rather than the crisp *whack* that denoted solid contact. His suspicion was confirmed a second later by the arc of the ball: too high, much too high.

The umpire called the infield fly rule, preventing the runners from advancing on the play. Eventually the ball landed in the shortstop's glove, not more than a few feet behind second base.

Data was numb. What had gone wrong? What *could* have gone wrong?

The crowd was all but silent. Certainly there were none of the cheers he'd heard earlier.

The dugout, too, was quiet. As Data reclaimed his seat, Jackson made a clucking sound with his mouth.

"Some hook," remarked the shortstop.

"Hook?" echoed the android.

"Number Two," said Cherry, who was sitting on the other side of Data. "You know—Uncle Charlie."

The android just shook his head in bewilderment.

"Curveball," explained Jackson. "I know you don't see too many of those in the minors, but up here you're going to see a lot of them. At least until you prove you can hit them."

Data looked at him. He resolved to learn more about this thing called a curveball.

On the next pitch Cordoban hit into a double play.

Chapter Nine

"HERE WE ARE," said Lyneea.

Riker's eyes focused again and he looked around, remembering where they'd been headed. Sometime in the last several minutes a light snow had begun to fall.

Only the Imprimans, Riker remarked to himself, would consider near-constant precipitation and sub-freezing temperatures suitable conditions for an open-air marketplace. Which accounted for the dearth of offworlders strolling through the place.

The merchants had set up their booths on either side of a single winding lane that somehow made its serpentine way from one end of the square to the other. Not the most efficient use of space, perhaps, but it did make the shopping experience a little more intriguing.

The merchandise was all native, all Impriman, from the antique rugs that seemed to be hanging everywhere to the spices that laced the air with strange, compelling scents. Rare animals sat grunting and screeching in their cages, wines and liqueurs poured like tawny waterfalls from dusky bottles, and the snow hissed where it fell into the flames of exotic oil lamps.

Riker had only been here twice during his first stay on Imprima. Once with Teller and Norayan and once by himself, just before he left. But for the life of him he couldn't remember why he'd come alone. Had he meant to buy something? He couldn't recall.

In any case, the market hadn't changed much. More than likely the rest of Besidia had been built around it, and it would probably go on long after the walls that defined it had turned to dust.

"You—the human!"

Reflexively, Riker turned his head. He was relieved to see it was only a spice merchant beckoning to him.

The fellow's eyes were sharp. With Riker's broader build, it was easy to see that he wasn't Impriman—but to know he was human, the merchant had to have gotten a good look inside his hood.

"Whatever it is," he told the man, "no, thank you."

"But I have what you've been looking for." The merchant's eyes seemed to smile all by themselves.

"And what's that?" asked Riker.

The Impriman held up a finely tooled wooden box. "The thing that all young men crave—the love of their fair companions."

Then he looked past Riker to Lyneea. And if his eyes had been smiling before, they suddenly seemed to laugh out loud.

"Ah," he said. "My mistake. It's you, my lady, who must buy this spice."

Lyneea looked at him as if he were crazy. "Ply your wares elsewhere," she advised, her voice as cold and businesslike as ever.

But the merchant didn't give up easily. "Come," he told her, "don't be shy. A woman may yearn for love, too, may she not?"

Lyneea pulled gently but insistently at Riker's sleeve. "Let's go," she said, not loud enough for anyone else to hear.

Under different circumstances, Riker might have played the situation for the obvious humor in it. Hell, he might not have been able to resist.

But they were here to find Teller's killer. He wasn't able to forget that, nor did he want to.

"All right," he told her. "I don't have any desire to linger here either."

"Then don't," she said, continuing to tug. "The last thing we need is to draw undue attention to ourselves."

"I'm walking, see? I'm walking."

"So you are." Finally she let go of him, after they were well past the spice merchant and his remarks. A moment later they negotiated a bend in the lane and the man was gone altogether.

"Touchy," he said, "aren't we?"

She snorted, keeping her eyes straight ahead. "I prefer to call it impatient."

"It couldn't be that you were a little embarrassed, could it?"

Lyneea turned and scowled at him.

"I guess not," he said. "Sorry I even mentioned it."

Abruptly she grabbed his sleeve again. "Look," she told him.

He followed her gesture to a booth about halfway down the lane on the right. The merchant within was tall, heavyset—an unusual trait among the Imprimans—and thickly bearded—no less unusual.

Behind him, on a wooden frame, all manner of ancient weapons were displayed: long spiked maces, a javelin with a nest of deadly hooks surrounding a cruel point, swords with blades so curved they looked like bloodthirsty question marks. On the table before him were knives—thirty, maybe forty of them, some still in their original sheaths.

Riker grimaced. "Nice stuff. I guess that's our antique weapons dealer?"

Lyneea nodded.

The merchant was haggling with a couple of middle-class types over a rather plain-looking sword. Madraga employees, in town for the carnival? Or retainers, like Lyneea? If so, their jobs were probably a good deal simpler than hers was right now.

The merchant turned the sword over in his hands, no doubt pointing out how finely it was balanced. His customers shrugged and made disparaging gestures. The merchant held the weapon up to his oil lamp, which limned the blade's edge with a soft, rosy light. His customers shrugged again and passed remarks to each other, shaking their heads.

And so on.

Of course, Riker and Lyneea had to wait for this charade to end before they could move in. They didn't want to start asking questions in front of people who might be another madraga's retainers. Particularly if they were retainers for Rhurig—and of course, unless they wore their madraga's color, one never knew.

At last the middle-class pair decided to move on—without buying the sword. The merchant cast them a long, disapproving look before he turned and restored the piece to its place on the frame behind him.

"Time for some new customers," said Lyneea. "Let me do the talking."

He looked at her. "Don't I always?"

They had just started for the booth when Riker noticed that they weren't the only ones. And the other group was closer.

"Wait," he told Lyneea, putting a hand on her shoulder.

She must have seen them, too, because she didn't balk, either at the warning or at the hand. She just stood there.

"Riker," she said.

"What?"

"Do you see what I see?"

He took a closer look at the figures in front of the weapons dealer's booth. And all at once he realized what Lyneea was talking about.

"The emblem," he said.

"The emblem," she confirmed. "I can't tell for sure with his hood pulled up, but I'll be quite surprised if that isn't Kobar."

Riker studied the man Lyneea had pointed to, the third official of Madraga Rhurig. He was taller than his two companions, rangier. And there was something about his bearing— an arrogance? An attitude of superiority?

This was the man who had murdered Teller Conlon. This was the maggot who'd killed his friend.

Suddenly, he wanted very much to return the favor.

Calm down, Riker. You're not some chest-beating savage. You're the first officer of the USS Enterprise. *Let your feelings get in the way here and all you'll do is put Kobar on the alert.*

"Riker? You're being awfully quiet."

"I'm catching up on my beauty sleep."

"Well, catch up while you're looking at a rug or something. We can't just stand here and gape."

"No," he said, "I suppose not."

The nearest booth was that of a pet merchant. The man peered at passersby from behind a corgodrill— something like a small ape with luxuriant rainbow-colored plumage covering its neck, shoulders, and arms. The corgodrill, known for its pleasant disposition, was sitting on the table picking parasites out of its fur.

As they approached, the merchant straightened. "Can I help you?" he asked.

"Not really," said Lyneea. "We're just taking in the sights."

"Then look no further," he told them. "The greatest sights in the entire world are on display at Griziba's booth." His grin was so ingratiating it made Riker's teeth hurt. "Now . . . was it the corgodrill that caught your eye? He's a wonder with children." The man pointed to a plump, cobalt-colored lizard. "Or perhaps a nice menigirri. It eats very little, and its scent has been known to help the digestion——"

"That's very nice," interrupted Lyneea. "But we're just looking. Really."

The merchant nodded. "I understand. You wish to see something less docile." He leaned toward them over the table. "Something you can train to dissuade unwanted visitors. I have just the thing."

"It's all right . . ." Lyneea began, but the merchant had already disappeared under his table.

Riker was keeping one eye on Kobar, so he really didn't pay too much attention when the fellow came up again. Nor did he notice what he came up *with*.

"Here," said the merchant, pushing a cage in their direction. "As you know, one so very young is not easy to come by. It will give you many long years of loyal service."

Suddenly something small and dark lashed out through the bars of the cage. Probably it would have gotten Riker's attention even if it hadn't been inches from his hand.

Just in time, he withdrew the endangered appendage. And as if in parody, the dark thing snapped back into its cage.

Riker inspected his hand. He found tiny rents in the back of his glove, but no damage to the flesh beneath.

"Many pardons," said the merchant. "But as you can see, he is quite effective. Imagine him guarding your domicile someday."

Then the animal pressed its small black muzzle against the bars in front, and Riker realized what it was the man was peddling.

132

"An isak," he said. He recalled his experience in the tavern, not without a certain amount of apprehension.

"Of course," said the merchant. "What else can strike so quickly? And with such strength?" He smiled. "A couple of months from now, he would not have fallen short of his mark."

Riker grunted, eyeing the beast even as it eyed him. "How reassuring," he remarked.

"Indeed," said the petmonger. "Then you will take him?"

"Look," Lyneea cut in. "They're moving away from the booth."

Riker looked. Sure enough, Kobar and his compatriots had finished their business with the weapons merchant. Judging by the package beneath Kobar's arm and the smile on the merchant's face, they had come to terms on some item or other.

"Let's go," he told Lyneea.

"Just a moment," she said. "We mustn't follow too closely."

"That will be fifty credits," said the petmonger. "And a bargain at that, if I may say so."

"Perhaps some other time," Riker told him. "When I'm feeling masochistic."

"Ah," said the merchant, "but he will not *be* here some other time. Isakki are rare at any age, and as I have indicated—"

"Now," advised Lyneea, and started walking.

"You do not understand," said the petmonger, still appealing to Riker. "This is a once-in-a-lifetime opportunity! You cannot pass it up."

"No doubt we'll live to regret it," said the human, and using his long strides to advantage, he caught up with his partner.

"I have a good feeling about this," decided Lyneea. "A *very* good feeling."

"You think he'll lead us to the seal now?" asked Riker.

She nodded. "If we can believe our tailor friend, Kobar loves his knives better than he loves his own mother. He'll want to keep his new acquisition in the safest place he knows of—along with his other valuables. A certain seal, for instance."

"Somewhere in town? Or at his madraga's estate?"

"The more I think about it, the more I'd say it's in town—for Rhurig's protection. Why keep the evidence where it might incriminate the whole madraga? In Kobar's hands, it can hurt only him—a risk he'd probably assume for the sake of his kinsmen."

"But Kobar's their third official," said Riker. "It will make for a considerable scandal if he's caught with Fortune's Light. Why not put some retainer in jeopardy instead?"

"Probably because a retainer would not be trusted with such an important task," Lyneea told him, "even if he or she was capable of performing it. Obviously Rhurig has gone to great trouble to stop the merger. It is worth a certain amount of risk to make certain the seal stays hidden. And besides, Kobar may have insisted on handling this personally."

"Then why is he out buying knives for his collection," asked Riker, "instead of keeping watch over the seal?"

Lyneea turned to glance at him. "Because," she said, "he is who he is. Even a madraga official may be governed by something other than logic."

Remembering Norayan's tale, he could hardly disagree. "Good point," he muttered.

"Hold on," said his partner. "Something's wrong."

Up ahead, Kobar and his companions had stopped. The third official was holding up his package, and one of the others was pointing to it. Remarks were exchanged, which Riker and Lyneea had no hope of overhearing. Kobar frowned.

"He's not happy with his purchase," observed Riker.

"Apparently," said Lyneea. "Maybe they've decided it wasn't such a good deal after all."

"So we make ourselves scarce again."

"You're catching on," she told him.

Kobar and his friends started back the way they'd come. Their discontent was increasing step by step, if the expansiveness of their gestures was any indication.

"Just one thing," said Riker. "Let's not find another pet dealer, all right?"

"It's a deal," agreed his partner.

She'd already started toward a nearby winemonger's booth when they heard the first small cries of surprise. Then came the full-blown screams and the rush. And before Riker knew it, the crowd was carrying him back, separating him from Lyneea.

A moment later he got his first look at what prompted the riot: the isak cub that had been shown to him earlier. Apparently the damned thing had gotten out of its cage and was trying to make a meal out of somebody's ankles—*anybody's* ankles.

In their haste to avoid the snapping, snarling little beast, the marketgoers were leaping onto some tables and overturning others, while the merchants were doing their best to keep their booths intact and their wares from spilling to the ground. It was chaos such as the marketplace in Besidia had probably never seen—and might never see again.

Riker tried to work his way out of the press. He grabbed for one of the poles supporting a basket merchant's display, missed. Someone fell, starting a domino effect, and by the time it got to him it had the weight of a half-dozen bodies behind it. Like a swimmer overtaken by a slow but inexorable wave, he went down, inadvertently taking a couple of others with him.

Nor could he easily get up again. Not with his legs

pinned under an equally helpless Impriman, who was in turn pinned by somebody else. And to make matters worse, other marketgoers were trying to climb over him, in order to put as much distance as they could between themselves and the skittering isak. There were curses, grunts, even a couple of misplaced blows.

Twisting and squirming, Riker managed to pull his legs free—but there was still no place to stand. So he did the next best thing. He worked his way over to the first booth he saw and slithered underneath its leather-draped table.

Once he'd pulled his feet in after him and the heavy coverings had fallen back into place, Riker allowed himself a shudder of disgust. *Crowds.* He was grateful for the relative quiet, the relative peace afforded him by his shelter.

In fact, he almost hated the idea of coming out again into the swirling madness of the marketplace. But he couldn't forget that he'd come here for a reason. After a couple of seconds' respite, he crawled out on the other side of the table.

Riker had fully expected to have to excuse himself to the proprietor. After all, he was hardly an invited guest.

But the merchant cast him no more than a sideways glance. He was too busy attending to a couple of marketgoers who'd found themselves sprawled across his knife collection.

Abruptly, Riker recognized the face. It was the weapons dealer they'd observed in his dealings with Kobar. Small world, wasn't it?

Perhaps a bit *too* small right now, and a bit too crowded as well. He had to find Lyneea. And also the ones they'd been following, before they got away.

Riker had already risen to one knee and was starting to get up the rest of the way when he realized that the weapons dealer's wasn't the only familiar face around here. Nor would he have to look very far for Kobar.

Just a few inches, in fact—because Kobar, having pushed himself off the knife table, was staring Riker in the face.

There was an excruciatingly long moment in which their eyes met and locked. An eternity, it seemed, in which something less than peaceful flickered, then flared, and finally flamed in Kobar's gaze.

"You," he spat. "You're the other human. Norayan's other companion!"

Riker realized then that his hood had fallen away. Hurriedly he put it back on.

"Sorry," he mumbled, turning away. "Don't know what you're talking about."

"You're right," cried Kobar's friend, who had also recovered quickly enough, it seemed, to place Riker's face. "It's the one . . . what was his name? Reeker? No—*Riker.*"

By that time, the human was slipping away—and trying to slip out of Kobar's thoughts at the same time. If he moved fast enough, maybe he could lose himself in the crowd again. No, better—get out of the marketplace altogether.

How had Kobar and his companion remembered him? It had been five *years,* and *he* didn't remember *them.* Apparently his friendship with Norayan had been scrutinized more closely than he'd realized—at least by some.

Riker brushed aside a double layer of leather and emerged in the next booth, where the crowd had already brought the table down. The rug dealer who ran the place was protecting his best pile of merchandise with outstretched arms. Seeing a narrow space between the backs of two other booths, the *Enterprise* officer started for it.

"Not so fast, human!"

He couldn't help glancing at the source of the command—it was that insistent. Nor was he sorry afterward that he had turned around. For if he'd practiced more restraint, he might not have avoided the knife that came whizzing at him end over end. As it was, it embedded itself in a support pole not more than a hand's breadth from his cheek.

Kobar and his companions—the three of them had been reunited, it seemed—were standing at the entrance to the booth, beside the overturned table. And each had an exotic-looking knife in his hand.

"What are you doing?" asked Kobar. "Following me?" He took a step forward, making tiny motions with the point of his blade, as if he were carving something. "Admit it, Riker."

"Just calm down," Will said, giving up on the idea of escape. By the time he squeezed himself through the opening he'd spotted, each of his adversaries could have taken a nice leisurely shot at him. And one of them was bound not to miss. "I think we have some sort of misunderstanding here."

By that time, the isak threat seemed to have abated. Those who only moments before had been scrambling for shelter were now attracted to the drama in the rug merchant's stall.

"Misunderstanding, you say?" Kobar shook his head. "I don't think so. I believe I understand perfectly."

Not perfectly, Riker thought, but well enough to put two and two together. To realize that the Federation might have sent someone to Imprima to investigate Teller's disappearance. To recognize that Riker's presence at the marketplace was hardly a coincidence. And to know that if the human was following him, he might also have caught on to his friend's murder.

Of course, to figure all that out, Kobar had to be guilty as hell, not only of the murder but of the theft of Fortune's Light as well. Riker had satisfied himself of that fact—a limited accomplishment if he didn't live to tell of it.

And judging by the look in Kobar's eye, he had every intention of silencing his accuser before he could make any accusations.

Riker looked past his antagonist, scanned the faces in the crowd. Where in blazes was Lyneea?

"Why don't you tell me what the problem is," he suggested. "Then we can work it out."

There was no point in confirming the Impriman's suspicions. If he had any doubts, Riker was going to nurture them.

Kobar smiled. "Can we? I doubt it."

"Surely you're not thinking of killing an unarmed man?" Riker lifted his chin to indicate Kobar's companions. "All three of you?"

That drew a murmur from the clutch of onlookers. Kobar's smile faded, and he pointed his knife at the weapon stuck in the support pole.

"Take it out," he said. "Then you'll be armed, too. And I promise my friends will stay out of it."

Riker didn't want to accept the weapon. If he did, it would mean a fight to the death; that was the nature of street duels on Imprima.

And the advantage would almost certainly be Kobar's. Riker could tell from his comportment that he'd done this sort of thing before—obviously with success.

Of course he'd never fought *Riker* before. But even if the human came out on top, his victory would be a Pyrrhic one. Killing an official of Madraga Rhurig would draw attention to him, blow his cover wide open, and maybe make further investigation impossible.

Not to mention the fact that Kobar's friends would want to avenge his death. That, too, was the nature of street duels on Imprima.

"Come on," Kobar jeered. "What are you waiting for?"

Riker shook his head slowly. "No," he said evenly.

Kobar's eyes narrowed. "I always suspected you humans were cowards." He spat. "Now I've got proof."

But Riker wouldn't take the bait. He just stood there.

Not that he wouldn't have *liked* to take up the knife. He was itching to give Kobar a taste of what he'd done to Teller. *But we can't always do as we like, can we?*

"No," he said a second time, as much to confirm his own resolution as to announce it to his enemy.

What blossomed in Kobar's eyes looked like genuine anger. Coming forward, closing the rest of the gap between them, he shifted the knife to his left hand. Then, with his right, he dug his fingers into Riker's tunic, grabbing a fistful of the thick material.

"You'll fight me," said the third official of Madraga Rhurig. "No matter how cowardly you are, you'll fight me, or so help me I'll gut you where you stand."

They were almost nose to nose now, Kobar's gaze getting hotter and hotter. The human returned it as calmly as he could. *Easy, Riker. It's still three against one. Your best chance is to wait this one out.*

Then he felt the knife point in his ribs. At first there wasn't much pressure behind it. But after a couple of seconds, it began to dig in.

"Well?" said Kobar.

Would he carry out his threat or was it a bluff? The human wasn't sure.

Even in the cold of the open-air market, he could feel a drop of sweat trickling down the side of his face. Riker's mouth went dry as the knife point moved abruptly, cutting through his tunic. It must have cut flesh as well, because he felt a sharp, burning pain.

For a moment, he believed that Kobar would gut him after all, that the old Riker luck had finally given out. Then the Impriman let up on the pressure. Opening the fingers of his right hand, he let go of Riker's tunic.

Finally he turned his back on the human and walked

out of the booth, wiping blood—Riker's blood—off his knife onto his trouser leg.

It's over, the human told himself. *And it seems I've won.*

Suddenly Kobar turned and regarded him again. He spoke to his companions without looking at them.

"Drag him out of there," he snarled. "He may think he can avoid this, but he can't."

Looks like I spoke too soon, Riker chided himself.

Without hesitation, Kobar's friends came to get him. Each of them took an arm and dragged him out of the rug merchant's booth.

Nor did he resist much. What for? It would only have postponed the inevitable.

With the crowd packed in like this, he couldn't run. Lyneea could have helped, but where *was* she? Hadn't she noticed yet what was happening here?

As Kobar's companions thrust Riker forward, the crowd cleared away and formed a circle around a portion of the market's winding lane. It was big enough for what Kobar had in mind, but barely.

"Last chance," the Impriman warned him. He gestured to one of his friends, who held out his knife, handle first.

Riker didn't take it. *Don't give in now,* he told himself. *You'll find another way out of this.*

"Suit yourself," said Kobar. And subtly altering his grip on his weapon, he advanced on the human.

The attack wasn't meant to be clever. It was intended to humiliate with its straightforwardness.

But Riker didn't intend to be humiliated. Or, for that matter, to be skewered on Kobar's point.

At the last moment, he sidestepped the attack and, for good measure, struck Kobar a two-handed blow that sent him staggering.

The Impriman looked at him with newfound respect. "So," he said. "You *can* fight."

Will didn't reply. It was more important to concentrate on staying alive.

Kobar took another swipe at him—this time, one with a little more thought behind it. Riker had to jump back quickly, using all the space the crowd would give him, then shuffle sideways to avoid the real attack. For a trained duelist almost never intended his first assault to be his best one, and Kobar was obviously a trained duelist.

Sure enough the Impriman followed up with a long, hard lunge, expecting to hit flesh and bone. But with Riker already on the move, his point found nothing but empty air.

Cursing, he rounded on the human again. Riker kept dancing along the perimeter of their space, brushing against the ring of onlookers as he moved.

Kobar feinted. Riker refused to be deceived, refused to react and yield the advantage to his adversary.

Another feint, better than the first, but the human didn't swallow this one either. Kobar was getting impatient, Riker decided. He would be less cautious, less picky about his openings.

He was right. Kobar didn't wait long to strike again. He started his attack slowly, hoping to lull Riker into overconfidence, then put all his weight into a sudden rush.

It was a rash thing to do when time was on his side. But Riker wasn't about to tell Kobar that. Timing it so that his adversary just missed him, he whirled and chopped down on Kobar's wrist.

The Impriman cried out in pain. His weapon fell to the ground.

When he went for it, Riker kicked it between the legs of someone in the crowd. Kobar took the opportunity to slam into the human's midsection, carrying him off his feet. As they fell together, Riker grabbed his adversary's tunic and planted a heel in his solar plexus. Then, as he rolled backward, he pushed his leg out and sent Kobar flying.

In a fraction of a second Riker was on his feet, not because he feared a reprisal from Kobar—he had landed pretty hard if his grunt was any indication—but because Kobar's friends were still in the first rank of onlookers, and both still had knives.

In another fraction of a second, he'd located one of them. The Impriman was starting forward, weapon in hand. Riker braced himself.

Where was the other?

The human never saw the blow. The next thing he knew, his cheek was pressed against the frozen mud of the lane, and there was a ringing in his ears.

Someone turned him over, dropped down on top of him. The same someone pinned Riker's shoulders to the ground with his knees. Snowflakes fell into his face, big and soft and dreamy. He tasted blood as he recognized the face looming above him: it was Kobar's.

"Filthy muzza," the Impriman spat, his clenched teeth making the words hard to understand. His eyes flashed green fury. "Filthy muzza of an offworlder bastard. Here's what you get for putting your nose where it doesn't belong."

As if from a great distance, Riker saw him raise the knife. It occurred to him that he should try to grab it, but he couldn't seem to reach high enough. For a long time it hung there like a sickle moon, Kobar's features twisting with rage just below it.

Then the Impriman spat out a curse—and plunged the knife into the ground beside Riker's ear. The human rolled his head to look at it, barely grasping its significance.

Kobar lowered his face to Riker's. When he spoke, his voice was little more than a whisper, but his words had a cutting edge to them.

"Go back," he said, "and tell your friend Norayan that

she's wrong. I didn't kill him, no matter how many times she accuses me." He raised his lip in a sneer. "No matter how many Federation muzza she sends after me."

With a last shove, he got to his feet and walked away. His companions joined him as he made his way through the crowd.

From his vantage point in the first row, next to the Sunset dugout, Geordi looked around at the frozen ball park—the frozen fans, the frozen players, the frozen umpires and hot dog vendors and video cameramen. Even the frozen clouds in the sky.

"Data," he said, "this is *great*. I mean, this is *some* program."

"I cannot take credit for it," the android responded. "As I indicated earlier, it was conceived by Commander Riker before he went planetside."

Geordi leaned over the restraining wall and trained his gaze on the Sunset pitcher. "That's the fellow who gave you trouble, eh?"

Data nodded. "That is indeed the fellow. I propose to have him repeat the pitch he threw to me—the one I popped up."

"Popped up?"

"Propelled the ball in a more vertical than horizontal trajectory," interpreted the android. It was rare for him to have to explain jargon to Geordi; the significance of the moment did not escape him. "It is not the desired result of a swing."

The chief engineer of the *Enterprise* nodded. "Gotcha. Okay, let's take our positions and get a gander at this—what did you call it?"

"Curveball," said Data. "Hook. Uncle Charlie. Number Two . . ."

Geordi held up his hands to signify surrender. "All right already. Whatever it's called, let's see it."

The android entered the batter's box, spread his feet, and held his bat aloft. "Ready?" he called to Geordi.

"Ready," came the answer.

"Computer—resume program."

All at once, everything came back to life. The crowd yelled and cheered, the players in the field went into their crouches, and the clouds started crawling across the blue heavens.

As before, the Sunset pitcher set himself, rocked back, and fired the ball. Data just stood there. After all, he'd already had his chance to hit this pitch. The replay was just for purposes of demonstration.

Once again, the ball seemed to come in slower than it should have. And now that he wasn't distracted by the motion of his swing, Data noticed something else: just before it reached home plate, the ball appeared to dip—rather precipitously.

"Ball *two*," ruled the umpire.

"Stop program," commanded the android.

The program stopped. A flock of geese, on a diagonal path high above the diamond, stuck to the sky.

Data turned to Geordi. "Was that of any help?"

His friend still seemed to be eyeing the pitch, though the ball was now frozen in the catcher's glove. After a moment or two Geordi climbed over the wall and trotted out onto the field.

"I want to see it again," he said, "from closer up. Also the pitch that preceded it—the one you said was faster."

Data issued the required instructions, and the computer complied. As Geordi looked on, the holodeck reenacted both of the pitches that Data had seen in his unproductive at-bat.

Geordi harrumphed, stroking his chin. "I think we've got two issues here," he announced. "The first one has more to do with you than with the ball."

"Me?" said the android.

"Yup. With all that whirling and twirling, you expect that pitcher to be throwing the ball as hard as he can. But he's *not*. He's actually releasing it a little earlier, with a little less velocity. Of course, you don't know he's going to do that—so you swing too soon."

Data thought about it. "Or perhaps just begin to stride before I have to."

"Or perhaps just that," agreed Geordi. "You should wait a little longer before reacting. That way, a slower pitch won't fool you. And with your strength and speed, you'll still be able to handle a fast pitch."

"Wait longer," repeated Data. "I will remember that."

"But that's not all there is to it," Geordi added. "Remember, I said there were *two* issues involved here."

"Ah," responded the android. "So you did."

"The second one," said Geordi, "has to do with the flight of the pitch. Whoever named that thing a curveball knew just what he was talking about—it really does curve. In this case, down and into the batter, although that's not to say it can't curve in other directions as well."

"I *thought* I saw the ball drop just before it reached me," recalled Data. "And you say it moved toward me as well?"

"That's what happened all right. And it had something to do with the way the ball was spinning."

"Spinning," repeated the android. "How interesting."

"*Very* interesting. And also, as far as I can tell, quite impossible."

Data looked at him. "But it *happened*."

Geordi shrugged. "I can think of two principles that might be at work here—but neither one would explain that curve."

"Perhaps," said the android, "if you went over them with me . . ."

"Sure," said the chief engineer. "Maybe you can find something I've overlooked." He paused, frowning. "Okay, theory number one. If the weight of the ball was distributed unevenly, the spin imposed on it could create eccentricities in its trajectory. However, judging by this specimen I'm holding in my hand, there aren't any serious disparities in weight distribution, so that shouldn't be a factor."

Data pondered that. It was true—the balls he had handled in the field had actually been quite well balanced. If they'd been otherwise, he certainly would have noticed.

"Theory number two," resumed Geordi. "Friction. The stitches that protrude from the ball, finding resistance in the molecules that constitute this atmosphere, could work to turn the object away from the straight course dictated by momentum. But for that to happen in any significant way, the air would have to be several times denser than what we're breathing. Or the stitches would have to be many times larger, to invite more resistance."

Data could find no loophole in either analysis. And yet there had to be an explanation. He said so.

"No doubt there *is*," said Geordi. "And I'll think about it some more. But for now I'm stumped."

"Stumped," echoed the android. He searched his memory for the word. "Ah. *Stumped*. Stymied. Thwarted. Frustrated . . ."

"All of that," admitted Geordi. "In the meantime, you'll have to do the best you can."

He followed Geordi's gaze into the Icebreaker dugout, where the android's teammates were frozen in various poses. Terwilliger, his foot planted on the dugout's second step, was leaning forward on his knee. His face was half turned away from the goings-on at home plate, as if he couldn't bear to watch—as if he *knew* that Bobo would find a way to keep him from his victory. Jackson, nestled in the shadows, looked on with what appeared to be only mild interest. Cherry was leaning on the bat rack, scrutinizing the pitcher through narrowed eyes.

"Didn't those guys know anything?" asked Geordi. "About the curveball, I mean?"

"Not very much," said the android.

His friend regarded him. "Look, Data, maybe it's none of my business, but . . . well, why is this so important to you? Commander Riker no doubt intended this to be *fun*—relaxation. And here you are, putting an awful lot of effort into something that no one else will ever know or care about."

"Perhaps," said the android. "And I must admit, I have asked myself the same question, without being able to come up with a satisfactory answer." He looked back at Geordi. "In that respect, I suppose, the curveball and my motivation have much in common."

Geordi smiled. "Okay. To each his own." He jerked a thumb in the direction of third base. "Are you going to play some more now?"

Data shook his head. "It strikes me that there may have been some scientific research concerning the curveball, back in the twentieth or twenty-first century. I would like to conduct a search for it before proceeding to the next inning."

Geordi nodded. "Then I'll walk you as far as engineering. I've got a shift starting in ten minutes, and it doesn't look good for the boss to be late. Sets a bad example."

"I understand," said Data. "Computer—save program, please."

Riker tried to sit up, found it harder than he would have thought. The ringing in his ears wasn't getting any better, and he could still taste the blood in his mouth. But he'd be damned if he was going to lie there on the hard, cold ground any longer. With an effort, he rolled over and got up on all fours. Then, slowly, he pushed himself to his feet.

"Riker. Are you all right?"

He turned. "Lyneea," he said dully.

She held his head steady, looked into his eyes. "I think you've got a concussion," she told him.

"Great." It sounded as if someone else had said it.

She took his arm. "Come on. Let's get out of here." She pointed to a narrow street that led off the market square. "Can you walk by yourself?"

He nodded. They walked. And what was left of the crowd let them through.

At one point Riker took note of the petmonger they'd seen before, the one whose isak had gotten loose and caused all the furor. Ironically, his was one of the few booths left untouched by the uproar. And by the looks of things, he'd even managed to recover the vicious little beast.

A moment later they were in the street that Lyneea had pointed out. There were a couple of shops here, but neither seemed to be open. The street itself was deserted —unusual, Riker decided, considering its proximity to the marketplace.

Lyneea turned him toward her, looked into his eyes again. She frowned, nodded. "Definitely a concussion."

"Feels like someone packed my head with mud," he admitted. Then a memory cut through the fog. "Where *were* you?"

"Watching. And hoping I wouldn't have to intervene. After all, that would have neutralized my usefulness."

He felt something like anger crawl up his gullet. "Neutralized your . . . I could've been *killed.*"

Lyneea shook her head. "Not a chance. I'm too good a shot—remember the isak pit?" She turned Riker's face to one side, looked at it critically. "You look terrible," she decided. "We should get you to a doctor."

He took her hands away. "No doctor," he told her. "There's too much to do."

"Is there?" she asked. "What, for instance? Kobar will be on his guard now. He'll never lead us to the seal."

Riker thought about that, or tried to. It wasn't easy.

The ringing in his ears was starting to abate, but he still felt as if his brain had grown a size too large for his skull. And now there was a new pain, in the area of his temple—no doubt the point of impact of the knife handle, or whatever had hit him.

Then it came to him: it was something Kobar had said. Something about . . .

"He didn't do it," blurted Riker.

Lyneea looked at him. "I beg your pardon?"

"Kobar. He didn't murder Teller."

"What makes you so sure?"

"For one thing, he could have killed me just now if he'd really wanted to. He could have eliminated someone who was almost certainly on to his crimes. But he didn't. What does that tell you?"

Lyneea shrugged. "That he's a fool?"

"No. That he may be innocent—of the murder and maybe even of the theft." He paused, trying to pull it all together in his mind. "Kobar said something to me after he stuck his knife in the ground. He told me that Norayan was wrong about him. Apparently she'd accused him of killing Teller, and he was passing a message to her through me."

His partner's brow wrinkled ever so slightly. "I thought Norayan didn't know your friend was dead."

Riker grunted. "According to what she told me, she didn't. But what if she really *did* know? What if she went looking for Teller in the maze, and found him lying there—as we did?"

"Then she lied to you. But why would she do that?" A pause. "Unless . . ." She licked her lips. Had some of the color drained from her face? "Riker . . . couldn't Norayan have *planted* that patch we found? The one that led us to Rhurig—to Kobar?"

With hindsight, it *did* seem like a coincidence—didn't it?

"For what reason?" he asked out loud. "Because someone else killed Conlon? Someone she didn't want us to know about?"

His mind had finally kicked into gear, and his mouth along with it. But it took a couple of moments for his emotions to catch up—for him to realize the implications of what he was saying.

They looked at each other. For their own individual reasons, neither of them wanted to believe it. To Riker, Norayan was a friend. To Lyneea, she was an official of the madraga that the retainer had sworn to defend with her life. But if she was guilty of deceiving them . . .

God. What if Norayan herself was the killer?

"Let's say it's all true," Lyneea told him. "Let's say that Norayan led us to Kobar to keep us off the real killer's trail. Why would she first alert Kobar by accusing him of the crime?"

Riker shook his head. "Maybe to make him act the part of a hunted criminal, to make his behavior more convincing to us." Something else occurred to him. "Or maybe to turn him on us, to take us out of the game."

Lyneea's temples worked. "So we wouldn't live long enough to find out she'd deceived us."

The human nodded. "And the rest of Criathis wouldn't suspect a thing. Kobar's a known hothead. It wouldn't be so farfetched if he killed an offworlder, and maybe a Criathis retainer as well, without knowing it."

His partner scowled. "What about Fortune's Light? Could Norayan have been in on the theft of that, too?"

Riker met her gaze. "It's hard to believe, I know. But is it any less believable than the rest of this?"

It hurt to say these things. However, it hurt even more to think that Norayan was trying to kill them.

Maybe Teller wasn't the only one who had changed. *Maybe.*

"Unless we're jumping to conclusions," said Lyneea.

Her scowl deepened. "Or was that what we did back in the maze?" She sighed. "What about that oath of secrecy that Norayan swore you to? That sounded like something of genuine importance to her."

The human had to agree. "Maybe she was telling the truth about her affair with Teller and lying about the rest of it."

"But if that was the case, why let us in on her association with Conlon and the maze? Why not just let us blunder around and leave her secret a secret?"

Riker pondered that one. "Could it be," he suggested, "that we were close to the truth and didn't know it? That Norayan had to lead us on a wild-goose chase and take some chances because otherwise we would have found her out?"

Lyneea had a queer expression on her face. It had some surprise in it and some respect and maybe a couple of other things. "You know," she said, "you're not such a liability after all."

He wanted to smile, but his temple was throbbing too badly now. "Thanks" was all he could muster up.

"Don't mention it." She looked away from him. "So now," she said, "there are two questions staring us in the face—assuming, of course, that Norayan is truly hiding something about the murder or the theft or both."

"Number one," said Riker, picking up the thread, "what were we looking at that made Norayan so nervous? What were we doing that we should start doing again?"

"And number two," continued Lyneea, "whom was she protecting?"

Lyneea seemed to think, as Riker did, that Norayan could have committed the murder herself. But, like Riker, she didn't want to drag it into the open—not yet. It was the one possibility that neither of them was quite willing to countenance.

The human pulled his tunic more tightly about himself. Somehow it seemed colder here in this narrow street.

"Let's go back," he suggested, "to the time before Norayan's visit. We had just tailed Bosch to his place at the Golden Muzza, right?"

Lyneea's eyes lost their focus a little as she remembered. "You think that Bosch was mixed up somehow with Norayan?"

"Maybe. In any case, I think we should call on him again—that is, if he hasn't decided to change his address."

Lyneea nodded, her gaze still focused elsewhere. "What if it wasn't Bosch? What if it was the Pandrilite that made Norayan nervous?"

Riker thought about it. The Pandrilite's story had seemed plausible enough, but . . .

"We've got him under wraps on that blaster charge," he said. "It can't hurt to ask him a few more—"

Suddenly Riker felt something hit him in the back—*hard*. He turned instinctively and saw a cloaked figure fleeing in the direction of the marketplace.

Lyneea cursed and clutched at him, and at the same time he felt something long and stiff in his shoulder, something that didn't belong there, something that was beginning to hurt. Numbly he looked down at the right side of his chest and saw a bloody knife point sticking out of his tunic.

"My God," he whispered. The pain was getting worse with each passing moment. Already it felt as if there were a hot poker inside him, searing his flesh with agonizing slowness.

He staggered against the nearest wall, Lyneea still holding on to him. There was fear in her eyes, rampaging wide-eyed fear.

The stain on his tunic was spreading quickly; he was

losing blood at an alarming rate. A few drops fell into the slush at his feet, making tiny black pools.

Lyneea swallowed. "Hang on, Riker. I'm going for help." Her voice was calmer than she looked—it must have taken quite an effort.

"No," he told her. Not that he didn't agree he needed help. Only the help he had in mind was orbiting hundreds of kilometers above them.

Digging into his tunic with his left hand—he had lost feeling in his right—he scrabbled about for his communicator. The pain was getting unbearable, but he clenched his teeth and forced his fingers to close about the device. As he withdrew it, he slid down along the wall to his knees, despite Lyneea's efforts to hold him up.

Will activated the communicator with thumb pressure and got as far as "Riker to *Enterprise*" before the damned thing squirted out of his grasp. He tried to pick it up out of the slush, but he was cold, so cold suddenly, and his fingers wouldn't do what he wanted them to.

He looked up at Lyneea for help, saw her narrowed eyes, and knew what she was thinking: a violation of the high-tech ban, a breach of her vows as a retainer. Technically she was wrong, but he had neither the strength nor the time to explain it now.

"Please," he rasped. There was a blackness at the edges of his vision that was beginning to eat its way inward. "Please . . . Captain Picard on . . . on the ship."

Lyneea's mouth was set in a straight, hard line. The kind of help he wanted went against everything she believed in. It meant defiling, for the sake of an offworlder, what her people held sacred.

But there was no way to get any other kind of help in time to save his life. If she'd doubted that before, she had to see it now.

"Please," he whispered again, reaching for the communicator with useless fingers. The pain was sheer agony now; it was closing down on him like a vise. And still Lyneea stood there, looking for all the world like a beast caught in a trap.

The moment seemed to stretch out forever. Before it ended, Riker lost consciousness.

Chapter Ten

FORTUNATELY, Beverly Crusher had been in sickbay when the call came from the bridge. In a matter of seconds, she'd scraped together everything she needed and headed for the turbolift.

It wasn't until the lift doors closed and the compartment was headed for Deck Six that she began to gather her thoughts as well. And to replay her conversation with the captain, picking out the bits of information she thought she might need, skirting her personal feelings of hope and dread as best she could.

"You'll be taking a chance, Doctor, you know that?" Picard had said. "Whoever made Will a target may make you his next one. And we won't be able to beam you back until . . ."

Then the lift stopped and the doors opened and she was rushing down the corridor to Transporter Room 1. Crewmen hugged the bulkheads on either side of her, careful not to get in her way. Apparently she wasn't the only one who'd been informed of the emergency.

The transporter room doors parted without a sound. Inside, Chief O'Brien was waiting for her. Also Worf—with a bundle in his hand.

"I thought I was going alone," she told him.

"You are," he snarled, obviously none too pleased about the fact. He unfurled the bundle with a flick of his wrist, showing her the heavy dun-colored tunic she'd have to wear over her medical garb.

"Oh," she said, "that's right. Don't want to attract too much attention, do we?"

The wardrobe change seemed to her a waste of time—one they could hardly afford now, if Riker's wound was half as bad as reported. After all, if someone had bothered to stab him, wasn't the Federation's presence in Besidia probably known already?

Nonetheless, she put down her supply pack long enough to pull the tunic on over her head. Then she recovered her pack, bounded up onto the transporter platform, and gave the order: "Energize."

Chief O'Brien complied. Her last shipboard sight was that of Worf, his body unnaturally rigid as he resisted the impulse to leap onto the platform beside her. His eyes flashed black fire, and she had no trouble understanding their message: *Do not let him die.*

Then the transporter effect took over.

Picard paced in front of the command center, trying to hope for the best. The Impriman's message had made it sound bad for Riker. Very bad.

Hell, the mere fact that it was she who'd had to use the communicator, and not Riker himself, had been enough to indicate the gravity of the situation. Her report had only underscored what he'd already known in his bones.

He thanked God he'd gotten advance clearance for additional beam-downs. Otherwise Dr. Crusher would still be waiting in the transporter room while some Besidian bureaucrat waded through red tape. As it was, all it took was a brief message, and the teleportation barrier was lifted long enough to allow the doctor to beam down to Riker's side.

Not that Picard felt at all good about sending Crusher down there. Apparently someone was on to Riker's mission, someone who wouldn't hesitate to use deadly force in opposing it. And if they could cut down someone as resourceful as Will Riker, what chance would a mere doctor have against them? Granted, she had a Criathan retainer to watch over her, but that kind of protection had already proved insufficient.

As the captain pondered these things, the lift doors opened and Lieutenant Worf came out onto the bridge. Without so much as a glance to either side of him, the Klingon assumed his regular position at Tactical, relieving the officer who'd manned the post in his absence.

Normally Picard would have dispatched someone else to give Crusher the tunic they'd been holding for her in ship's stores against just such an emergency. Certainly there were personnel more convenient to the task.

But Worf had requested that he be allowed to do it, and Picard had allowed it. How could he not? Riker was one of the few real friends the Klingon had, not just on the ship, but anywhere. If he wanted to feel that he was helping in some small way, who was the captain to deny him that?

Picard gazed at the main viewscreen and the curved sweep of Impriman planetscape that dominated it. By now Dr. Crusher would have set to work on Riker. By now she would have a good idea if she'd arrived in time.

And so might Troi, if she was monitoring the doctor's emotions. Picard turned to his counselor, queried her with a glance.

Was it his imagination, or was Troi looking a little haggard? Perhaps a trifle paler than usual? If so, it was understandable. The Impriman's message had hit them all like a point-blank phaser blast.

"Nothing to report," said the Betazoid, answering his silent question. "Dr. Crusher is still uncertain of the outcome."

Her voice was even, untainted by the emotions that must be echoing inside her. Picard admired her for that.

"Thank you, Counselor."

So they were truly in the dark. They would get the news, good or bad, only when the doctor completed her ministrations.

Damn. Why couldn't the Imprimans have let him beam Riker *up*—instead of Crusher *down?* Or should he have disregarded their cultural taboo and beamed his first officer up anyway, thereby affording him the resources of a state-of-the-art sickbay instead of those few items that Crusher could fit in her pack?

No. That would have been a serious violation of Impriman law, perhaps serious enough to end their economic alliance. And though Picard himself might have cared a good deal more about Riker than about relations with the Imprimans, the Federation wouldn't have seen things quite that way.

So we wait. And hope.

Data was thoughtful as he made his way to engineering. But his mind was not on the engine enhancement program to which he and Geordi had been assigned.

He was still thinking about curveballs.

Unfortunately his research had failed to turn up anything conclusive. Over the years numerous authorities, ranging from physicists to mathematicians to philosophers, had tried to explain the behavior of the curveball. And none of them had posited a more credible theory than those put forth by Geordi.

Just after the end of the twentieth century a Californian by the name of Ray Sparrow, who identified himself as a priest in the Church of the Center Field Bleachers, speculated that the pitch performed as it did because the ball's spin approximated that of the free electrons in the Mind of God.

While original, that theory didn't help the android

much. It was difficult enough, sometimes, for him to interpret the intentions of the captain, without trying to understand the thinking of a divine being.

As the doors to engineering slid aside at his approach, Data gave up his ruminations, or at least assigned them a lower priority in the positronic heirarchy of his intellectual functions. After all, duty came first, and the captain himself had asked him to work on the engines.

Engineering was unusually quiet, he noticed. Normally it was one of the more affable sections on the ship—no doubt a reflection of Geordi's personality, just as the security section was shaped by Worf's intensity, and sickbay by Dr. Crusher's dedication.

Just now, however, the only sound here was the drone of the engines. Hardly anyone looked up to see him enter. And those who did looked distracted, almost grim.

Nearing Geordi's office, he saw that its doors were open and that the engineering chief was inside, hunched over his personal work station.

Geordi did not appear to be working. His screen was alive with power-transfer schematics, but he was paying no attention to them.

Data knocked on the door frame as an alternative to catching his fellow officer by surprise. It was something he'd seen done by Commander Riker on more than one occasion.

Geordi turned partway in his seat and looked at him. "Hi, Data. I guess you've heard, huh?"

The android regarded him. "Can you be more specific?"

Swiveling around the rest of the way, Geordi cursed under his breath. "Of course. How would you know? You haven't been on duty." He got to his feet, crossed the open space between them, and put a hand on Data's shoulder.

"Commander Riker's been hurt," he said.

The android cocked his head. "Hurt?"

"Knifed. I didn't get all the details, but apparently it's bad. Very bad."

Data absorbed the information instantaneously, but it took a while for the implications to strike home.

"Do you think he will die?" ventured the android.

Geordi looked as if he had a bad taste in his mouth. "I don't know. I don't think anyone does—not even Dr. Crusher, and she's with him." His Adam's apple moved up and down. "I called the bridge a couple of minutes ago. That's when I got the news."

Data nodded slowly. "I see." He paused. "That is, I comprehend."

He wanted to say more. He wanted to be able to say he was worried or fearful or anguished—and mean it.

But he couldn't. He was only an android.

"Wesley was right," said the chief engineer. "He was telling us how dangerous that place can be. Besidia, I mean." He shook his head. "And the worst part is that I made fun of Wesley's concerns. I told him Commander Riker could get through anything."

The android observed the emotion in Geordi's face. Was that sorrow? Or guilt? Or a combination of both, perhaps?

"He still may," suggested Data. "You did say he was alive, did you not?"

Geordi sighed. "That's what I said, all right."

The android didn't know quite what to do next. But he knew what he *didn't* want to do, and that was leave.

"May I remain here," he asked, "until we learn the outcome of Commander Riker's situation?"

The engineering chief smiled. "Sure. In fact, I wish you would."

"Thank you," said Data. He took a seat on the opposite side of the room.

And in shared silence they waited.

* * *

It was cold in the narrow street, but Crusher barely felt it. She was too intent on nurturing the spark of life that still burned in her patient.

She looked up at Lyneea. "The knife," she said, "is going to have to come out."

The Impriman nodded soberly. "You hold him," she said. "I'll do it."

Crusher put her tricorder down and took Riker by the shoulders. His head lolled; his face was ashen.

The doctor thanked God he wouldn't feel the procedure. Introducing Riker to a hefty dose of painkillers was the second thing she'd attended to. The first had been to give him something for the shock.

"I've got him," she told Lyneea. With more strength than Crusher would have given her credit for, she slipped the blade out in one motion.

Blood gushed, but not as badly as the doctor had expected. Apparently the weapon had missed the major blood vessels. Lucky.

Sure. *Real* lucky.

Working as quickly as she could, Crusher applied the dermaplast she'd brought in her pack. First to Riker's back, where the wound gaped larger. Then to his chest.

That would stop the flow of blood. Judging by his pressure and by the pool of crimson slush in which they were kneeling, he had little enough to spare.

Next she brought out the equipment that would actually heal the wound. Not that she expected to be able to do it here in the street, but if she could get the process off to a good start, there would be less chance of infection.

After a few minutes she noticed Lyneea's expression. The Impriman looked angry. At her?

"Something wrong?" she asked.

Lyneea frowned and looked away. "These instruments are forbidden here," she said. "This is carnival time."

"Would you rather I let him die?" said the doctor. She

understood the reference, thanks to her discussions with Wesley about Besidia. "It was you who called for help," she reminded Lyneea, glancing at the communicator that lay beside her tricorder. "With a device, I might add, that is no less technologically advanced."

Lyneea swallowed.

Riker moaned softly. Crusher brushed aside the matted hair on his forehead and got another look from Lyneea—but this one, she realized, had nothing to do with technology. And she suddenly knew why the Impriman had broken her people's law to aid the human.

"We've got to get him out of here," said Lyneea, ignoring the penetrating quality of Crusher's scrutiny. "It's a miracle someone hasn't come down the street and seen us already."

The doctor nodded. "But we can't carry him very far by ourselves." She would have preferred not to move him at all, but she recognized the danger in remaining out in the open.

Lyneea took a quick look around. Her search seemed to end at a boarded-up door between two shops. Rising to her feet, she took a couple of quick steps and slammed shoulder-first into the door. There was a cracking sound as it yielded partway. When Lyneea followed with a sharp kick, the door swung inward, revealing a shadowy interior.

"We can hide the two of you in here," she told Crusher, "at least until I can get some help from my madraga. Then we can find a better place."

There didn't seem to be any other options. "Agreed," said the doctor.

As gently as they could, they picked Riker up and carried him through the open doorway.

Beverly Crusher's words were like cool water to a man dying of thirst: "He's going to be all right."

A cheer went up from those on the bridge, a wave of gladness that swelled and broke, washing away the fear that had tainted their spirits.

At one of the aft stations a crew member murmured thanks to her deity. Up at the conn, Wesley thrust a fist into the air.

Troi looked at the captain, seated beside her. He looked back, his eyes hard with pride—in Will Riker's penchant for survival, in his chief medical officer's ability to perform miracles, indeed in everyone and everything that had contributed to this happy result.

"You look tired," observed Picard.

"I am," she said. "A little."

"And this was not your shift. Why don't you get some rest? I think we'll be all right without you for a while."

Troi nodded. "You don't have to tell me twice."

The captain was beginning to extract details from the doctor as Troi rose and headed for the turbolift. On the way, out of the corner of her eye, she caught a glimpse of Worf. For a moment, as their eyes met, she could have sworn she saw a smile on his face. But before the counselor could be certain, he returned his attention to his instruments.

Stepping into the lift, Troi called for the level where her quarters were located. The doors closed and she was alone. The lift began to move.

Will . . .

Normally it took her quite some time to pick out a single presence from the midst of a large population, even if that presence was a familiar one.

But not this time. From the moment she had received word of Will's injury, she'd been with him.

Was it because of the relationship they'd once had? Or the different kind of closeness they'd come to enjoy here on the *Enterprise?* Or perhaps something else entirely?

She would probably never know. After all, empathy

164

was not a science; it could not be reduced to terms and equations.

And once she had linked up with the first officer and felt his agony and his terror—yes, even Will Riker could feel terror—she could not bring herself to break the contact. She had endured what he endured, suffered what he suffered, been racked by the same dark miseries, fought the same desperate fight.

In her life she had touched greater pain, but never as openly or as willingly. She had glimpsed deeper despair, but never had she embraced it as she embraced his.

And even now, with the first officer reportedly out of danger, she still could not break the link. For beneath the mantle of sedation, the agony was still with him, balanced against the force of his desire to survive. And it would be that way for some time.

Why had she exposed herself? Why had she made herself so vulnerable?

Certainly it didn't help him that she shared his pain. There was no way he could know or, knowing, be aided by the knowledge.

But that was not the point, was it? The point was that he not be alone, that he not endure this all by himself.

The point was that she show the universe someone cared about this being. In some inexplicable way that was very, very important to her.

Needless to say, the experience had taken its toll. It had worn her down, cut her to the marrow of her soul.

Yet through it all she had remained the picture of composure. It was her job to remain calm in the face of adversity, to set an example for others, and she had done what was expected of her.

After all, she was the ship's counselor. She was supposed to be able to handle this sort of thing.

But even a counselor had to vent feelings such as these, to let out the suffering she had taken in. Even a counselor had to have a breaking point.

A little more than halfway down to her quarters, the lift doors opened and a crewman stepped in. What was his name? She couldn't remember.

"Counselor," said the man, as the doors slid shut behind him. "Any news about Commander Riker?"

Will . . .

She nodded, doing her best to fashion a smile. "Dr. Crusher just sent word. Commander Riker will pull through."

A grin spread over the crewman's face. "That's good news," he told her. "Hell, that's *great* news."

"Yes," she said. "It is, isn't it?"

Two levels down, he departed and she was alone again. But not truly alone, for another crewman could walk in at any time.

Finally the lift came to a stop at her destination. A familiar sight greeted her: the corridor that led to her suite.

Normally it was a busy place at this time of day. As luck would have it, it was deserted now.

She was grateful.

The entrance to her residence was programmed to respond to her approach. It obeyed that programming and she breezed inside, hardly noticing when it sealed itself off in her wake.

Will . . .

She headed for her bedroom. Only after she'd reached it and another set of doors had closed behind her did she allow herself to crumble.

Slumping against the wall, she felt the sobs well up from deep within her. And she cried as she had seldom cried before.

Chapter Eleven

"YOU KNOW, Will m' boy, it's too bad."

"What is?"

"That we couldn't have brought some of that Dibdinagii joy juice back with us."

Will smiled. "It packed a punch, didn't it? Like some of the stuff we used to drink on a dare back home."

"Nothing like this synthehol they're producing now. The Ferengi are traders, not revelers. They wouldn't know a fine liqueur if they drowned in one."

"Maybe not. But when there's no fine liqueur to be had, synthehol's a damn sight better than . . . uh, Teller?"

"Yes?"

"Do you mind if I ask what you're doing?"

"I'm taking off my boot. What does it look like?"

"In the officers' mess? Is this some custom you picked up from the Dibdinagii?"

"I picked up a custom, all right. But it has nothing to do with footwear."

Teller turned his boot upside down, and a slim leather pouch fell into his lap. He tossed it in the air, caught it.

"Joy juice," he announced. "Dried and sterilized, of

course, so it wouldn't set off the biofilter alarms." He
plunked the pouch down on the table.

"In your boot. I don't believe it."

*"I keep all my valuables in my boots. An old Conlon
family tradition, starting with me. Because no one ever
thinks to look there."*

*"But this is contraband, Teller. If they catch you with
this, you'll be drummed out of Starfleet."*

"True—if they catch me. Which they won't."

He walked over to an automated food unit and ordered
two glasses of water. It took him a moment to mix in the
powder. Then he came back to the table.

"Care to join me, Will?"

"You're crazy. Out-and-out crazy."

"One drink, then I toss the rest away. How's that?"

"To prove what?"

Teller shrugged. *"That all things are possible. That a
man can do anything if he just sets his mind to it."*

"And you'd risk your career for that?"

Another shrug, a light in his eyes. *"Of course, if you're
too frightened of getting caught . . ."*

"Frightened isn't the word. Try 'petrified.'"

"Then I guess I'll be drinking alone."

There was something contagious about Teller's particular madness. Riker had learned that a long time ago.

"All right." He glanced over his shoulder at the entrance
to the mess. *"Do it. Just be quick about it."*

*"Quick as you please. Here you go. Whoa—wait a
second."*

"What now?"

"A toast, of course." He raised his glass. *"To the art of
the possible."*

"Sure. To that."

They drank.

"Ah. Now, you can't say that didn't hit the spot."

"It hit all the spots. Now get rid of that pouch."

"Hey, I keep my bargains, Ensign Riker. No one ever said a Conlon went back on his—"

"Teller! Someone's coming!"

"You've got ears like a bat, Will, you know that?" Teller crossed the room. "Are you sure you're not part Ferengi yourself?"

The sliding-aside of the door, a dour look. "Gentlemen." A pause. "The two of you look like cats who've swallowed canaries."

"Beg your pardon, sir?"

A slowly spreading frown. "Don't beg, Mr. Conlon. It isn't becoming. But as long as you're wrestling with that food dispenser, you can get me a cup of coffee. Make that a strong cup—it's been a long shore leave."

"Aye, Captain. Three cups of coffee, coming right up."

The smell of fresh-brewed coffee. Sunlight on his eyelids, a pinkish orange incandescence. He opened his eyes and saw the room.

The first thing he noticed was the fire in the hearth. But something was wrong. Wasn't the hearth in the wrong place? He looked around. This wasn't the room he'd been in before, the hotel room where he'd first met Lyneea. This was somewhere else.

A door opened behind him, and he tried to turn in response. He never quite got all the way around—a sharp pain in his shoulder stopped him.

That was when he realized he had a portable regenerator strapped to his shoulder. He looked at it stupidly.

"Ah. You're awake."

It wasn't Lyneea's voice, but he knew it all the same. *No. That can't be,* he told himself. *She's up on the ship.*

Then Dr. Crusher came around the couch he was lying on, and he had to admit that it could be. Hell, it *was*.

And that would explain where the regenerator had come from.

"How do you feel?" she asked, pulling a chair over to sit beside him. In one hand she held a cup of coffee.

The word "fine" started to come out of his mouth. Then he felt his shoulder, worked it in its socket, and suffered that darting pain again. "This hurts," he told her. As he looked into her bewitching green eyes, he remembered why. "The knife, right?"

She nodded. "The knife."

"Then Lyneea called the ship after all." He grunted. "How about that?"

"But not without a lot of soul-searching," Crusher pointed out. "She wasn't too happy about using your communicator, what with that high-tech ban they have around here. And when I took out my tricorder . . . forget it. I thought she was going to bite right through her lip."

Riker regarded her. "You shouldn't be here. It's too dangerous."

"You should have thought of that before you went and got yourself skewered."

"You can't go back, you know. Not until the end of the carnival."

The doctor rolled her eyes. "Believe me, I know. I've only been told half a dozen times, by everyone from the captain to Lyneea to those two strong-arm types who lugged you here in the middle of the night."

Of course. They'd had to get him off the streets somehow, and there were no mechanical conveyances in Besidia.

"This isn't where we were staying before," he noted.

"No. They thought it might not be safe there any longer. Also, this place was closer to the market. It was hard enough to carry you *this* far."

Riker took it all in. "Where's Lyneea now?" he asked.

Crusher shrugged. "Damned if I know. She muttered something about time running out—and then ran out herself."

Time running out? He didn't like the sound of that.

He sat halfway up—and winced at the searing pain that erupted in his shoulder. "Damn," he breathed, easing himself back down onto the couch.

"Serves you right," she told him.

"How long have I been lying here?" he asked.

The doctor set aside her coffee, leaned over and searched through a pack on the floor, finally extracting her tricorder. "Almost two days, thanks to the dimexidrine."

"Two . . . *days?*" he echoed.

Crusher straightened, looked him in the eye. "Why? Did you think you'd have come this far in less time? Or without the aid of a sedative?" She placed a forefinger against his chest—and none too gently. "Listen to me, Will Riker. I know exactly what you're thinking."

"You do?"

"Yes. You think you're going to leap up and go after Lyneea, as if you were fully recuperated, but you're not. Forty-eight hours ago you were knocking at death's door. There wasn't enough blood left in you to sustain a good-sized rodent. Plus you had a nasty concussion." She sighed. "I practice medicine, Commander, not magic. It's going to take time for that shoulder to heal properly, even with the regenerator working nonstop. And then some more time for you to get your strength back. In sickbay it might have happened a little faster, but not much. You're not made of duranium, Mister. Remember that."

He smiled a little at the doctor's speech. Of course she had a point. In this condition he wouldn't be much help to Lyneea. And she had the strong-arm types if she really needed help.

Crusher set her tricorder and held it near his shoulder. Judging by her expression, his progress met with her approval.

"How am I doing?" he asked.

"Could be worse," she told him.

What was it Lyneea had said to him in the beginning? Something about Imprimans taking care of their own problems?

Well, she'd finally gotten it her way. With Riker laid up, Lyneea could conduct the kind of investigation she preferred, without having to play nursemaid to an offworlder. Especially one who thought he knew her world because he'd been here once for a couple of months.

On the other hand, he *had* made some contributions. He'd saved her life when Bosch was about to draw a blaster on her in his room. And if it hadn't been for his stubbornness, they might never have found Teller's body.

But then, he'd also fallen for Norayan's ruse, and he'd nearly lost his life to the Pandrilite in that alley. And wasn't it Riker who'd blundered into Kobar, putting him on his guard—and maybe drawing the attention of his would-be assassin in the process?

"You look pensive," observed Crusher. "Can it be I've actually drummed some sense into you?"

He looked up at her. "Did Lyneea find out anything about the knife thrower? Like whom he worked for?"

The doctor put the tricorder away and shook her head. "No."

Good. Then he could continue to believe it wasn't Norayan.

Apparently Lyneea believed it, too, or she wouldn't have called for help from Madraga Criathis. Because if Norayan had hired the assassin, and if she knew Riker was convalescing here, relatively defenseless . . .

He eyed the door warily and wished he had a phaser close at hand instead of a regenerator.

"I heard about your friend," said Crusher. "The captain told me."

Riker frowned. The loss of Teller had subsided to a dull ache in his gut.

"Things happen," he remarked. "You just never think they'll happen to you or to the people you love." He met her gaze. "Who else did the captain tell?"

"Only those who might have had to beam down at some point. Me. Worf." She paused. "I guess that's it. Oh, and Deanna probably knows, too—but then, that's Deanna."

Riker found the mere thought of Troi soothing. But he put it aside. He didn't feel much like being soothed now.

"Listen," he said, "I'd appreciate it if you wouldn't make too much of Teller's death when we get back. Especially under the circumstances."

The doctor nodded. "I understand."

For a moment or two there was an awkward silence. Then Crusher spoke again.

"You know," she said, "Wesley was afraid something would happen to you."

Riker cracked a smile. "Was he?"

"Yup. It seems he was studying Impriman culture, particularly as it relates to Besidia and the Trade Carnival, and he decided that this was a pretty dangerous place." Her eyes twinkled. "Actually he started out trying to figure out why Starfleet had sent you down here. And though he never quite came up with the answer, he did unearth some interesting items along the way—in addition, I mean, to his conclusions about it being dangerous."

Riker's smile widened. He couldn't help it. "Such as?"

"Well, there was something about a parade on the last day of the carnival. All the locals dress up as clowns and serenade the officials of each madraga."

"I've seen it," said Riker. "It's quite a show. And some of them do a little more than serenade—but that part wouldn't be in the library files."

"What else?" Crusher asked herself. "Oh, yes. The maze, up in the hills above the city? Wesley was telling me how all the tunnels are color-coded, so you can find your way in and out, and . . ."

Riker stopped hearing her. He'd fixed on the word "color-coded" and was unable to get past it.

Why? He knew about the color codes. Damn, he'd seen them only a couple of days ago.

And then it came to him. Like a hawk out of a gray Alaskan sky: The codes would have been useless to his friend. Teller was color-blind.

Which meant that if he'd been hiding in the maze and not just dumped there after he was killed, or if he'd had to stage a rendezvous there, or even if he'd just been using the place as a cache for Fortune's Light, he must have had another way of getting in and out. And if the seal was hidden there, he would have needed a way to find it again after he concealed it.

Crusher waved a hand in front of his face. "You've got that faraway look again, Commander. Something I said?"

He took her hand in his. "Doctor, I've got to get back to the maze."

Her mouth became a straight, hard line. "See?" she said. "I knew you'd try this. That's why I kept you under for so long."

"You don't understand," he told her. "I think I just figured out how to find the seal."

"Good for you. When Lyneea returns, you can tell her all about it. I'm sure she'll be only too glad to test out your theory."

"But we don't know when she'll be back or, for that matter, even *if* she'll be back. You heard her say that time is running out? Well, it is. Lyneea won't call on us until she's done everything she can to help Criathis. And even then she may decide we're not worth the effort."

For a moment the doctor seemed to waver in her resolve. Then she shook her head. "Forget it, Commander. You're still weak. You can barely use that arm. And your assassin friend is still out there; maybe next time he'll be more thorough."

"I appreciate your concern," he told her, "but this is something I have to do." Taking a deep breath, he tried to sit up again. This time he made it. "For Teller." Pivoting on the couch, he planted his feet on the floor.

Crusher was faster. She placed herself in his way.

"Use your head," she told him. "What are you going to do? Resurrect your friend by risking your own life?"

"No," he agreed, gathering himself. He really *was* weak. "I can't make his past go away, and I can't bring him back from the dead. But I *can* make amends for him—by returning the seal to Madraga Criathis."

"If you live long enough."

Riker glanced out the open window at the snow-covered street below. Was the doctor right? Was there someone out there waiting for him?

Hell, hadn't he wondered about that himself before she'd ever mentioned it?

"I'll take my chances," he told her. And with that, he got to his feet.

But Crusher wasn't budging. "Don't make me pull rank, Will. Don't make me order you to stay here."

Riker looked down at her, smiling gently. "It won't matter if you do, Doctor. This isn't about Starfleet. This isn't even about Criathis. It's about one man's obligation to another man. I wasn't a very good friend the last few years, or I would've seen how Teller was changing. But I'm going to be a good friend now."

He put his hand on her shoulder. "It's not just Teller I'm making amends for, Beverly. It's me, too."

Crusher frowned. "Silver-tongued Will Riker."

"Not this time," he assured her. "This time, it's straight from the heart."

She searched his face, came to a decision. "Yes, I suppose it is." She grunted. "All right, Commander. You win. But if you're going somewhere, I'm going with you."

And snatching up her pack, she began checking to make sure that everything was secure.

He hadn't anticipated that. His first reaction was to assemble reasons she couldn't go. But there were more reasons for *him* not to go, so he decided to keep his mouth shut.

Besides, he mused, she'd probably be as safe with him as she would be if she stayed in the suite alone. Which was to say, not very.

Her pack slung over her shoulder, Crusher straightened again. "Ready when you are," she told him. "Back to the maze?"

He adjusted his sling to make it a little more comfortable. "Back to the maze," he confirmed.

Stretching out on his bed, Picard took a deep breath. After a moment or two he felt himself start to relax.

It had been a close call for his first officer. He didn't like close calls, particularly when he had no control over them.

As his body unwound, so did his mind. And some of the ship's business that had been submerged during the emergency started to float to the surface.

The captain sifted through it. And stopped when he got to Data's recent attraction to the holodecks.

It was a development he'd barely noticed at first. But the android was hardly a creature of habit, so anytime his behavior grew repetitive, it drew Picard's attention.

And given the substance of Data's *last* obsession with the holodeck . . .

Perhaps it was something that needed looking into. Filing the thought away, he went on to the next bit of command minutiae.

Rain clamored on the dugout roof, dripped off the edge of it in wind-twisted cascades, and collected in puddles on the worn concrete steps. It had begun in the

Icebreakers' half of the fifth inning with a light sprinkle, which the umpires decided would pass.

The umpires were incorrect. By the top of the sixth the skies had become bloated with black-bellied clouds, which looked no less menacing after the stadium lights were turned on. Then came the wind and the sheeting downpour, and by the time the ground crew rolled out the tarpaulin, the pitcher's mound and the base paths were the color of rich, dark cocoa.

Now Data knew what the clubhouse man had meant when he'd questioned the weather before the game. Apparently he'd seen this kind of meteorological phenomenon before.

In any case the android didn't have to sit through the delay. He could have stopped the program and picked it up again after the deluge was over. Certainly he wasn't honing his prowess as a baseball player by huddling in the dugout.

But only a couple of the other Icebreakers had retreated into the clubhouse. Most of them remained out here despite the swirling wind and the rain, speaking in soft voices and regarding the vast, empty field. Occasionally they would laugh, and the laughter would ripple down the bench from player to player until it was finally lost in the *shusharush* of the elements.

This was part of the experience, Data told himself. Part of what Commander Riker had built for himself, and as such, he could not overlook its possible value.

Still, as time passed, and the players' exchanges became more and more like those that had gone before, the android found his mind drawn elsewhere. It kept returning to matters outside the holodeck and, in particular, to the goings-on in Besidia.

Why *had* the first officer been called down there? And was he truly out of the woods now, as Dr. Crusher had informed the captain? Or, as Wesley seemed to think, did other dangers await him?

Throughout the worst of the storm, Denyabe had been sitting next to Data, his fists jammed into the pockets of his warm-up jacket. He hadn't spoken a word to the android or anyone else. He just followed the clouds in their passage and smiled from time to time.

So the android was unprepared when Denyabe elbowed him in the ribs—or what *would* have been his ribs if he'd truly been Bobo Bogdonovich, and not Dr. Soong's creation.

"Hey," said the second baseman. "You look down. Like your best friend just died."

Data looked at him. *How perceptive,* he thought. Especially in view of the android's limited capacity for facial expression.

"In fact," he told Denyabe, "a friend was severely injured recently. But I am told he is recuperating."

The second baseman nodded. "Good." He turned back to the field, where the rain had lightened to a drizzle and the wind seemed all but spent.

Just when Data thought their conversation had come to an end, Denyabe nudged him again and pointed to something. The android followed his gesture past the left field wall to the mountains rising in the distance.

"See that?" he asked.

Data wasn't sure what he was referring to. He said as much.

"The light," said Denyabe. "The sun's trying to come out—way up in the mountains."

The android saw it now, though he was a little surprised at the acuity of his teammate's vision. Most humans could not see well at such great distances.

"It's the Light," said Denyabe.

"The Light?" echoed the android.

"Yes. The Light, the golden radiance that pierces the clouds at the end of a storm." The second baseman's eyes narrowed. "Back where I come from—or anyway, where

178

my people come from—it's supposed to be an omen of good luck. The Light touches you, the goddess Fortune lays her hands on your shoulders, and you're blessed. You'll become wealthy, you'll have a big family, you'll be surrounded by love and happiness. The same with the land. Where the Light falls on it, the crops will grow strong and tall."

Out among the mountains, the shafts of light were easily visible now. As the storm receded, they seemed to be approaching the stadium.

"An interesting theory," said Data. "And probably one with some basis in fact. Light, after all, is a—"

Denyabe stopped him with a shake of his head. "No. It's a lie. The goddess Fortune, the Light, the promise of wealth—all lies." He smiled at the android. "Fortune doesn't turn double plays. She doesn't knock me in from second base. And she sure as hell doesn't grow crops." He hawked and spat. "Wealth? I'll tell you what wealth is. It's you and me, here and now. It's people working on something together—something they can be proud of." He grunted. "People can't depend on Fortune, Bobo. They've got to depend on one another." A pause. "You understand?"

Data nodded—slowly at first, tentatively, and then with more assurance. He hadn't comprehended all of it, to be sure. There was still much for him to ponder. But he had grasped the essence of it.

The second baseman winked. "All right, then. You remember all that and maybe you'll hit a home run today."

The android winked back—it seemed to be the appropriate response. "I certainly hope so," he said, as the ground crew trotted out to uncover the playing field.

Even though Riker had some idea of where he was going this time, the passageways were still narrow and confusing, and he needed his wits about him. The color codes wouldn't help him much if he read them incorrectly.

"How's the arm?" asked Crusher, a few steps behind him.

"It isn't throbbing as much as it did before," he told her. "The effect of the cold, maybe?"

"Or else your regenerated nerves are deteriorating. But more likely it *is* the cold." She looked around. "You know," she said, "this place seemed a lot more romantic when I was listening to Wesley describe it. It's hard to be enchanted when you're so concerned with staying alive."

Riker was concerned, too. He'd been looking over his shoulder since the moment they left their hotel suite. There had been no sign that anyone was following them—but then, a real professional would have been sure not to leave one.

And now that they were in the maze, it would have been easy to kill them as Teller was killed—and just dump their bodies in the hole beside his.

"Are we getting close?" asked the doctor.

"Very close," he told her. "In fact, if memory serves . . ." They negotiated a sharp bend in the passage and there it was—the pit created by the cave-in. "We're here," he said.

It was no different from a dozen other pits they'd passed on the way—at least, at first glance. Crusher said so as they approached.

"Nonetheless," Riker insisted, "this is the one."

They shone their beamlights down into the darkness. To her credit, the doctor didn't gasp at what she saw within. She didn't make a sound. In fact, her only overt reaction was a flaring of her chiseled nostrils.

Teller was just as he and Lyneea had left him. Perfectly preserved by the cold, more like an ivory statue than the remains of a man.

"I'll go first," said Crusher. "You're going to need some help getting down."

Nor was the irony of role reversal lost on the first officer. Normally Riker, with his greater strength and agility, would have been giving the doctor a hand. But this was no time for machismo.

"You've got to hang on to that flat rock," he instructed, indicating the stone with his beam. "Then drop. There's a slope below it."

She walked around the hole until she had a better view. "I see it," she told him. Then, stashing the beamlight in her tunic, she latched on to the rock and lowered herself over the brink. A moment later he heard the crunch of her boots on the gravel.

"All right," she called softly—out of deference for the dead man? "Do your best. I'll try to keep you from hitting anything."

Riker stowed his own beamlight. He sat carefully on the edge of the cave-in and took hold of the rock with one hand. Then he let himself slip in and down.

His purchase on the rock was tenuous at best; he couldn't hang on for very long, and he wound up dropping at an awkward angle. But Crusher was there to help straighten him out when he landed.

Together they slid down the incline. Somehow they managed to keep their feet.

"Thanks," he told her.

"Don't mention it," she said. "I didn't spend all that time healing your shoulder to let you go and wreck it again."

The body was at the base of the slope. They knelt down beside it.

"What are we looking for?" she asked.

He tried not to think about what they were doing. He couldn't shake the notion that it was one step removed from grave-robbing—if very necessary grave-robbing.

"A communications device of some kind—that is, if I've guessed right about Teller's method of finding his way through the maze. And even if it's here, it won't be easy to locate. Lyneea searched him pretty thoroughly and didn't find a thing."

"Then it's not in his pockets," concluded Crusher.

"No. Not in any *obvious* pockets, anyway." He played the beamlight on Teller's footwear. "Try those."

"His boots?"

"Just a hunch. I don't think Lyneea looked there."

The doctor removed the dead man's right boot and reached inside it. Immediately she turned to regard Riker, and a grim smile played at the corners of her mouth.

"There's something here all right," she told him. "A couple of somethings, in fact." A second later she drew out a plastic rectangle.

"A chit," said the first officer, recognizing it easily. He trained his light on it. "A valuable one at that—you don't see too many of this denomination." And the thing was black. "Issued by Madraga Rhurig."

"What does that mean?" asked the doctor, delving deeper with her narrow fingers.

"Probably Teller's payoff, or at least the first installment. And since it came from Rhurig, that's probably who hired him to steal the seal."

Crusher plucked out something else then—an object the size and shape of the chit but thicker.

As Riker illuminated it, she turned it over in her hand. It was silver, with four fingertip-size plates and three tiny but separate readouts above them.

"He had a pocket sewn inside his boot," explained Crusher, still looking a little incredulous. "This fit right inside it, along with the chit."

"It looks Maratekkan," he observed. "They're good at miniaturization." He pulled his glove off with his teeth and held out his good hand. "May I?"

She gave it over. Cradling it in his palm, he fingered one of its plates. Immediately one of the readouts became illuminated; numerals appeared.

"Coordinates?" ventured Crusher.

"That's what they look like," he agreed. When he touched another plate, the first readout died and a second one sprang to life. It displayed the same sort of numerals.

The third plate triggered the bottommost readout, but that one was blank, as if it hadn't been programmed. That left the fourth plate, which was set below the first three and centered.

Riker had an idea what it was for. Touching the first plate again, he reactivated the original set of numerals. Then he tried the fourth plate.

Suddenly the thing started beeping. Not loud—in fact, if it hadn't been for the silence all around them, they might not have heard it at all. But it was loud enough.

Riker nodded, gripped the thing tighter. He looked at Crusher.

"A homing mechanism," he told her. "The louder this beeping gets, the closer one is to one's objective."

"I see," said the doctor. She tapped the topmost readout with a fingernail. "It looks as if it's got two active settings. You think that one of them will lead us to . . . what's it called again?"

"Fortune's Light."

"Right. And the other setting, I imagine, would indicate the way out."

"That would make sense," said Riker. "Teller probably planted a transmitter near one of the exits."

"So what are we waiting for? Let's follow the audio signal and—"

A sound. They froze at the same time and exchanged glances by the glow of the beamlight.

It could have been one of those skittering things, Riker told himself. There were enough of them down here. But somehow, he didn't think so. The sound had been too heavy, too substantial. And it had been isolated, with nothing before or after it—as if whoever made the sound had realized it, and stopped before he could make another one.

Riker jabbed a forefinger at the opening above them; Crusher nodded. They had to get out of there or they'd be easy targets for whoever had followed them.

With a touch of his thumb, he eliminated the beeping. Then he pressed the device into the doctor's hand and led her up the slope.

"You first," she whispered, as she stashed the thing in her tunic. She braced herself and held out her hands.

He shook his head. "No."

If Crusher went first, at least one of them had a shot at getting away. If they wasted time trying to get *him* out, they might both be caught.

And he couldn't allow that. They had just found the key to recovering Fortune's Light; it was important that it not be lost again.

The doctor glared at him, but gave in. There was no time to protest and she knew it.

This time, Riker held out his hand—just one, unfortunately, but Crusher was a slender woman. It would have to do.

Placing her boot in his palm, grasping his good shoulder for balance, she launched herself up toward the crossways-lying rock. Riker couldn't add anything to her effort—it was all he could do to keep his hand steady against the thrust of her heel.

But it turned out to be enough. And once the doctor had a good grasp on the rock, she managed to wrestle her way out of the pit. It wasn't easy for her—far from it. But she managed.

"All right," she gasped, leaning her head over the brink. "Come on. There's nobody around—not yet."

She held out her hand to him, but they both knew it

was a token gesture. If he was going to get out, it would be under his own power. And he had to make it on the first try; after that, with his strength at low ebb already, the odds would drop precipitously.

Setting his teeth, Riker eased his arm out of the sling. His shoulder complained, sending shoots of fire through the muscles in his back. He did his best to ignore them.

Hell, he told himself, *this is nothing. If you can't take this, you might as well give up the whole idea.*

Taking hold of the rocky projection he'd used once before, he gathered himself and sprang for the crosspiece. His hands hooked around either side of it. In the same motion, he swung his legs up and past, until they found the lip of the pit.

Agony. Like talons shredding the newborn nerve ends in his shoulder. Like acid searing the raw, half-formed flesh.

No time to breathe. No time to think about what would come next.

As Riker readjusted his grip on the rock, pushed with his feet and twisted, he cried out—he couldn't help it. He thought his shoulder would give out before he could reach the top. He thought he would find himself on his back next to his friend, hopeless, having spent the last of his strength.

He was wrong on all counts. On the other side of the blinding pain was Crusher. And the hard, reassuring ground that surrounded the pit.

"Come on," she was saying, trying to get him up off his back. "Let's *move,* Commander."

Cursing inwardly, he allowed her to help him to his feet. Then, slipping his bad arm back inside the sling, he started off with her down the passageway.

It was getting late, he noted. Up above, the sky was approaching the color of twilight.

Behind them, there were footfalls—distinct now, unmistakable. It gave them a greater sense of urgency as they negotiated a bend in the corridor and rushed through the gathering gloom.

They had a head start, he told himself. They could probably elude whoever was pursuing them.

But more than likely, there were *other* pursuers in the maze. And maybe a few outside as well, waiting for them to emerge.

A blaster would help to even the odds. It would help a *lot*.

Making up his mind, Riker stopped dead in his tracks. A moment later, the doctor stopped too—and looked back.

"What's the matter?" she breathed.

"Nothing. Just hoping our friend is well armed, that's all."

"What does *that* mean?"

"We need a blaster," he explained. "And I can't think of another way to get one." Slowly, as silently as he could, he worked his way back to the twist in the passageway.

When he reached it, he listened. The footfalls were getting louder. Closer. Suddenly they stopped.

In the vicinity of the pit? Perhaps to see if anything had been disturbed?

After a moment the sounds of progress picked up again. Riker noticed how quickly night was falling, how eagerly it was rushing to fill this place. But that was all right. Their pursuer would take that much longer to spot them.

And by then, he hoped, it would be too late.

The scrape of boot soles on gravel, a little nearer now. Nearer still. He exchanged glances with the doctor as she clung to the wall behind him. She frowned, unable to conceal her anxiety.

Turning back to the twist in the corridor, holding his breath, Riker closed his fingers into a fist. Just another moment. Just one more second. But his timing would have to be perfect.

As their pursuer turned the corner, Will took a swing at him. But the man was shorter than he'd expected, and the blow was only a glancing one.

It gave the Impriman a chance to strike back—and strike he did. Something hit Riker in the jaw—hard enough to stagger him. As he recovered, trying to protect his injured arm, a light came out of nowhere to blind him.

"Run," he told Crusher, sweeping her behind him—and knowing all the time how useless the gesture would be. He didn't stand a chance against a blaster. And the doctor wouldn't get very far in the time it would take Riker to fall.

Anyway, Crusher wasn't running. She was apparently going to stand her ground.

"If I'm going to die," she answered, throat tight, "I'm going to do it with dignity." And she stepped up to stand alongside him.

He was proud of her for that.

"Chits and whispers," said the voice behind the light. "Why did you have to go and surprise me like that?"

He knew that voice. And he'd never been so happy to hear it as he was now.

"Lyneea," he said.

"You're damned right," she told him, lowering the beamlight a little. She rubbed her temple with the fingers of one hand. "What were you trying to do? End our partnership in one fell swoop?"

He chuckled, massaging his jaw where she'd struck him. "I might ask the same of you. What in blazes are you doing here anyway?"

"Keeping an eye on you, of course. Did you think I'd leave you all alone, without protection?"

"You mean you were waiting outside the hotel? Watching over us?"

187

"That's *just* what I mean."

He thought about it for a moment. "But not *just* to protect us—right? You were hoping the assassin would show up—and try again."

"Obviously. I had no other leads."

Riker sighed. "I've got to hand it to you," he said. "Sentimental you're not."

"And cooperative *you're* not. What kind of insanity possessed you to leave your suite? Do you know how much more difficult it is to protect someone on the move?"

"You could have stopped me," he suggested.

"But that would have ruined the plan. We would have lost the element of surprise."

"Ah," he said. "I forgot—sorry."

"Excuse me," said Crusher, "but could we continue this elsewhere? I mean, our assassin friend may be closer than we think." She looked around, shivered. "I'd feel a whole lot safer on the *outside* of this maze."

Lyneea nodded. "Very sensible, Doctor." She regarded Riker. "You would do well to take a lesson from her."

The first officer cursed beneath his breath. Just what he needed—arguments from both sides.

Suddenly something clattered against the stones beneath their feet. As the echoes died, Lyneea played her light beam over it.

"What's *that?*" she asked. "More high-tech contraband?"

Riker bent and picked it up. "Just the thing that's going to lead us to Fortune's Light." And with a flick of his finger, he activated the device. It started beeping again.

The expression on Lyneea's face was worth the soreness in his jaw.

188

Chapter Twelve

"AND THAT," said Riker's intercom voice, "is the long and the short of it."

Picard drummed his fingers on his desk, stood, pulled down on his tunic, and strolled thoughtfully across his ready room.

"Allow me to iterate," he told his first officer, who had seldom seemed so far away as he did now. "Disregarding the severity of your wound, you hoodwinked Dr. Crusher into letting you go off on what is commonly known as a fishing expedition, despite the suspicion that whoever tried to kill you the first time would almost certainly try again. Once in the maze, you were rewarded—beyond any reasonable expectation—with the discovery of a homing device, which you believe has been programmed with the location of Fortune's Light. And now you wish to test that theory again, despite the severity of your wounds and the all-too-obvious fact that more able-bodied personnel are available." The captain cleared his throat. "Is that a fair summary, Number One?"

Silence for a moment. "I don't think I'd use the word 'hoodwinked,' sir." More silence. "Not exactly."

Picard regarded his aquarium. Sometimes he wished he could place some of his officers in that tank; certainly they'd be easier to keep tabs on. And they would have considerably fewer opportunities to take foolish chances with their lives.

Then again, there were extenuating circumstances. One could not forget that Riker had lost a close friend recently. That kind of experience had a way of jarring one's values.

"Will, you are obviously playing a very deadly game down there. Would it not be wiser to have someone *healthy* working with Lyneea?"

Picard could almost hear his first officer bristling. And hadn't he known what the answer would be, even before he posed the question?

"I'm still the best man for the job, sir. Unless, of course, that was a thinly veiled order."

The captain grunted. "No, Number One. It wasn't an order."

"Then I'd like to see this through, sir."

Picard nodded. "What about some help? A small security contingent?"

"Not necessary," advised Riker. "We're just going to find out where the seal is hidden. And Teller wouldn't have hidden it anywhere he couldn't easily recover it."

Picard mulled it over. "No," he agreed, "I suppose not." He paused. "But there is still the matter of that assassin. And who can say he's working alone? His employer could have hired others as well."

"I've thought of that myself, sir. But a group of offworlders would just draw too much attention. Remember, we're still trying to keep the seal's disappearance a secret. Besides, if someone's really determined to get me, an entourage isn't going to help."

The captain frowned. "All right. We'll do it your way—for now. But I will take the precaution of preparing an away team, in the event you should need help."

"Fair enough," said Riker.

Picard considered the aquarium again. "What about Dr. Crusher? What provisions have you made for her safety?"

"She'll be well protected," the first officer told him. "Lyneea has arranged for Madraga Criathis to provide some retainers. They'll be guarding the doctor's hotel suite from the inside as well as the outside."

"Good. At least one of my people will come out of this alive."

Riker didn't respond to the gibe.

"Incidentally, Number One, does your partner down there know of this conversation? Or will you be continuing to communicate in clandestine fashion?"

"No," said Riker. "She knows all right. In fact, sir, she's standing right here. I've already explained about that loophole in the high-tech ban, and she agrees—for the time being, anyway—that it's a gray area. So I don't expect any restrictions on our communications."

An exchange followed—one that Picard couldn't hear very well. "I beg your pardon, Commander?"

"Uh—nothing, sir. Lyneea was just reminding me that we have to go. The merger ceremony is scheduled to take place in fourteen hours."

"I understand, Number One. But remember—stay in touch."

"Will do, Captain."

Picard thought for a moment, then exited his ready room. As the more brightly lit, more spacious environs of the bridge opened up before him, he turned toward Worf at Tactical.

The Klingon had already looked up from his instruments, as if he'd sensed that an order was coming.

"Lieutenant Worf, be ready to beam down to Besidia on short notice."

"Trouble, sir?" asked Worf.

Picard shook his head. "Not yet, no. But I anticipate

it." He glanced at the Ops station, where Data usually sat. It was occupied by Lieutenant Solis. "Isn't this Commander Data's shift?" he asked.

"No, sir," responded the Klingon. "Commander Data's shift ended twenty minutes ago. He is presently"—Worf punched up the information—"in Holodeck One."

The captain noted that. "Mr. Worf, I would like Commander Data to be ready to help out as well. Please convey this to him. In person."

The security chief must have wondered at the order, but he didn't hesitate to obey it. Before Picard could make himself comfortable in the command center, Worf had disappeared into the turbolift.

After the rain delay the Icebreakers put a new pitcher on the mound. As Data understood it, the first pitcher's arm had tightened up, and it was feared he would no longer be effective. Or that he would strain his arm if he continued to pitch. Or both. The answer depended on which infielder he consulted in his search for insight.

As luck would have it, the new pitcher threw to only two batters. The first one walked. The second one tripled into the gap in left center field.

The Icebreakers' third pitcher was a little more stingy. But with two outs, he allowed a single over second base. The Sunset runner came in from third with the go-ahead run, making the score three to one in favor of the Phoenix team.

Terwilliger sat and fumed in one corner of the dugout. No one went near him—neither players nor coaches. No one dared. For as Jackson explained to Data while the fourth Icebreaker pitcher was warming up, Terwilliger felt responsible for the unfortunate turn of events.

"Why should that be?" asked the android. "He was not on the field. We were. If anyone is to blame, we are."

Jackson shook his head. "He's the manager." He

frowned at the sky and its tattered clouds, perhaps wondering why the rain had to come when it did. "If he had put in somebody else, the game might still be tied. Who's he going to blame—the public address announcer?"

The last out for the Sunsets came on a curveball, Data noted. A curveball that was popped up to Galanti at first.

The android sympathized with the batter.

The pitching coach, a large, red-faced man, stood and clapped his hands as the players came in from the field. "All right," he roared. "Let's get 'em back. Let's get something started here."

Data was only too glad to comply. As the leadoff hitter, he lingered in the dugout only long enough to deposit his glove and secure a bat. Then he bounced back out and headed for home plate.

The Sunset pitcher was in back of the mound, already twirling the ball in his bare hand while he waited for his teammates to find their positions. By the time the android took his place in the batter's box, the infielders were already set. A few seconds later the outfielders reached their destinations as well, and the pitcher ascended to the rubber.

"Play ball," called the umpire.

The pitcher went into his motion. Data crouched slightly and drew the bat back. The first time the ball became visible, whipping around from behind the pitcher's back, the android riveted his attention to it. It flew straight and true.

Not a curveball, he observed—and was pleased by the fact. Keeping his eye on it, he prepared to drive it over the fence. After all, he had no trouble hitting fastballs.

The ball came whizzing toward him. Data began to step forward, to put his weight into his swing.

There was only one possibility he wasn't prepared for. And of course, *that* was the one that presented itself.

Instead of hurtling over home plate, or at least in that

general direction, the ball came right at Data. Before he could avoid it, it had plunked him on the shoulder.

Out on the mound, the pitcher kicked at the dirt. "Take yer base," barked the home plate umpire.

For a moment, Data just stood there. He felt as if he'd been cheated somehow, as if that fastball should have been sailing out of the stadium now, instead of lying motionless at his feet.

But rules were rules. A batter hit by a pitch had no option but to go to first base. Reconciling himself to that reality, the android dropped his bat and started down the base path.

"Wait a minute," stormed Terwilliger, charging out of the dugout. The team trainer, an older man with a thick crop of white hair, was right behind him.

Data was a little surprised by the manager's concern. Until now, Terwilliger had not shown any great affinity for him.

Perhaps, he mused, his gruff manner was a charade. A mask he used to conceal his true affection for his players.

Then he realized that the manager wasn't heading for him. He was heading for the umpire.

"Time out," called the man in blue, turning to confront Terwilliger.

"What kind of bullhinkey is *this?*" growled the manager, coming up just short of a collision. "You're gonna let them throw at my cleanup batter?"

"Give me a break," said the umpire. "He was leading off, and Cordoban's up next. They'd be *crazy* to throw at him. The ball just got away."

Data could hear their words clearly and distinctly, despite the growing clamor in the stands. It was one of the benefits of being an android.

"They *threw* at him, I tell ya!" Terwilliger turned his cap around and put his nose in the other man's face. "I want that pitcher tossed out on his behind!"

The umpire was obviously trying to remain composed. But he also wasn't giving an inch. "I'm not throwing him out," he said, "so forget it."

By this time, the other Icebreakers had been drawn to the top step of the dugout, and it did not take the talents of a Deanna Troi to divine their hostility.

"Then I'm protesting the game," yelled Terwilliger, his eyes bulging. "This is a mother-lovin' *outrage!*" And he turned to the crowd along the first base line, raising his arms as if in appeal. The spectators responded with an ear-shattering roar. Next he turned to the other side of the field. Another roar, louder than the first.

"I know what you're trying to do," said the umpire.

"Oh, yeah?" said Terwilliger, rounding on him. "And what's that?"

"You're trying to get me to throw you out. So your team'll get riled up and do some damage."

"What's wrong with that?" snarled Terwilliger, kicking dirt on the other man's shoes with all the energy he could muster.

"Nothing—except I'm not going along with it."

"Why not?" asked the manager, flinging his hat into the pile of dirt. "Don'tcha have any self-respect?"

"Because it isn't fair," maintained the umpire. "Besides, if I toss *you* out, then McNab's going to want to get ejected, too." McNab, Data knew, was the manager of the Sunsets.

Terwilliger chomped and swore. "You mean I've got to bring *family* into this? Is that what you're telling me?"

The umpire's features hardened.

"I hate to do it," snapped the manager. "I *really, really* do."

"Then get back to your dugout," instructed the man in blue.

"Not on your life," said Terwilliger, planting his index finger in the umpire's chest. And he proceeded to reel off a string of derogatory remarks the likes of which Data had never heard. The android believed that even a Klingon would have been shocked.

By the time Terwilliger had finished, he was the color of molten lava. And the umpire was heaving him from the game—only figuratively, of course, though he looked as though he'd have liked to do it literally.

"Come on," said the Icebreakers' trainer, taking Data by the arm. "By the way, you're not hurt or anything, are you?"

The android shook his head. "No. Thank you." And still mulling over what had transpired, he allowed the older man to escort him to first base.

"What an actor," chuckled the trainer.

"An actor," repeated Data. "You mean Terwilliger?"

"Sure do. He was just itching for an excuse to come out here. If you hadn't given it to him, he'd have had to make one up." He chuckled again. "It's moments like these that make me put off retirement."

Suddenly the crowd grew loud again. Data turned, expecting to see Terwilliger milking his ejection.

But that wasn't the case at all. In fact, Terwilliger seemed to be as riveted as everyone else as a powerful figure strode out onto the field.

"Blazes," said the trainer. "Who's the guy in the Halloween costume?"

"That is not a guy," explained the android. "That is Lieutenant Worf."

Worf was halfway across the diamond when he noticed the uniformed men pouring out of the stands. Before he'd gotten much farther, he realized their purpose: to detain him.

"Where do you think you're going?" asked one.

"Hey *you*," called another. "We're talking to you. Don't make it hard on yourself."

Yes. *Definitely* to detain him.

Instinctively, Worf rose to the challenge, whirling and bracing himself. As his nearest pursuer charged him, the Klingon stepped aside like a matador and used the man's momentum to send him sprawling. The next two came at once; the first took a kick to the solar plexus, the second a fist to the jaw.

However, the paired maneuvers left Worf vulnerable, precariously balanced. And as the rest of his uniformed adversaries swarmed over him, he went down rather unceremoniously. Nor was it easy to get up again; holodeck simulacrums were every bit as heavy as they looked.

Kicking and smashing, tearing and slithering, he did his best to work free of the tangle. Anyone else would have acknowledged that he was fighting a losing battle— but Worf was not *anyone*.

"Damn you, hold still," yelled an adversary.

"Hey, George . . . I don't think that's a mask."

"Of *course* it's a mask. Nobody's *that* ugly."

Worf struggled with renewed fury. *Ugly,* was it? He would show these slugs how *ugly* a Klingon could . . .

"Pause," said a voice—one that Worf recognized.

Suddenly the comments stopped. And so did his adversaries' attempts to subdue him. With as much dignity as possible, the Klingon climbed out from under the pile.

He found Data waiting for him with an outstretched hand. The android looked more than a little apologetic.

"I hope you are not injured," he said. "I would have stopped the program sooner, but you appeared to be enjoying yourself."

Worf ignored the hand and got to his feet. "Who *are* they?" he asked, looking back at the mound of simulated humanity. "I did not know you were partial to combat programs."

"I am not," answered Data. "The main activity here is

something called a baseball game, a spectator sport of the twenty-first century." He indicated the uniformed ones. "These security guards are present to keep the crowd from endangering the players and, of course, one another."

Worf couldn't believe his ears. "*These,*" he said, "are *security* guards?" He grunted—a sound that another Klingon would have recognized as an expression of disdain. "They dishonor the title. A dozen of them could not subdue a lone intruder."

"To be fair," said the android, "they were unaccustomed to dealing with an intruder like you."

The Klingon allowed the truth of that, but it did not raise the guards in his esteem. He believed that security personnel should be prepared for anything. Then another question occurred to him.

"Why did they attack me," he asked, "and not you?"

"I am disguised by a persona function," explained Data. "When the simulacrums look at me, they see someone called Bobo Bogdonovich—the role Commander Riker intended to play when he created this program. You, on the other hand, are extraneous to this milieu. Since the security guards did not recognize you, they attempted to remove you from the field." A pause. "Nor could your Klingon appearance have helped matters any. In the twenty-first century, mankind had not yet seen a Klingon."

Mankind's loss, mused Worf. As for the persona function, he probably should have thought of that himself—though in his own holodeck programs, he wove in no such protection. After all, it was essential that his enemies recognize him if they were to engage one another in battle.

But this was all beside the point. He had come here for a reason, and he apprised Data of the fact. *Without* any further pleasantries.

"The captain sent me. He wants you to be ready in

case it becomes necessary to join Commander Riker in Besidia."

That seemed to pique the android's curiosity. "I thought Commander Riker was incapacitated."

"He is. Apparently, he has decided to forge ahead anyway."

Worf did not disguise his admiration, though he would have expected no less of Riker. The first officer was not easily daunted.

Data nodded. "I see. You may consider me alerted."

The Klingon rumbled his acknowledgment of the fact and turned to leave.

"Lieutenant?"

Worf looked back, saw the inquisitive expression on the android's face. He hoped that the question would not be a long one, though experience had taught him to expect otherwise.

"Certainly you could have contacted me via the ship's intercom," said Data. "Is there some reason you chose to deliver your message in person?"

"Yes," said the Klingon. "I was ordered to do so." Then, before he could be interrogated any further, he exited the holodeck.

As soon as Worf was gone, Data commanded the computer to resume the program—but at the point just prior to the Klingon's unannounced visit. At once the stadium came back to life.

"It's moments like these," said the trainer, "that make me put off retirement."

"Indeed," replied the android.

On the playing field, things were beginning to settle down again. The Sunset pitcher was back on the mound, the defensive players had taken up their positions, and Cordoban was approaching the plate.

The trainer was still descending the dugout steps when the pitch came. Cordoban hit it hard to the right of the shortstop, who dove to knock the ball down. Then, after picking it up with his bare hand, he threw it to second base—just in time to beat the sliding Bobo.

However, Cordoban reached first base before the relay throw. So the Icebreakers still had a runner at first—just a *different* runner. And, of course, there was one out.

As Data returned to the Icebreaker dugout, he was surprised to see Terwilliger's face peering out of the stairwell that led to the clubhouse. Hadn't the manager been ejected from the contest?

He asked Denyabe about it. "Come on," said the second baseman. "You're kidding, right? Even in the minors, managers don't leave when they're ejected. At least they didn't when *I* was in the minors."

It was another nuance of the game that Data had been unprepared for. He filed it away with all the others.

The next batter up was Augustyn. To the delight of the fans as well as his teammates on the bench, he doubled down the right field line. That put runners on second and third with only one man out.

Jackson batted after Augustyn. He worked the count to three balls and two strikes before lofting the next pitch deep to center field. Data judged by the accolades all around him that it was deep enough for Cordoban, the runner on third, to tag up and score.

In the end it accomplished more than that. When Augustyn tried to tag up as well, the Sunset center fielder made a poor throw to third. The ball squibbed into the Sunset dugout, and Augustyn was waved home.

Once again, the score was tied. It made for a jubilant moment in the Icebreaker dugout when Cordoban and Augustyn came trotting down the steps, with Jackson on their heels.

No one even seemed to care when Cherry struck out to end the inning.

* * *

The turbodoors opened, admitting Worf back onto the bridge. Picard turned and their eyes met.

"All is in readiness," said the chief of security, in response to the unspoken question. "Commander Data has been briefed."

Picard nodded. "Thank you, Lieutenant." He paused, and the Klingon remained where he was, perceiving that the captain required something else. *How well you have come to know me, Worf.* "I would like a word with you. In my ready room."

Rising out of his command chair, Picard headed for his private office. He strode past the Klingon; the doors slid aside and they entered.

As he rounded his desk, the captain gestured to the seat on the other side of it. "Please," he said. "Sit."

Worf sat. He regarded Picard with hooded eyes, but said nothing. It was the human's prerogative to speak first in this situation, and they both knew it.

The captain leaned back in his chair. "I must confess," he said, "I am more than a little curious as to what Data is doing in that holodeck. Which is why I had you relay my orders in person . . ."

Suddenly a soft beeping came from the vicinity of the door. Sighing, Picard responded: "Come."

When the doors parted, Geordi came striding in, as full of energy and enthusiasm as ever. "Just wanted you to know," he said, "that those enhancements are already paying dividends. I just—"

He was halfway inside the cabin before he noticed the captain wasn't alone.

"Oops," blurted Geordi. "Sorry, sir. I didn't know you had company."

"That is all right, Commander. Actually I was going to call you as soon as Worf and I were finished. You might as well pull up a chair and join us."

Geordi glanced at the Klingon, shrugged. "If I'm not

interrupting, sure." And with that, he slipped agreeably into the chair next to Worf's.

"We were talking about Mr. Data," remarked Picard. "And his fascination with that holodeck program." He indicated his security chief. "I just sent Worf to visit him in the holodeck—to alert him to the possibility that he may be needed on an away team."

"In support of Commander Riker," supplied Geordi.

"Precisely. Of course, I could have sent the order via ship's intercom . . ."

The engineering officer nodded. "But you wondered what Data was up to."

The captain made a steeple of his fingers, taking the time to choose his words carefully. "I am not a busybody," he said finally. "Normally, what people do in their off-duty hours is their own business. However, the last time Mr. Data spent so much time in a holodeck, he was helping his android prodigy to select a species and a gender. I do not want something like that happening again without my knowing it."

Geordi waved away even the suggestion of it. "Not to worry," he said. "First of all, this program wasn't even Data's idea."

Picard looked at him. "Then whose idea was it?"

"Commander Riker's. It's a baseball game he plucked out of the history books. Data just adopted it—with permission, of course."

The captain smiled. "Baseball, eh?"

Geordi tilted his head. "You're familiar with the sport, sir?"

"I have a nodding acquaintance with it," Picard said. He thought for a moment. "But why has Data become so absorbed in it?"

"You know," replied Geordi, "I asked him the same question, more or less. He said he'd thought about it a lot, but didn't have an answer."

Picard grunted. "Care to venture a guess—either of you?"

Worf just scowled. Apparently, the experience had been a bit too alien for him.

Geordi was somewhat more daring. "This is only a guess," he warned, "but I think Data feels . . . well, a kinship with the characters in the program."

"Kinship?" echoed the captain. "How so?"

Geordi's brow wrinkled. Obviously he hadn't thought this all the way through yet. But he went on anyway, groping for the logical conclusion. "Because they're man-made," he said at last. "Because they're like him."

Picard shook his head. "Only on the surface, Commander. Mr. Data is an autonomous life-form. He is not dependent on some external mechanism for his existence."

"Isn't he?" Geordi wondered out loud. "In fact, aren't we *all?* Let's say the ship suddenly vanished out from under us. How long would we last in the vacuum of space? Of all of us, Data would be the only survivor. And even he would succumb eventually—if not to cold and radiation, then to the inexorable tug of Imprima's gravity."

The captain drew a breath, let it out. "I see what you mean, Commander. And your point is well taken."

Picard was touched by a feeling of déjà vu. Hadn't he had this conversation with someone once before?

Or was it a conversation he'd had with himself—sometime during the many hours he'd spent trying to define intelligent life, if not for the Federation, then at least for Jean-Luc Picard? Since the day he entered space, his most heartfelt beliefs on that subject had been turned on their ear more than once. And Data had done much of the turning.

Worf was looking at Geordi with narrowed eyes. "Commander, are you suggesting that Data's loyalty may be divided?" Naturally, that would be of concern to the head of security, whether he believed it or not.

"Not at all," said Geordi. "I'm just saying that Data feels a responsibility to these characters. He doesn't want to let them down, any more than he would want to let *us* down."

"In what way might he do that?" asked the captain.

"Data wants to help them win the game, sir. That's something they didn't do historically. But he seems to feel they have a victory coming to them." He stopped, stroked his chin. "One of them in particular—the manager, a fellow named Terwilliger."

"The manager?"

"An administrative position. He's like . . . well, like a captain, if you want to stretch it a little."

Picard digested that. "So Data wants simply to do a good deed. To rectify, in some sense, the way history has maltreated this individual. And the rest of the team as well."

"That's it in a nutshell," Geordi agreed. "To tell you the truth, I don't know if he has a prayer. History can be a pretty tough opponent. But he's got to try. If he just gives it his best shot, I think he'll feel he's done his bit for his teammates. He'll feel he's earned their respect."

The captain leaned forward again. "Well," he said, "one certainly can't fault him for that. Particularly when he's got his superior's reputation at heart, eh?"

Geordi chuckled. Worf's scowl deepened.

"Tell me," said the captain. "Would I like this . . . what did you say his name was? Terwilliger?"

"That's right, sir," said the engineering chief. "Terwilliger. But as for liking him . . . I don't think so. Not from what Data told me."

Picard had expected otherwise, but he refrained from saying so. "Very well then, gentlemen. Carry on."

As his officers departed, the captain stood. Perhaps it was time to pay a visit to Holodeck One himself.

Chapter Thirteen

"HEY—YOU! How the hellja get in here?"

Picard considered the smallish, wiry man in front of the primitive viewscreen. What was that technology called again? Television? Yes, television.

"Actually," said the captain, holding out his hands in a gesture of helplessness, "I dropped in to visit an associate. Perhaps you know him—Bobo Bogdonovich?"

He was glad he had obtained some details from the computer before entering the holodeck. Fortunately, the program was an open one, neither Riker nor Data having been inclined to close it.

"Bogdonovich?" echoed the wiry man, his anger and surprise giving way to curiosity. "He give you a pass or something?"

"Why, yes," said Picard. "As a matter of fact, he did." He pointed to a rectangle of blue sky balanced at the top of a short flight of steps. "He's not up there, is he?"

The man screwed up his face. "Of course he's up there. What didja think? They're playin' a damned game, right? And he's one of the players, so where the devil *else* would he be?"

The captain smiled. "Thank you," he said, and started for the patch of blue.

"Just hold on there a second, buddy." The man interposed himself between Picard and the exit. "You can't just go out there, no matter *what* kind of pass you have. That's the dugout, fer cryin' out loud."

The captain took stock of the situation and realized it might be a difficult one. "Suspend program," he said. Abruptly the wiry man fell silent, though his mouth remained open, in mid-argument.

As he straightened his linen sport jacket, Picard walked past the frozen figure and up the stairs. Shading his eyes against the brightness of that blue sky, he almost bumped into someone huddled on the topmost step—someone apparently trying to peek out of the aperture without being seen himself.

The man was in a uniform; logic dictated that he was part of a team. But he was certainly no athlete—not with that belly hanging over his belt. A suggestion bobbed up from the depths of Picard's memories. Wasn't there something called a batboy in these baseball games? Maybe that was this one's function.

No. Batboys were youngsters, weren't they? And this grizzled specimen was anything but young.

Negotiating a path around the man, the captain came out on the dugout level. From here he could see the playing field—a stretch of green that, from his eye-level perspective, seemed to go on forever.

"Greetings, sir."

Picard looked up and saw Data standing to one side of the dugout. He was dressed in the same uniform as the man on the stairs. One hand held a leather mitt; the other dangled by his side.

The captain smiled by way of acknowledgment. "Hello, Data. I hope you don't mind my coming by. I just wanted to, er—"

"To see what I was up to," suggested the android.

"That's right."

"Then Mr. Worf's report was insufficient?"

Picard chuckled. "How did you know I sent Worf?"

"He told me so," explained Data. "Though perhaps not in so many words."

The captain nodded. "You know, Data, you really are becoming quite perceptive."

"Thank you," said the android. "But truthfully, your intent was not difficult to deduce. After all, given my recent efforts with Lal in one of the holodecks—"

"Yes," Picard interjected, not wishing to rehash a topic Data might find painful. Or was it *he* who might find it painful? "I see that you have anticipated my concern."

The android nodded. "But perhaps not far enough in advance. When I began spending so much time here, I should have apprised you of what I was doing. I should have set your mind at ease."

The captain shrugged good-naturedly. "Water under the bridge, I say. And in point of fact, it was more than concern that drew me here. It was curiosity as well."

Data looked at him. "Curiosity, sir?"

"Indeed. You see, I have heard bits and pieces about this program. From Mr. Worf, of course. And also from Commander La Forge. I thought I should see it for myself—that is, of course, if you don't object."

The android shook his head. "Certainly not. After all, it is only on loan to me in the first place." He paused. "Do you wish to participate in the game? I could alter the program to—"

"No, Data. That will not be necessary." He looked out at the sea of humanity in the stands, gestured across the field. "I think I'll just take a seat and watch. Like everyone else."

"As you wish, sir."

"But first, perhaps you could point someone out to

me." He surveyed the faces in the dugout. "Someone named Terwilliger, I believe. The man in charge of your team."

"Of course," said the android. "That would be the individual just behind you. The one hiding in the stairwell."

The captain turned to take a second look at the man. It was no more impressive than the first.

"*This,*" he said, "is Terwilliger?"

"Yes," maintained Data. "The manager of the Fairbanks Icebreakers. And now, sir, if you don't mind, I would like to see the program continued."

Picard forced himself to regain his composure. "Sorry," he said earnestly. "I will find a seat immediately."

Climbing out of the dugout, he wandered out near the pitcher's mound and scanned the stands for an empty chair. Not an easy task, considering how full the place was. Spotting a vacancy just a couple of rows behind the third base line, he headed in that direction.

It was no trouble at all to vault the rail that separated the spectators from the field. And though made of hard plastic, the seat was more comfortable than it looked.

"All right," called the captain. "Resume program."

Suddenly the stands were awash with the sounds of the crowd. In the seat to Picard's right, a child looked up at him wide-eyed.

"Daddy," he said, tugging at an elbow on the other side of him, "there's a man there."

The youngster's father glanced at the captain. "That's right, Robby. There's a man there."

"But, Dad, he wasn't there before."

"Sure he was. He just got up to get a hot dog or something."

"I don't think so, Dad. I think he *wasn't there.*"

"Ssh," hissed his father. "Look—Giordano is up. He tore the cover off the ball last time. And—what is it, Katie?"

"Daddy, I have to go."

"Jeez, Katie, can't it wait? Giordano . . ."

Picard grunted softly. *Children*. He turned his attention back to the game.

As it happened, Data was standing closer to him than any other player, guarding the third base line, as one was supposed to do in the late innings. What's more, the captain noted, the android looked comfortable at his position—slightly crouched, weight forward, as if about to charge home plate, his glove low to the ground.

Having observed that much, Picard peered into the Icebreaker dugout, where he was able to catch a glimpse of Terwilliger's less-than-noble visage. He shook his head.

The man hardly looked like the sort who could lead. But then, not every great leader looked the part.

Just then the crowd moaned—a huge sound, almost frightening if one was unprepared for it—and got to its feet as if it were one colossal entity. Unable to see, Picard got to his feet as well—in time to see a Sunset player rounding the bases.

Apparently he had missed something. A home run, if the Sunset player's leisurely trot was any indication. There were boos from the crowd, to which the base runner responded by doffing his cap. The boos got louder.

Hardly an example of good sportsmanship, the captain mused. On either side.

And then he noticed a flurry of activity along the Icebreaker bench. He jockeyed for a better look. Finally, peering between two other spectators, he saw what was happening.

It was Terwilliger. With a bat. And he no longer seemed interested in concealing himself. Rather, he was intent on destroying a water cooler at the far end of the dugout.

The process didn't take long. A moment later, the

cooler's water-filled container exploded with a loud crash, sending water and glass flying in every direction.

Picard looked at Data. The android must have sensed his scrutiny somehow, because he looked back— apologetically, as if it were he who had annihilated the water cooler. The captain consciously softened his expression.

"Freeze program," he said quietly.

As before, everything came to a halt. He climbed past the statuelike spectators, vaulted the rail again, and approached Data.

The android anticipated his remarks: "It is his nature, sir. And it *was* the go-ahead run."

Picard glanced at the Icebreaker bench. It was a study in chaos—an umpire standing at the top step, gesturing dramatically. Terwilliger holding the bat aloft, as if threatening to strike the umpire next. The players and coaches clustered at the opposite end of the bench, having sought protection there from the exploding water cooler.

"Data," he said, turning back to his fellow officer, "there is *no* justification for such behavior. Certainly not from one who has been designated a leader." He took the time to choose his words carefully, and the android remained patient, if troubled-looking. "As I understand it, your . . . affinity for this program has much to do with that man. But I fail to see how he inspires such dedication. Such loyalty." He frowned. "Without question, you are entitled to your opinions. However, it concerns me that you have selected this Terwilliger as a role model. Is he really worth your time? Your respect?"

The android shook his head. "It is not a matter of respect, sir. It never was."

Picard regarded him. He searched those golden eyes, that childlike countenance.

"No? Then what is it that inspires you so?"

Data's brow wrinkled ever so slightly. "I believe, Captain, that it is called compassion."

That put matters in an entirely different light. Picard nodded, then breathed a small sigh of relief. He had feared that the android might be losing his moral perspective, enthralled by some inexplicable fascination with Terwilliger.

But it was quite the contrary. The android's moral perspective was coming along quite nicely.

"Sorry," the captain said. "Again. I should have known better than to doubt you, Data."

"Do not give it a second thought," replied the android. "It is easy to jump to conclusions, sir."

Picard wondered if he'd been rebuked. *What the hell. I deserved it, didn't I?*

"I am going to return to the stands now," he told Data.

"That would be best, I believe."

And they went back to their respective positions.

They had set out immediately after Riker made his report to the captain. The streets were dark and deserted, hushed, blanketed by a newly fallen snow. The only sound was the homing device's soft but insistent beeping.

After some trial and error, they were able to determine the general direction of the signal's source. And to follow it, along silent, winding streets that seemed to resent their intrusion.

Riker had never seen Besidia at this hour. There was a certain calm, an elegance almost, that he would never have associated with the carnival town.

Lyneea seemed different, too. Softer, more vulnerable. As if she wasn't quite awake enough yet to be as hard-boiled as she would have liked.

Slowly but surely the signal took them away from the heart of the city. Away from the shops and the hotels and the taverns into the residential neighborhoods, which became more and more well-to-do as they progressed.

And finally it led them here—to this eight-foot-high stone wall that blocked their passage.

Riker stood before it, Teller's homing device nestled in the palm of his gloved hand. Snow was falling; a couple of fat flakes hit the tiny digital display and clung there, turned ruby red by the illumination.

He touched the device's lowermost plate with the forefinger of his other hand. The thing started beeping again, a little louder than the last time they'd activated it.

Lyneea nodded. "This is where it wants us to go, all right."

The human considered the barrier. He could see shards of broken glass embedded in the concrete at the top of it. A primitive but effective way of ensuring privacy.

He grunted. "Who would go to the trouble of putting up a wall here?"

"Who indeed," added Lyneea, "but a madraga?"

"Then this is part of an estate," said Riker.

"So it would seem. And only one madraga has holdings in this part of town." She looked at him. "Terrin."

He nodded. Now that he knew who owned the place, he began to recognize the grounds. He'd been here before, of course, though he'd never approached the estate from this side.

"That's interesting," he said, "considering Terrin's the madraga that Criathis is merging with."

Lyneea nodded. "Your friend hid the seal under the noses of the people most likely to be offended by its absence."

"But why would he do that?"

His partner shrugged. "We can only speculate. Perhaps he just appreciated the irony. Perhaps he planned to expose the seal's location at some point, thereby making it look as if Terrin had stolen it, and ensuring that the merger would never go through." She bit her lip. "At any rate, an interested third party, such as Madraga Rhurig, wouldn't really have cared if it had the thing in its possession—only that Criathis *didn't* have it. Conlon could have been paid just to hide it until the merger fell apart."

Riker pondered the possibilities. "Good point," he told her. He regarded the wall. "But there will be plenty of time to sort this out *after* we recover Fortune's Light."

"Agreed. Can you make it over the wall?"

"With a little help." He slipped his arm out of the sling.

"You've got it."

Planting herself by the base of the barrier, Lyneea bent down to give the human a step up. He took advantage of it, balancing on her back before finding a space relatively free of glass shards and clambering up as best he could. Once again he remarked inwardly on her deceptive sturdiness.

"Up?" asked Lyneea.

"Up," he answered. "Need a hand?"

"No."

His offer refused, he slithered down the far side of the wall. The snow had drifted deeper here; it was up to the tops of his boots. He replaced the sling.

A moment later Lyneea joined him. She landed like a cat, gracefully.

They looked out on the rolling fields that constituted the grounds of the estate. The place was pristine, beautiful, interrupted only by a few tall, stately trees. In the distance there was a stone house, not all that big but classically intricate in its design.

It brought back memories.

"Let's try the device again," said his partner.

Riker activated it, expecting to hear the beeping. There wasn't any. But a change had come over the digital display. It now showed only three numerals: seven, four, and three.

"What's the matter?" asked Lyneea. "Don't tell me the damned thing's broken."

"I'm not sure," he told her, "but I think it switched over to another mode—automatically." He looked around. "Maybe because we've gotten within a certain radius of the transmitter."

He took a few steps away from the wall, and the three became a two. Another few steps, and it turned into a zero.

"Anything happening?"

"As a matter of fact, yes. I've got a three-digit number here, and as we get closer to our objective, the number decreases. Or at least, that's how it looks."

"Then theoretically," said Lyneea, "when it gets down to zero, we will have reached the seal."

"That's right."

"So what are we waiting for? Let's go."

Riker went. And as he did, the number continued to decline. The display read five-nine-nine before he realized the direction in which they were going.

"You know," said Lyneea, "we're heading toward the house."

"I've noticed," he told her. "But it's not as if we've got a choice. Let's just be as careful as possible, and hope we're not spotted."

It made sense, didn't it? Using the house as a heading now, he kept his eyes open for Imprimans, checking the homing device only from time to time. The number kept on diminishing at a steady rate.

"At this rate," observed Lyneea, "we'll be *in* the house before we're finished."

Riker estimated the distance. He shook his head. "Not quite. I think we'll wind up by that tree there." He pointed. "The last one."

She made a derisive sound. "That's *almost* in the house, isn't it?"

214

"Want to turn back?"

His partner scowled. It didn't make her any less lovely, he noticed. "I'll shut up," she assured him.

By the time they reached the vicinity of the tree, they were down to a single digit on the readout. And then, as they got near enough to touch it, the digit became zero.

"All ashore," said Riker.

"I beg your pardon?"

"An old Earth expression. It means we've reached our destination." And still no sign of a guard or anyone else. They'd been lucky so far.

Lyneea pointed to the ground at their feet. It was a smooth patch, nestled between two of the tree's immense roots and covered, like everything else in Besidia, with snow. "Here?" she asked.

"Here."

She removed a pouch from her belt, knelt, and emptied its contents on the frozen ground. It was a small sharp-bladed shovel that came in two parts. As Lyneea put them together, she surveyed the spot.

"He couldn't have buried it too deep, right? That would have taken too much time."

Riker shrugged. "I don't know. If he was using a blaster, it might not have taken much time at all."

She looked up at him. "Now *there's* a cheery thought." Then she shook her head. "No. A blaster would have scarred these roots. And I don't see any scars." She jammed the shovel blade into the earth. "Why don't you keep an eye out while I do some work?"

As she bent to the task, the human surveyed the grounds of the estate. They were as tranquil as deep space, as serene as an uninhabited planetoid. A light breeze tickled the hair on his chin where it jutted out from his hood.

The house might have been empty, it was so quiet— though, more likely, it was just that no one was up yet.

On the side of the structure that faced them there was a large oval window. Inside it Riker could see the well-appointed library that he and Teller had once visited.

He watched the window for a couple of seconds, just to make certain no one was looking out at them. Satisfied, he turned away.

But as he did so, he glimpsed a movement out of the corner of his eye. Ducking instinctively behind the tree, he took another look.

This time there was no mistaking it. Someone was on the other side of the window. And not just anyone.

A Ferengi.

"Damn," he said.

When Lyneea saw him take cover, she'd hunkered down a little lower herself. "What is it?" she asked. "Have we been seen?"

Riker shook his head. "That's not what made me jump." He jerked a thumb in the direction of the house. "There's a Ferengi in there."

Lyneea regarded him. "Are you certain?"

"Take a look for yourself."

She peeked around the side of the tree. And cursed.

"There aren't supposed to be any Ferengi on Imprima," said Lyneea. "Under penalty of law."

"But there's one here," said Riker. "Smuggled in somehow as the guest of Madraga Terrin."

She took a breath, let it out. It dissipated on the wind. "Treachery," she concluded.

Riker nodded. "Terrin hasn't fared well under the Federation treaty, has it?"

"Not as well as when we were trading with the Ferengi. But that was the whole point of the merger—to put Terrin in a better position to benefit from the Federation agreement."

"Obviously the Ferengi made them a better offer." He thought about it. "Terrin is the wealthier party in the merger, isn't it? So its first official, Larrak, would be first official of the newly merged entity as well. With that kind of power, he could cut any number of deals with the other madraggi."

"Enough to vote the Federation out and the Ferengi back in."

"Not exactly what Criathis had in mind, eh?"

"Far from it."

He had a thought. "And Terrin may have killed Teller as well. If he came here to bury the seal and screw up the merger, and noticed the Ferengi as we did . . ."

"They'd have killed him for it. Without a second thought," said Lyneea. "Just as they'll kill us if they find us here." Her eyes narrowed. "But then, what was Conlon doing in the maze?"

"That's probably just where they chose to dump him. They couldn't have anticipated that Norayan would think to look for him there." He pursued the thought to its logical conclusion. "It was just dumb luck that she found his body. And those settings on the device, for getting out of the maze—they must have been left over from his lovers' trysts."

As they spoke, another figure came into view on the other side of the window. He was taller than the average Impriman, and even slimmer. Nor had he changed much in five years.

"Larrak," spat Lyneea. "And he's greeting the Ferengi."

"That cinches it," said Riker. "We've got to alert Criathis." He started to move away, but she grabbed his good arm.

"What about the seal?" she asked.

"Leave it here for now. What's the difference? When Criathis finds out what Larrak has in mind, they won't want to go through with the merger anyway. Then, when all the dust clears, you can recover it at your leisure."

Lyneea frowned. "Fortune's Light isn't something that's needed only for the merger. Nor is it merely a family heirloom. It's the heart and soul of the madraga —the most precious thing we own." Her frown deepened. "We can't just let it lie in the ground, not when we're so close to recovering it."

He sighed, moved back toward the tree. "All right. Let's just be quick about it."

"That *was* my intention," she told him.

She resumed digging. In the meantime, Riker watched Larrak and the Ferengi. Fortunately they were too engrossed in their conversation to take any notice of what was going on outside.

After a while, Larrak poured a liquid—probably a liqueur—into a couple of ornate goblets. The Ferengi said something, and they put their goblets together in a toast.

It made Riker's stomach turn. To murder someone for the sake of profit . . .

"Ah," said Lyneea. Thrusting her blade into the earth one last time, she put her weight on the handle and used it as a lever. A moment later, something rose from the earth with great reluctance. It was small, covered with some rough variety of hide.

"You were right," he noted. "He didn't bury it too deep."

"A fact for which I am most grateful." Laying aside her shovel, she began to unwrap the package. Suddenly she raised her head and looked around. "What's that?"

He tried to follow her gaze. "What's what?"

"That sound. Like . . . oh, *no.*"

Now he heard it, too, and recognized it immediately.

"Isakki," he snapped.

A couple of seconds later he saw them. Four or five of them, deadly black streaks on the otherwise flawless fields of snow. A couple of Terrin's retainers ran behind them, struggling to keep up. And they were all coming from the spot where he and Lyneea had climbed the wall.

"We've got to get out of here," he told her, pulling her up off the ground. *"Now."*

She resisted just long enough to grab up the seal. Then she ran along behind him.

Riker didn't know where he was headed. He just knew that he didn't want to be caught in those powerful jaws. And the only place that seemed to offer shelter was the house.

"What are you doing?" asked Lyneea. "There may be more retainers inside!"

And more isakki as well, if his last visit here was any indication. But he didn't have time to stop and think about it.

Their only chance was to get into the library, somehow neutralize Larrak and the Ferengi, lock the doors against pursuit, and contact the *Enterprise.* Then the captain could send for the authorities, who would be more than a little interested in their report of a Ferengi in Besidia.

As they skirted the side of the house, he could hear the isakki bearing down on them. And the strident shouts of the Imprimans in their wake.

Come on, he told himself. *All we need is a door.* As he recalled, this structure had only one entrance, and that was in the front. Snow crunching beneath their boots, they skidded around another corner.

The isakki growled, closing the gap with dizzying quickness. Riker's blood pounded in his ears.

Yet another corner. Surely after this one . . .

And there it was—the front door. An oversize specimen carved out of dark wood and inlaid with precious metals. It was set into an overhanging stone archway.

Now, with any luck, it would be unlocked.

It was.

Riker ushered Lyneea inside. Then, together, they shoved the door closed behind them. Finding a dead bolt, he slammed it home.

A moment later they heard the skittering of claws on the outside of the door, and the shrieks of the frustrated animals, and the shouts of the two retainers.

Riker took a deep breath, let it out. But before he'd finished, Lyneea was pulling him away.

"Come on," she told him. "If they've got blasters, that door is history."

She was right. There was no time to waste. They had to get to Larrak before he could hear the commotion and prepare himself.

Behind them was a corridor that seemed to lead into the center of the house; Riker didn't remember for certain. They followed it.

The inside of the place was still a lot like the outside. The walls were made of large gray stones; the ceiling was a tight latticework of assorted woods polished to a high gloss.

The corridor ended in a hub from which six other spokes extended. Five led to closed doors. The sixth showed them the entrance to the library.

Riker could see Larrak standing in the opening, his back to them, as yet unaware that there was anything wrong.

Lyneea pulled her projectile weapon out of her tunic. Somewhere along the line, she had stuffed Fortune's Light into the pouch at her belt; it dangled there heavily.

They exchanged glances. "You take Larrak," she whispered. "I'll handle the Ferengi."

He nodded.

Then they were off, pounding down the hallway as fast as they could. When they'd gotten about halfway, Larrak turned and saw them coming.

A brief cry escaping his lips, he ducked and rolled out of sight. A moment later Riker burst into the room, Lyneea half a step behind him.

Too late he saw that Larrak and the Ferengi weren't the only ones waiting for them.

Lyneea was blasted before she could get off a shot, but she wasn't hit hard enough to lose consciousness. As Riker helped her to her feet, he saw those responsible for the blast—a quartet of armed retainers. Their host peeked out from behind the quartet. He smiled.

"Welcome to the estate of Madraga Terrin," he said. "I don't believe we've been properly introduced."

Chapter Fourteen

THE FIRST OFFICIAL of Madraga Terrin scrutinized the seal. It glittered with red, green, and blue sparks as the gems embedded in it took turns catching the light. Larrak looked appreciative, as did the retainers who stood by the walls and the Ferengi who leaned against a massive bookcase across the room.

"I am forever in your debt," said Larrak, turning his gaze first on Riker and then on Lyneea. "Who would have thought that my merger was in jeopardy? Imagine if you had been a trifle less clever and the seal had remained hidden for a while." He shook his head. "All my maneuvering, all my planning . . . worthless." Gently, almost reverently, he placed Fortune's Light on a small wooden table near the window. Right next to Teller's homing device. "I don't know what I would have done."

Apparently, Riker mused, Larrak still didn't recognize him, although they'd sat in this very room together once before. Was it the beard? Or was it just that Teller had been the memorable one?

"You could show your gratitude," he suggested, in

response to Larrak's speech. He shifted his weight in his chair, but it only made the ropes that held him cut more painfully, and his partially healed wound was already a throbbing misery. The Ferengi seemed to be enjoying his discomfort, he noticed. But Larrak was his main concern. "You could let us go."

Larrak chuckled. "I could, yes. But then you might be inclined to tell someone about my friend Ralk." He indicated the Ferengi with an outstretched arm, and Ralk nodded his grotesque head. "That would put an end to my plans more surely than the lack of a seal." He shook his head. "No, I think I'll keep you here for a while. At least until Fortune's Light is returned—surreptitiously, of course, so Criathis won't suspect that I had anything to do with its disappearance. That way, there will be no questions, and everything will proceed according to schedule."

"And after the merger ceremony?" asked Riker.

"Save your breath," Lyneea advised him. "After the ceremony, he'll kill us." She glared at Larrak. "He would have killed us already if he wasn't so superstitious. It's supposed to be bad luck to bloody your hands on the day of a business transaction, and our host believes in luck more than most people."

Larrak considered her waspishly. "I see that I'm no stranger to you. I wish *you* were as familiar to *me.*" He approached Lyneea, his retainers straightening just a hair as their attentiveness increased. "Not that you're a complete mystery." He reached out to caress her cheek, then saw the fire in her eyes and thought better of it. "A retainer, no doubt. I'd heard that Criathis had some females on its payroll, and you're proof of it."

Lyneea said nothing, but her expression spoke volumes.

Larrak turned his attention to Riker. "As we all know, humans are rare on Imprima. Given the fact that you were searching for the seal—as evidenced by your little excavation effort—and in the company of a Criathan retainer, I'd say you're here in an official capacity." He shrugged. "Probably on loan from the Federation vessel that's been in orbit the last several days—yes?"

Riker didn't give him the pleasure of an answer. He could feel Lyneea looking at him approvingly.

"You need not respond," said Larrak. "I have gotten this far without your help. I believe I can reconstruct the rest as well." He looked to the Ferengi. "Shall I give it a try, Ralk?"

The Ferengi laughed. It was more like a series of barks.

Larrak let the echoes die before he continued. "The Federation trade liaison strikes a deal with one of the madraggi opposed to the merger. Rhurig, maybe, or Lycinthis. The liaison steals the seal, or arranges to have it stolen, and plants it on Terrin's grounds. His price? Who knows? Probably enough to buy himself a nice retirement somewhere—but well worth it to the madraga who hired him."

He nodded, smiling to himself, as if his understanding was deepening even as he spoke.

"You two are assigned to catch the Federation's liaison and to recover Fortune's Light. At some point you find a homing device and wonder if you can use it to find the seal. It leads you here, to the grounds of Madraga Terrin. Something of a surprise, I expect. And while you're digging for your buried treasure, you find something else you don't expect—a Ferengi in the estate house." He paused. "Close enough?"

He didn't get an answer, but by this time he probably didn't expect one.

Larrak made a clucking sound with his tongue. "Really. Did you think no one would notice your footprints? At least the liaison had the sense to do his dirty work during a snowstorm." He grunted. "Not that it did him much good. He, too, you see, was fascinated by Ralk.

Otherwise he might not have come closer to the house—and we might not have noticed him."

The Ferengi laughed again. The sound grated on Riker's ears, but Larrak appeared to appreciate it. Birds of a feather, the Starfleet officer mused.

Larrak snapped his fingers, and one of his guards left the room. "I must confess," he said, "I was concerned when I found a Federation liaison snooping around my grounds. I wondered how word of my association with Ralk had leaked out. Now, of course, I see that I can set my mind at ease. He wasn't here about Ralk. He was here to bury the seal, wasn't he?"

Reminded of Fortune's Light, he retrieved it, along with the homing device that lay beside it. For a moment he held them both in his hands, considering them, as if weighing one against the other. Then he dropped the homing device and crushed it beneath his boot.

"Fortunately," said Larrak, "it's carnival time, and there's a ban on modern communications systems. Or you could have contacted Criathis once you realized where the seal was hidden."

Riker tried not to wince. He could have kept the *Enterprise* up to date on their progress, but in his eagerness, he'd chosen not to.

A moment later, Larrak's retainer returned with a long, flowing garment in his hands. It was precisely the color of human blood.

"Ah," said Terrin's first official. "My ceremonial robe." As he accepted it, he gave the retainer the seal. Once again, the man left the room.

"Just for the record," said Riker, "you did kill Teller Conlon, didn't you?"

Larrak donned his robe with a flourish. "For the record, yes." Smoothing the front of the brocaded garment, he turned to Lyneea. "How do I look, my dear? Fit to lead this world's newest and most powerful madraga into a golden age of prosperity?"

Larrak smiled. Lyneea spat at him. For a second or two his good humor fell away and he looked as if he might strike her. Then his smile returned.

"Tut, tut," he said. "I expected better breeding from a retainer of Madraga Criathis."

And with that he made his exit.

The captain stayed for the uneventful balance of the sixth inning and then excused himself. He had never been a real devotee of the game, he explained. And his concern about Data had been laid to rest.

In the top half of the seventh, the Phoenix hitters went down in order. It might have been otherwise but for a spectacular play in right field, in which Augustyn climbed the wall to rob the batter of a home run.

As Data took his seat in the dugout, he recalled the computer's verdict on Bobo Bogdonovich: three official at-bats, one single, and one run batted in. Of course, he had already had two of those at-bats, plus one that didn't count statistically—the one in which he got hit with the pitch.

And history had already nailed down the outcome of his last time at bat—when he would end the game by flying out to deep center field. But somewhere in between, he would have to get up again.

After all, he was the sixth hitter scheduled. That meant that even if all three Icebreaker batters failed to reach first base in the seventh, he would still come up in the eighth. It would work out for him to be the last out of the game only if the Icebreakers batted around—and he came up twice in the process.

However, the computer had been specific: only *three* official at-bats. And his fly out would be the third. So whatever he did in the seventh or eighth inning would have to constitute an *un*official at-bat.

Data rifled through his memory for the circumstances

that would make a time at bat unofficial: a walk, a hit batsman, a run-scoring sacrifice via a fly out or a bunt . . .

The Icebreakers' first batter, Maggin, hit a line drive single through the middle.

The following batter, Denyabe, got a base hit as well—this one a grounder between the first and second basemen—and on the play, Maggin made it to third.

Things were looking up for the Fairbanks team—a fact that was reflected in Terwilliger's expression, which was decidedly less hostile than usual as he watched from the shadows. With two men on and no one out, it seemed they might win this game after all.

Of course, Data knew better. If history had its way, his teammates would find a way to leave those runners on base.

The next two batters managed to do just that. Sakahara hit a pop-up to the first baseman, too shallow to score Maggin from third. And Galanti could only produce another dribbler to the pitcher, who was able to freeze Maggin with a glance before throwing to first for the out.

There were men on second and third now, but with two outs. Worse, Galanti had pulled a hamstring trying to beat the throw to first. He had to be helped off the field by a couple of coaches, the trainer following solemnly in his wake.

If Data had wondered when he'd get a chance to bat again, he wondered no longer. He'd been watching Galanti's efforts from the on-deck circle. And as the first baseman was helped into the dugout, he approached the batter's box, spurred by the encouragement of his teammates. And, of course, the muffled curses that came from the clubhouse stairs.

As Commander Riker would have put it, the deck was stacked against him. But if there was a way to thwart history, to drive in Maggin and perhaps Denyabe as well, Data vowed to find it.

Unfortunately he never got the chance. The Sunset manager, no doubt wary of Bobo after his performance in the first inning, opted to walk him intentionally—and thereby fill the bases for Cordoban, who had had better days with the bat.

Nor did the manager end up regretting the move. For on a two-and-oh pitch, Cordoban hit a soft fly to right field.

Three outs. End of threat.

In the dugout, at the top of the clubhouse stairs, Terwilliger didn't say a word. It was as if all the fire had gone out of him. As if he could read his future and it was no different from his past.

After all, there were only two innings left. And scoring opportunities like that one didn't materialize very often.

Noting that it was time for him to return to duty, Data saved the program and left the holodeck.

"You won't get away with it," said Lyneea.

"Of course we will," returned Ralk. He turned away from them as he crossed the room, casually considering its decor.

Probably estimating the value of the furnishings, Riker mused. It had been some time—a few hours at least—since Larrak had left them to proceed with his plans for the merger ceremony.

Lyneea pressed her case. "Criathis will become suspicious when the seal turns up at the last minute. They'll put a stop to the merger."

The Ferengi shook his head, standing with his back to them as he regarded an Impriman globe. "No. They won't." He spun the globe, sending the continents flying by with dizzying speed, and glanced at the captives over his shoulder. "They will be happy to see it and relieved to

228

avoid the disaster they anticipated." He smiled, exposing his short, sharp teeth. "It will not be a problem." He stopped the globe's rotation with a long, knobby finger. "Besides, you need not concern yourselves with the outcome. Either way, you will die."

Riker laughed—the loudest and most obnoxious laugh he could muster.

Obviously it was not what Ralk had expected. His brow furrowed, displaying his irritation.

"Do not make that sound," said the Ferengi. "It offends my sensibilities."

Now *that* was a switch.

"I can't help it," said Riker. "You think you've thought of everything, but you're in for a surprise."

That got Ralk's interest, though he tried not to show it. "Oh? What sort of surprise?"

Riker looked at Lyneea. "Should I tell him?"

She looked back. "Why not?" she said.

He turned back to Ralk. "Larrak's a businessman, just as you are. And just like you, he'd drop out of your mutual admiration society if he thought it was curtailing his profits. Right?"

The Ferengi's eyes had become slits. "Go on."

"Well, as soon as the merger goes through, Larrak's going to be privy to Criathis's records. And as a member of the team that put together the agreement . . ."

The slits suddenly opened wide.

"That's right. I helped take Imprima away from you. And I can tell you that Madraga Criathis has profited immensely from the deal—more than anyone on this world can possibly imagine. In fact, I'd call their profits obscene—though you might have another name for it." Riker smiled, giving himself some time to formulate his next statement. After all, he was making it up as he went along.

"How good is the deal you offered Larrak?" he asked.

"Very good," said Ralk.

"No doubt. But trust me on this—it pales by comparison to what he can make with the Federation, now that Criathis is becoming his plaything. Add to that the difficulties and the dangers involved in upsetting the status quo, the concessions and compromises Larrak will have to make to reinstate trade with the Ferengi, and then *you* tell *me:* which way do you think Larrak is going to go?"

There. That sounded pretty plausible, if he said so himself—even though he was lying through his teeth. Criathis wasn't benefiting from the trade agreement *that* much.

More to the point, Ralk seemed to have swallowed it. He took a couple of steps toward Riker and backhanded him across the mouth. For a moment the human forgot about his wound.

The three retainers in the room were starting to look fidgety. It was understandable. A few moments ago it had clearly been their duty to protect Ralk. Now, with a possible conflict brewing between the Ferengi and their employer, they weren't so sure.

Of course that was just the icing on the cake. Riker's real goal was to raise Ralk's temperature a bit. And then a bit more.

So instead of cursing, he just grinned. "Someone once told me you Ferengi are stronger than you look. I guess he was just kidding."

His face twisting with hatred, Ralk belted him again. This time Riker tasted blood.

"Love taps," he got out. "But then, you don't really want to hurt me, do you?"

"Shut up," said the Ferengi. "Just shut up!"

"After all, I'm one of the humans who skunked you out of Imprima in the first place. I'm—"

As Ralk pulled back for a third blow, Riker rocked

forward and stood up, chair and all. The idea was to take the impact on his chest, where he was still wearing his communicator under his Impriman tunic—no one having thought to search him that thoroughly.

But the Ferengi's fist never landed. One of the retainers intervened, catching Ralk's wrist in mid-swing.

"That's enough," said the man, allowing the Ferengi to twist free. With his other hand, he shoved Riker backwards and, with a small adjustment on the human's part, hit Will just where he wanted to be hit. The chair landed on the floor, jarring his spine all the way up to his neck and sending shoots of agony through his shoulder. But he heard the muffled beep that told him the communicator had been activated.

He looked around quickly. Apparently no one else had heard it—not even Lyneea. There had been too much going on.

"All right," said the retainer who'd come between Riker and Ralk. "I'll have no more of that. The first official said we were to kill them"—a remark addressed to the Ferengi—"but that doesn't mean we have to torture them, too." He turned to Riker. "As for you, keep your mouth shut. We weren't told we couldn't hurry things along—if you know what I mean."

Riker nodded. "Sorry. It's just that being tied up and held at gunpoint makes me a little edgy. Not to mention being threatened with death."

The retainer muttered something and took his place by the wall again. Ralk cursed and went to stand by the window.

How long would it take before Captain Picard was alerted to the situation? And then how much longer before help might arrive?

"I mean," he went on, "I don't mind sharing a room with a Ferengi, despite what happened just now, but three retainers armed with blasters—all to watch me and my friend Lyneea? That's enough to make anyone nervous."

"You were told to shut up," Ralk reminded him. "You know, you are just like your friend, the trade liaison. He would not keep quiet either."

"Who was it that actually killed him?" asked Riker, taking advantage of the opening. "You, Ralk? Or Larrak?"

"Larrak," said the Ferengi. "Of course. It is a host's responsibility to dispatch spies." His lip curled. "Though in your case I may insist on doing it myself."

The retainers looked at him. They seemed to have other ideas.

But that wasn't his chief concern now. He was trying to buy time and, whether he lived or not, to log a record of Larrak's crimes with the *Enterprise's* computer.

"What gets me," Riker went on, "is Larrak's audacity. To even consider hoodwinking Criathis like that, making them believe the merger was honorable, when all the time he intended to overturn the agreement with the Federation and restore trade with the Ferengi."

"Business is business," said Ralk. "And despite what you say, Larrak will see that *we* offer the greater profit."

How far could he push it? He'd soon find out.

"Exactly how did Larrak spirit you in here, anyway? Did he pay someone to lower the transport barrier? Or have you been hiding here since before the carnival began?"

The Ferengi started to answer and then stopped himself. He eyed Riker suspiciously. "Something is going on," he decided. His mouth twisted as apprehension dawned. "He's got a communicator! He's talking to his ship!"

It didn't take Riker's guards long to reach him. Before they did, he blurted out the name of the madraga holding them and their location in the house.

Not that O'Brien would need it—by now, he'd certainly have logged their coordinates. But it might help Worf in planning his arrival.

A retainer—the one who'd stopped Ralk a few moments earlier—grabbed Riker by the front of his tunic. "Damn you," he said, "what was the point? You're only going to die that much quicker."

And stepping back, he leveled his blaster at the human's face.

Where the hell was Worf? Where was the familiar shimmer of coalescing molecules?

Suddenly, a blue-white phaser beam came out of nowhere. It slammed into the retainer just before he'd have pressed his trigger, sending him flying across the room.

Riker wrestled around in his chair—just far enough to see Worf and Data standing in the doorway, dressed in Impriman tunics. The two remaining guards noticed them at the same time.

Blaster rays and phaser beams crisscrossed in midair. Another retainer was propelled into the wall behind him.

The last one must have known he didn't have a chance. So rather than return the newcomers' fire, he opted to take out the captives.

As he took aim, Riker saw that he meant to kill Lyneea first. Frantically, he rocked forward and tipped his chair; when it fell, it took his partner's with it.

The two of them went over in an ungainly tangle of legs, living and otherwise. Before they hit the floor, Riker saw a shaft of blasterlight sizzle past his good shoulder.

Then someone—either Worf or Data—nailed the retainer with a phaser bolt. The man was knocked off his feet, landing heavily on one of his unconscious comrades.

"Ferengi," called Riker, even before he'd gotten his bearings. "Maybe armed."

A fraction of a second later, he heard a frenetic shuffle, as of escaping footsteps—followed by a scream and a triumphant Klingon snarl.

"Not armed," announced Worf. "But definitely Ferengi."

"Let me go," complained Ralk.

"Then *cooperate,*" advised Worf. And so saying, he thrust the Ferengi into a vacant chair—at least that was how it sounded.

Of course Riker could see neither the Ferengi nor his fellow officers. Lying on his back, still bound to his chair, all he could see was Lyneea, who had fallen on her side with her face mere inches from his.

Without meaning to, he looked into her eyes, something he'd never had the opportunity to do before, at least not so close up.

"Thanks," she told him, aware of the awkwardness of the moment. But a lot less ruffled by it than he would have expected.

"Don't mention it," he said.

Abruptly Data's face loomed above them. "I trust," he said, "that you are not hurt."

The first officer shook his head. "No, Data. But I'd appreciate it if you could untie us. I can remember being in more comfortable positions."

"As you wish," said the android. And replacing his phaser on his Impriman belt, he knelt to free Lyneea.

A coincidence that he was taking care of the female first? Or was Data developing a code of chivalry? Riker pondered the question as his partner's bonds were loosened.

Lyneea glanced at the android's phaser. "I suppose," she said, "there is a loophole in the high-tech ban regarding your weapons as well?"

Data looked puzzled. But Worf knew what she was talking about.

"Perhaps we stretched the rule," he offered. "But if we

had not, you would be in no position to raise the question."

She frowned at the Klingon's answer, but seemed to accept it. Riker marveled at the change in her; a couple of days ago, she would have made a point of confiscating the phasers. Would wonders never cease?

After loosening the last of Lyneea's bonds, the android moved to free the first officer. "Hurry," urged Riker. "We've got to get out of here in time to stop the merger ceremony."

Normally they could have made it to the ceremony site in no time—by beaming over. But direct beaming required them to be transported up to the ship first and then sent on to their ultimate destination. And with the transport barrier preventing anyone from leaving Besidia, that was currently impossible. Besides, Riker still had to come up with a plan to stop the merger, though the seeds of one were already germinating in his head.

"I am doing my best," said Data. "If I work any faster, I fear I may injure you in the process."

"It's all right," said the human. "After what I've been through, I think I can stand a few friction burns."

Obediently the android worked faster. But such was his skill that, despite Data's apprehension, Riker felt no discomfort except for the throbbing of his wound.

"What are you going to do with me?" asked Ralk.

"Nothing like what we should do," said Lyneea.

Worf looked to Riker. "Commander?"

"We can't just tie him up," he said, thinking out loud. "One of these retainers is bound to wake up soon and free him. And we still need him as proof of what Larrak was up to." He smiled at the Ferengi, noting how much Ralk looked like a fish on a hook. "I guess we'll just have to take him with us."

235

Chapter Fifteen

THE AMPHITHEATER was a plain brick building with a green-stained copper roof. It wasn't nearly as old as the Maze of Zondrolla or as elaborate as the estate house of Terrin. But its round shape, high walls, and considerable size made it imposing in its own way.

The single entrance to the place was guarded by retainers. Fortunately, Riker noted, they were in the employ of Madraga Criathis.

"There's no time to explain," Lyneea told them. "We've got to get in. *Now.*"

The retainer in charge indicated the unconscious figure slung over Data's shoulder. "But . . . that's a *Ferengi.*"

"I know what he is. And you know that my assignment is top priority. Now, are you going to let us through?"

The retainer cursed. But in the end, he had to trust Lyneea's judgment.

They followed a passageway that led underneath the first level of seats—all five of them, including the phaser-stunned Ralk, who had made the mistake of testing Worf's vigilance. The Ferengi was still deadweight when they arrived at an opening that led into the seating area.

Every madraga seemed to be represented in the crowd. Riker saw the yellow robes of Alionis, the black of Rhurig, the rich green of Ekariah. The blue, almost violet hue of Criathis. And of course, the red of Terrin.

As they emerged from the opening, heads turned—to see who had come so unpardonably late. There were retainers situated strategically at intervals, and not all of them belonged to Lyneea's madraga. Their heads turned as well.

In the center of the arena, on a massive white-silk-draped platform perhaps ten meters high, the officials of the two merging madraggi had begun their ceremony. They were ensconced at a semicircular table, at either end of which was an ornate brass stand supporting a purple velvet pillow. And resting on each pillow was an object difficult to see from this distance, except for a point of splendor where it caught the artificial radiance emanating from fixtures in the ceiling.

The seals of the two respective madraggi, one of them—the one near the twilight-blue robes—the newly restored Fortune's Light.

Riker's group headed down an aisle toward the first row of seats. There were stirrings among the onlookers—murmurs of curiosity and concern and even amusement. More important, the retainers in the audience had apparently decided the newcomers were up to no good; they were starting to converge on them.

Luckily none of the retainers was directly in their path. *Un*luckily, those closest to them wore a variation of the patch they'd found in the maze.

"Move," urged Lyneea.

They moved, down the aisle and over the rail at the foot of it. Fortunately, Riker was able to vault with one hand. When Data's turn came, he dropped the Ferengi into Worf's waiting arms.

By then the officials at the table had spotted them and halted their ritual procedures. Also, a number of retainers had dropped into the central area on the opposite side of the amphitheater.

There were three familiar faces up on the platform. One was Larrak's. Another belonged to Daran, first official of Criathis. The third was that of Norayan, Daran's daughter and second official.

Larrak stood up. Neither his face nor his voice revealed the emotions that must have been churning inside him.

"What is the meaning of this?" he demanded, loud enough to cut through the growing clamor in the seats.

Riker turned to Lyneea as they approached. "This time," he told her, *"I'll* do the talking."

She didn't object.

"Stop," called a voice from behind. Riker glanced over his shoulder and saw the retainers dropping over the rail.

Worf started to draw his weapon, but Lyneea grabbed him by the wrist. "Don't," she advised him. "We're here. They can't stop us now."

The first official of Criathis was on his feet now next to Larrak. His lack of comprehension was evident in his face—and it was hard to surprise someone of his station. Probably the last thing he'd expected to see today was a group from the *Enterprise* interrupting the merger ceremony, aided and abetted by one of his own retainers and carrying an unconscious Ferengi.

"Yes," said Daran. "What *is* going on here?"

At about the same time, Riker and the others were surrounded. The retainers had their projectile weapons in their hands, but they wouldn't shoot unless someone gave the order. And even then, they might not obey the command of anyone other than their own employer.

Riker had a moment of indecision. After all, Criathis's call for help from the Federation was to have been a secret—like the loss of the seal.

But he couldn't expose the criminals at this gathering without revealing his mission. Lyneea must have figured that out, too, though, and she'd made no move to stop him. He took that as silent approval.

Here goes nothing.

"You know me," he told Daran. His voice rang out, echoing. "My name is Will Riker. I'm the first officer of the Federation starship *Enterprise.*"

That sent a ripple of reaction through the crowd. Riker wet his lips, aware of Norayan's scrutiny, and Larrak's as well. He plunged on.

"Some days ago, First Official, you asked for my assistance. You said that someone had stolen your madraga's seal and you needed it back in time for this ceremony."

Norayan's father looked on, tight-lipped. Inside, he must have been fuming. But then, he didn't know the whole story—not yet.

"I found the seal, and I found out who arranged to have it stolen." Riker turned, aware of the opportunity for drama in the moment, and found the clot of black robes in the stands. He pointed to them. "Madraga Rhurig was behind the theft of Fortune's Light. They paid to have it disappear—so this ceremony might never take place."

The black robes became a sea of confusion. Some of them stood, crying out bitter denials. And a couple separated themselves from the rest, climbing over the rail to land on the arena floor.

Despite the robes, Riker recognized one of them as Kobar. But he did his best to ignore the fact, turning back to the semicircular table and those who sat around it.

"This is a serious accusation," said the first official of Criathis.

"Indeed," remarked Larrak. He was eyeing Riker, still unsure of the Starfleet officer's intentions—though he probably remembered who he was now. "Especially in view of the fact that Fortune's Light sits right there." He indicated the seal of Madraga Criathis on its pillow of purple velvet. "Are you suggesting that the seal before us is a fake?"

A bold move on Larrak's part, to be sure. He was forcing the issue of how Fortune's Light had been recovered—trying to get Riker to lay his cards on the table, if he had any.

But the human was too good a poker player to be manipulated.

"No. It is genuine. And it is here—but only because it was returned. The fact remains that it was stolen."

He looked to the first official of Criathis. Without his confirmation at this point, Riker could go no further. He hoped that the Impriman had enough faith in him to take some risks.

"That is true," Daran said finally, though with obvious reluctance. "Fortune's Light was taken from us. We recovered it only hours before the ceremony—and under mysterious circumstances."

By that time Kobar and his black-robed companion had reached them, and were shouldering their way through the assembled retainers. Curses flew, and most of them were directed at Riker.

"Son of a muzza," spat Kobar, his eyes wide with anger. "I should have killed you when I had the chance."

"No doubt," said Riker. "But that doesn't change anything. Your madraga still hired Teller Conlon to steal Fortune's Light."

"You're mad!" snarled the other man—and now the human recognized him. It was Kelnae, the first official of Madraga Rhurig, and Kobar's father. He was as loud and arrogant as Riker remembered him. He appealed to Daran. "This is *your* ceremony, First Official. Either silence this offworlder or be held accountable."

The Criathan was under terrible pressure. To his credit, he didn't let it show. Nor did he let Rhurig's ultimatum fluster him.

Daran addressed Kobar's father. "You're right, Kelnae. This *is* my ceremony, and I will see it conducted with decorum." He turned to Riker. "I take it you have proof?"

The human nodded. "I do." He glanced in the direction of Kobar and his father. "In the form of a confession —from the man who stole the seal for them."

That put Kelnae on the defensive. "More lies!"

"No," said Riker. "Do you want to hear it?" He pressed the communicator that he still wore beneath his tunic. A moment later he heard Picard's voice on the other end.

"Yes, Number One?"

"What do you think you're doing?" demanded Kelnae. "That is forbidden technology!"

Riker shook his head. "Not true. Nowhere in the high-tech ban is there a mention of Federation communicators."

"A technicality," said Kelnae.

"Perhaps," said Daran. "But that's something we can rule on later. For now, I would like to allow the offworlder to proceed."

"On whose responsibility?" asked the leader of the black robes.

"Mine," answered Daran.

"Commander? Are you there?"

"Aye, sir. I need you to play back the audio portion of Teller Conlon's confession."

"That will take a moment. I trust your listeners will not mind waiting?"

Riker looked at Kelnae and then at Daran. "Briefly, Captain."

"I see. In that case, we'll do everything we can to . . . ah, here it is, Number One."

The next voice they heard was that of Riker's friend. It was a voice tinged with regret.

"My name is Teller Conlon. I am the Federation trade liaison to Imprima. And I have conspired with the officials of Madraga Rhurig to steal Fortune's Light in an effort to prevent the merger between Madraga Criathis and Madraga Terrin . . ."

Riker found it hard to listen—even though the words were his, put together on their way here, and reshaped by the *Enterprise*'s computer to simulate the voice and speech patterns of his friend. The forgery was too good; it actually hurt to hear Teller admit his guilt.

More important, those around him were listening—including Daran and Norayan, Kelnae and Kobar. Only Larrak had reason to doubt. He knew it was highly unlikely that Teller would have logged such a confession and then buried the seal anyway.

". . . to be rewarded for my efforts with Rhurig wealth and passage offplanet . . ."

Riker had taken chances with some of the details. But he'd had to. If he'd made the confession too sketchy, it wouldn't have convinced anyone.

Still . . . if he'd gotten even one of the details wrong, Kelnae would see through the ruse. And Riker's bluff would be called.

"This can't be!" protested Kobar. "It's a fabrication!"

"No," said Riker, but he spoke to Daran, not Kobar. "It's no fabrication. And when the carnival is over and you can use advanced communications again, we'll be glad to show you the confession in all its holographic glory."

Teller's voice continued.

". . . that the seal be buried. But that was not enough. To make doubly sure it could not be used to facilitate the merger, it was to be buried on the grounds of Madraga Terrin—the last place Criathis would expect to find it, and the place where its discovery would do the most . . ."

Kobar made a short chopping motion with his hand—a gesture of dismissal. His emerald green eyes narrowed. "Come, Father. There's no need to stay and be insulted—especially by an offworlder and by a madraga that can't keep track of its valuables."

He started away. But Kelnae stayed.

". . . all of it," said Teller's voice. "I am not proud of it. But in some small way perhaps I have atoned for my actions."

"Father? What's wrong?"

Kelnae's eyes had lost their fire. He somehow seemed to have shrunk a couple of inches in height.

"Father . . . ?"

"The offworlder is right," said Kelnae. He darted a hate-filled glance at Riker. "I don't know how he got Conlon to confess. But he is right."

Kobar obviously hadn't been in on the crime. He was crestfallen.

"I can't believe—"

"Of course you can't," said Kelnae. "I never told you, Kobar. I knew you wouldn't countenance an alliance with the trade liaison—a man you hated—no matter how necessary it might have been."

"Then you admit to stealing the seal?" asked Riker.

Kelnae sneered. "Yes—freely." He turned to those on the silk-draped platform, and Daran in particular. "And now what? Would you punish me—for the theft of something that has already been returned to you?" He chuckled. "Who among us would not have done the same thing, given half a chance?"

A good question, Riker observed. And one that only one man present dared answer.

"The issue," said Norayan's father, "is not what others would have done. The issue is what *you* did." He regarded Kelnae from the considerable height of the platform. "And once that becomes common knowledge,

243

you may find Rhurig's fortunes taking a turn for the worse."

"And what about Conlon?" asked Kelnae. "What about the Federation? Will *they* be held accountable—or only Rhurig?"

Daran wouldn't look at Riker or at his fellow officers. "That remains to be seen," he said.

"Of course," said the first official of Rhurig. "By now, Conlon is long gone, no doubt. Secreted away, where Impriman justice can't touch him."

It was truer than the man might have imagined. But Riker didn't remark on the irony. It wasn't time yet to let *that* cat out of the bag.

Kelnae spat and started back toward the audience. His son made no move to go with him.

Kelnae stopped, waited. "Kobar?" he prompted.

The younger man didn't react.

Kelnae stood there for a moment. Then he shrugged and started walking again.

Kobar turned to Norayan. His face was hard with humiliation. "Had I known," he told her, "I would have prevented it. I swear it."

She nodded.

Riker noticed that Larrak was studying him. With apprehension? Or was that admiration? Either way, he took it as a compliment.

And Larrak hadn't even seen his next move.

"First Official," said Riker, addressing Daran, "I have a confession to make."

The Impriman's brows knit. He didn't look as if he would relish any additional surprises.

"A confession?" he echoed.

"Yes." Riker indicated Kobar with a gesture. "This man was right. The recording we just heard was a fabrication."

Norayan stifled her reaction. Back in the stands, the

area populated with black robes erupted in protest. But Kobar himself was silent, trying to preserve what was left of his dignity.

"I don't understand," said Daran.

"If you had checked the holograph as I suggested, you would have found that it was a fake." He held out his hands. "I apologize for the deception. But it seemed the only way to draw out First Official Kelnae."

Daran considered him. He grunted. "I can't say I approve of your methods," he noted. "But I must admit they are effective."

Norayan spoke for the first time. "What about the Ferengi?" she asked. "What is his role in this?"

Riker admired her timing. "Glad you asked. You see, Rhurig is not the only madraga that has committed crimes against Criathis and the laws of Imprima."

Daran leaned forward. *"Now* what?"

To Riker's surprise, Larrak remained quiet—relaxed, even—as if relieved that the confrontation had finally begun.

"Teller Conlon is not in hiding," said Riker. "He's dead—murdered by the man who sits beside you."

Again the crowd reacted. The second and third officials of Madraga Terrin added their indignant voices to the tumult. As the protests died down, Larrak shook his head. "That is ludicrous."

"You know better," answered the human. He turned back to Daran. "Larrak deceived you, First Official. You thought his goals were in line with yours, but that wasn't the case at all. After this merger went through, he planned to oust the Federation, against your wishes, and use his newfound power to bring back the Ferengi."

"Absurd," said Larrak.

"Preposterous," commented his third official—who might or might not have been in on the deal.

Riker pointed to Ralk, who lay inert on the floor at

Worf's feet. "This one was Larrak's contact with the Ferengi."

He went on to speak of how Teller had stumbled on Ralk's presence, and the price he had paid for it. He told of how he and Lyneea had tracked the seal down to its hiding place on Terrin's estate, how they were captured, and how it was Larrak who returned the seal.

"We escaped," he finished, "obviously. But not before recording the Ferengi's admission of what he and Larrak had done, and still planned to do."

Larrak chuckled. "You're lying. You have no such recording, because there were no admissions to make. And as far as the Ferengi goes"—he dismissed the prone figure with a gesture—"I have never seen him before in my life."

"The recording exists," insisted Riker. "If you like, I can play it for you."

"And it will be a fabrication," said Larrak, "exactly like the one we heard a moment ago."

The human shook his head. "Not this time, First Official. How could we have copied Ralk's voice when we don't have it on file? No, this time it's for real."

Maybe it was the logic of Riker's argument that convinced Larrak of the truth. Maybe it was the fact that the human had bluffed already and wasn't likely to try it again. Maybe it was his certainty that eventually there would be corroboration for Riker's claims. Or maybe it was just something in his voice.

In any case, the accusation had its effect. And not an entirely expected one.

For no sooner had the amphitheater stopped ringing with Riker's voice than Larrak had a blaster in his hand.

Daran saw it and tried to disarm him, but he wasn't quick enough. Larrak smashed him across the face with his weapon, sent him tumbling off the dangerously high platform.

Norayan had started to scream when he grabbed her and pulled her to him, using her as a shield.

Nor did anyone—neither the assembled retainers nor the *Enterprise* officers—have a chance to stop him. It all happened too fast. And who would have dreamed that a first official would bring a banned weapon to a merger ceremony?

So that was why he had kept silent all this time. He had an ace in the hole. The thought came to Riker instantaneously.

Then things got crazy.

One of the retainers must have decided he could stand up to a blaster with a projectile gun. It was a bad idea. Larrak demonstrated immediately that his weapon was set on kill. And then, just for good measure, he fired indiscriminately into the small crowd at the base of the platform.

The retainers scattered, including those of Madraga Terrin. Larrak's second and third officials took the opportunity to leap from their perch; likewise, the Criathan who'd been sitting on Norayan's right.

With Norayan in danger, Riker couldn't run for the seats, so he exercised his only other option. He dove for the base of the wide-lipped platform, where the silk drapes didn't quite reach, and where Larrak would be hard-pressed to get off a good shot at him.

He wasn't the only one who'd had that idea. When he looked around a moment later, he saw Lyneea beside him. Past her, he saw Worf and Data, and past them, Kobar.

His fellow officers had drawn their phasers. Lyneea had her projectile weapon in hand—for all the good it would do. And Riker had the blaster he'd "borrowed" back at Terrin's estate.

"Come out," cried Larrak. "All of you—where I can see you. Or I'll blast this woman right where she stands."

Riker looked at Lyneea. She motioned for him to comply, then signed that she'd circle around the back of the platform, using the drapes for cover.

Where had he heard *that* plan before?

"Now," cried Larrak, his voice an octave higher than it should have been. "I mean what I say."

"All right," answered Riker. "We're coming."

He motioned to Worf and Data. They nodded.

Kobar, however, had something else in mind. Like Lyneea, he started to make his way around the platform —but at the other end.

Riker tried to get his attention, to keep him from interfering with Lyneea's maneuver. But Kobar either didn't see him or chose to ignore him.

Reluctantly, Riker came out of hiding and with him, Data and Worf. They were careful not to step on the Ferengi, who was just starting to come to.

Larrak watched with satisfaction. "Drop your weapons," he told them. His blaster muzzle was pressed against Norayan's temple.

"Don't do it," she said. "Not for me, Will."

But he had no choice. He couldn't let Norayan die.

"You heard him," Riker instructed his companions. "Drop them."

The phasers made a couple of dull thumps as they hit the floor. Riker's blaster made a slightly heavier sound.

Suddenly Larrak's face twisted. *"No,"* he said. "There's another one—the female. Where is she?" He looked around him, but Lyneea was nowhere to be seen.

Riker thought about trying to pick up one of their weapons. Data's phaser was lying only a few inches from his foot, having fallen closer to him than his borrowed blaster.

But Larrak didn't give him a chance. He darted a look at Riker. "I want her in front of me," he bellowed. *"Tell* her that!"

There was a moment when anything could have happened. Then Lyneea showed herself, and Riker saw that she hadn't gotten very far. She was only at the end of the platform; she hadn't slipped around to the back yet, where she might have obtained a clear shot.

"Drop the weapon," said Larrak, "pitiful as it is."

She did as she was instructed. Not happily, but she did it.

"Move over with the others," he said.

Again, she complied.

"Nice try," breathed Riker.

"Not nice enough," she told him.

Of course Lyneea didn't know about Kobar. As far as she was concerned, he had fled in the wake of the retainers.

Larrak must have made the same assumption, more or less, because he didn't look nervous anymore.

Come on, Riker rooted silently. *Come on, Kobar*.

"And now," said Terrin's first official, "I will need transportation off Imprima."

"Where will you go?" asked Riker.

Larrak shrugged. "The Ferengi will take care of me. I can still be of use to them, as an adviser. After all, I know of other madraggi that might consider dealing with them."

Norayan winced at the pressure of the blaster muzzle against her temple. It made Riker want to do something stupid.

But he kept his temper. He had to keep Larrak occupied, he reminded himself. Had to give Kobar a decent chance to bring him down.

"It'll never happen," he said. "After this, no madraga will *touch* a Ferengi deal."

Larrak looked at him. "Nonsense. You are too naive. Now . . . transportation, if you please. Use your communicator. See to it."

The human frowned, in the interests of not looking too eager. "Riker to Captain Picard."

The answer was instantaneous. "We've been listening in, Number One. It sounds as if you've got a problem."

"It's Terrin's first official, sir. He's got a blaster and a hostage. And he means to kill her if he can't get offplanet transportation."

There was silence for a moment, as the captain seemed to mull it over. "It doesn't appear we have much of a choice, does it?"

"No, sir. We'll need to start the beam-up calibrations immediately. You know how long that can take, and I don't think our friend is in the mood to wait."

Picard's answer was crisp, without a trace of hesitation, even though he knew that there were no "beam-up calibrations" to be made. He'd worked with Riker long enough to know how his mind worked—and to understand that he needed time.

"Will do, Number One. I'll see to it personally."

Larrak heard all this, of course, and he didn't object. No surprise there—he wasn't a technician, he was a bureaucrat. What did he know about transporter technology?

"It'll take a few minutes," Riker told him.

"So I understand," said Larrak. "Just be warned that my patience isn't—"

That was when Kobar made his move—vaulting up onto the platform, grabbing Larrak and pulling him away from Norayan. Suddenly the blaster in Larrak's hand went off—though fortunately, not in the direction of Norayan's head, thanks to Kobar's grip on Larrak's wrist. It continued to spew destructive force as Norayan dropped out of sight, its beam ripping up the wood of the platform and digging a furrow in the floor in front of it.

Larrak and Kobar struggled for control of the weapon, the Terrin official proving that he was stronger than his appearance suggested. They lurched together, falling across the table, and suddenly the blaster was cutting a swath in Riker's direction.

By that time the first officer had already knelt and retrieved Data's phaser. As the beam came his way, plowing a trench in the floor, he was able to fling himself out of its path. Somehow he avoided further injuring his shoulder.

Rolling to his feet, he saw that Larrak and Kobar were still vying for control of the blaster. But Larrak was slipping something out of his robe.

A knife.

Riker cried out, but his warning came too late. The knife slipped into Kobar's side and he let go of Larrak's weapon. Slumping to the platform, he left Larrak standing all alone.

The Impriman was too easy a target to miss. Riker fired the phaser and knocked the blaster out of Larrak's hand. A split-second later Worf retrieved a phaser, fired it, and spun him around and off the platform.

Data was the first one around the platform. He was already kneeling beside Larrak when the others arrived.

"His fall was not fatal," reported the android, obviously pleased. "Though he may have broken some bones."

Amazing, Riker mused. It didn't matter to Data that Larrak was ready to destroy him a few seconds ago. The android couldn't bear a grudge if he wanted to.

Riker, on the other hand, was only human. When he looked at Larrak, all he could see was the man who'd killed his friend.

A flurry of retainers and attendants and kinsmen took the injured away. Daran was protesting; he was hardly hurt at all, he claimed. And Kobar, though exceedingly pale even for an Impriman, was conscious when they removed him—a good sign. At the end, Norayan was clasping his hand, smiling, expressing her confidence that he was too tough to die.

And if there was more affection there than gratitude, she would not have admitted it, even to herself. She was still second official of Criathis—and he was still the son of Kelnae.

Ralk, they found out later, had not been so lucky. After Riker had avoided Larrak's errant blaster beam, it had zigzagged in the Ferengi's direction. At least, that was the way it looked.

More than likely, the human told himself, Ralk had never known what hit him.

Chapter Sixteen

PICARD TOOK A SIP of his Earl Grey. "Then we're off the hook, Number One?"

Riker's voice came through loud and clear over the ship's communications system. "Aye, sir. The madraggi have recognized the validity of my loophole, which means that our communicators as well as our phasers are sanctioned under the high-tech ban. And Data, too."

"Data?" echoed the captain.

"Yes. Once the Imprimans realized he was an artificial being, he came into question as well. Anyway, that's all been resolved. Next year they'll be closing the loophole to keep out communicators and phasers. But Data will be welcome anytime."

Picard considered that as he placed his cup and saucer on his ready room desk. "You know, Commander, you took quite a *few* liberties during your stay down there. Not only with the high-tech ban, but with First Official Daran's trust."

"There was no other way, sir. And now that he's had some time to think about it, the first official is coming to see that. Give him another few days and we'll be firmly back in his good graces."

The captain grunted. Optimism was a good trait for a first officer, and Riker had it in abundance. "And he suffered no injuries as a result of his fall?"

"Just some bruises, sir."

"Good to hear. What about Larrak?"

"You mean his medical condition? Or what's in store for him?"

"Both," said Picard.

"Well, he's going to be convalescing for a couple of weeks, until that leg can start to mend. Then he'll stand trial for Teller's murder, for killing the retainers in the amphitheater, and for violating the trade agreement. All in all, I'd say he's going to be put away for a long time."

"Put *away,* Number One?"

"The Impriman penal system is not as forward-looking as ours, sir. They still believe in long-term incarceration."

That sounded a little barbaric, Picard thought. But then, it was their planet. They could do as they saw fit.

"Interestingly enough, Madraga Terrin will probably emerge from the trial unscathed. From the looks of it, the alliance with the Ferengi was a one-man operation. The other officials had nothing to do with it." A pause. "That is, from the *looks* of it."

"You're skeptical?"

"There's no proof one way or the other, sir. And I've got nothing left to bluff with."

That was for certain.

"Kelnae?"

"It'll never be proved that he ordered my assassination, though it's pretty plain that he was the one. He'll have his share of problems, though. The other madraggi won't take kindly to the fact that he arranged the theft of Fortune's Light. There'll be sanctions—the kind that will give Rhurig a great deal of trouble."

"And Kobar?" asked Picard.

Riker chuckled. "A real surprise, Captain. He showed

a lot of character in the amphitheater—a lot of pride. I think he's a better person than anyone has given him credit for being. He's still trying to cope with a reputation he no longer deserves."

"You seem to be quite an admirer, considering he had a knife at your throat not so long ago."

"But he didn't use it, sir, and that makes all the difference in the world. Did I mention that he's severed all ties with his madraga?"

"No." Picard found himself impressed as well.

"Kobar could have stayed with his father and continued to live the easy life. Even with all the problems Rhurig is going to face, the madraga won't go downhill all at once. But Kobar doesn't want anything to do with Kelnae's machinations anymore; the old man went too far this time."

The captain reflected on just how deceiving appearances could be. "Good for him. But what will he do? Cut off from his madraga, he'll be penniless, won't he?"

"Penniless indeed. That's why I made . . . a suggestion."

The words hung tantalizingly in the air. "All right, Commander, I'll bite. What suggestion?"

"You see, sir, when I went to visit him in the hospital —to let him know that there were no hard feelings and to compare knife wounds—it occurred to me that the trade liaison post is unoccupied."

Picard started to lean forward. "You *didn't*."

"I did, sir. After all, he's demonstrated that his ethics are beyond reproach—a quality the Federation may find crucial if it's going to continue relations with this planet. You've got to admit our credibility is somewhat threadbare at the moment. And besides, it may be intriguing to see how an Impriman deals with Imprimans."

Picard smiled. He was glad that Riker wasn't there to see it. "Commander, that is not your decision to make."

"Of course not, Captain. As I said, it was only a suggestion."

"And what was his reaction to this suggestion?"

"He turned me down. He said he'd sooner sell his soul than work for offworlders—though he didn't sound entirely convincing. With a little work, I think, we could persuade him to take the job."

Picard mulled it over. "I'll propose it to the appropriate authorities," he said finally. "And then, who knows? Stranger things have happened."

"Thank you, sir."

"No need, Number One. Incidentally, the carnival is scheduled to end in a few hours—and the transportation ban along with it. I take it you'll be returning at that time, along with your fellow officers?"

For a moment, silence. "The others will beam up, Captain. But if it's all right with you, I'd like to take some of that shore leave I've been accumulating. The ship has to stay anyway, to tie up the loose ends, and—"

"And you'd like to tie up some of your own?"

"Exactly."

Picard nodded, for the benefit of no one in particular. "Take all the time you need, Will."

"I appreciate that, sir."

Their communication over, the captain picked up his cup and saucer and returned them to the food processing unit. He had a long report ahead of him, and his Earl Grey had no doubt by this time gotten cold.

"Will?"

Riker turned at the sound of Norayan's voice. He was in the anteroom to the Criathan inner chamber, where the madraga's officials held their councils. Norayan was standing in the outer doorway—as if hesitant to come in.

"I'm glad you came," she told him.

He shrugged. "You called," he said, as if that were explanation enough.

"Let's go out on the balcony," she suggested, finally entering the room. Here in the chamber suite, it was proper to wear the dark blue color of her madraga, just as *he* had come in *his* proper attire—the red and black of a command officer in Starfleet.

As she went by, Riker offered her his arm. She took it—gladly, it seemed to him.

They walked through a narrow archway into the inner chamber proper, which was even more ornate than the anteroom and considerably larger. It was dominated by a great pink marble fireplace built into the wall on their right.

Before the hearth stood the simple wooden Table of Officials, around which the madraga's founders were said to have seated themselves. It was unattended now, its chairs neatly organized around it, as if it had not been used since the founders' passing.

But he knew better. It had been used the day before and throughout much of the night—to debrief Lyneea, to discuss the manner in which Criathis had been victimized and by whom, to decide what measures needed to be taken to patch up the damage, and finally to chart a new course for the madraga, now that it would not be merging with Terrin.

Apparently Riker's partner had been discreet in her report concerning Norayan's relationship with Teller. Otherwise, Norayan would have been stripped of her status as an official, and Riker would not have been meeting with her here.

Just to one side of the table, Fortune's Light resided in its modest display case. Without direct light to awaken its multifaceted glory, the seal looked almost ordinary.

Hardly worth one's life.

Norayan didn't stop to look at any of this—though when Riker had first known her, she used to beg him for descriptions of the inner chamber. Of course, in those days, he was an honored guest of the madraggi and she was only a madraga-dzin's daughter.

The exit onto the balcony was an archway as well. Norayan paused a moment to open the doors. Then they emerged into the brittle radiance of late-afternoon Besidia.

For a change, it wasn't snowing, though the city's slender, lofty towers bore evidence of the morning's flurries. Riker breathed deep of the cold air, enjoying it for the first time since he'd beamed down.

All that separated them from the streets below was an elaborate wrought-iron railing that had blackened with age. Norayan approached it and looked out over the carnival town.

"I've been a fool," she said simply.

He could have let her off the hook with just that simple admission. But it would have been dishonest. They knew each other too well to ignore what had happened.

"To put it mildly," he answered.

When she turned, she looked a little surprised. But only a little.

"You lied to me," he continued. "Worse, you used me."

She nodded. "I had to—or at least I thought so at the time. There didn't seem to be any other way . . ."

"To expose Kobar," he offered, "without making public your relationship with Teller."

She smiled sadly. "I was so sure it was Kobar who had killed him. He hated offworlders, and Teller in particular. Certainly they'd had their share of run-ins, and not all on a political level, nor was it a secret that Kobar had feelings for me—I imagine Lyneea told you about that. Perhaps he sensed that I was involved with Teller . . . I don't know." She shook her head. "From the beginning, I suspected that Rhurig was connected to the theft of the seal. When I found Teller's body in the maze, it all seemed to come together. Kelnae had hired Teller, I decided, to do Rhurig's dirty work. Then, once Teller had obtained Fortune's Light, Kobar saw an opportunity—a chance to have his political and personal ambitions furthered at the same time. All he had to do was stab poor Teller in the back."

Silence for a moment. A wind came up, chilled them, and was gone.

"And the patch?"

"Just after I returned from the maze, shaken with grief, Kobar came calling on me. As before, he professed his love for me, asked me to retire from my position with Criathis and marry him. It was too much of a coincidence; I became certain that he'd murdered Teller. When he moved to touch me, to embrace me, I ripped the patch off his shoulder and threw him out."

More silence. This time there wasn't even a wind.

Norayan hung her head. "I'm so ashamed, Will. I thought I was doing the right thing—giving justice a helping hand. Now I see how I stood in its way—and almost got you killed in the process."

A tear ran down her cheek. A *tear* from an official of Madraga Criathis!

Riker had stood about all he could stand. He took Norayan in his arms, sling and all.

"It's all right," he said. "It is. You said it yourself— you did what you thought was right. That's all any of us can do."

She looked up at him. "That's the kind of thing Teller would have told me."

He smiled. "Is it?" He tried to remember. "I guess maybe it is."

"You know," she said, "there is one thing I can't understand. In that moment when Teller had finished burying the seal and was about to leave—the moment when he noticed the Ferengi in Larrak's house—why didn't he just *go?* Was it simple curiosity that made him inch closer to the window, and ultimately get caught? Or was it something else?"

Riker thought about it for the first time. "A sense of duty, you mean? To the Federation?"

"I didn't know him when he served on those starships, Will. I don't know what he was like in those days. But is it possible that, in the end, he put your Federation first? That he would have come out of hiding, no matter what the penalty, to expose Larrak's scheme?"

Riker shook his head. "I don't know, Norayan. But I'd sure as hell like to think so."

With matters settled in Besidia and Commander Riker's mission accomplished, Data returned to Holodeck One. It was time to finish the game.

He had left in the eighth inning, with Sunset runners on second and third and two outs. The android recorded the last out himself, cutting off a sharply hit grounder between third and shortstop. His throw to first beat the runner by two strides.

The Icebreakers' half of the inning was nothing to boast of. Augustyn hit a line drive right at the Phoenix shortstop. Jackson walked, but Cherry struck out swinging and Maggin hit a little nubber to first.

In the top of the ninth, the Sunsets mounted another threat. Their first two batters reached base safely before the Fairbanks pitching coach, managing in Terwilliger's place, called for another pitcher.

The new man shut the door on the Phoenix team. There were two pop-ups and a meek ground ball, and suddenly it was the Icebreakers' last chance.

The Sunset pitcher had been effective until this point, but his manager wasn't taking any chances. As his team took the field, he called for his ace reliever.

"Tom Castle," said Jackson. "If you thought

Redding's curve was a killer, wait till you see *his*. Best hook in the league, if you ask me."

It was not good news—especially to Data, who would come up fourth in this inning. He could picture himself hitting the long fly ball that would give Phoenix the victory.

More than anything he wanted to avoid that. But it was looming more and more likely, the pieces all falling into place. When it came to the curveball, he was still not the hitter he wanted to be, despite Geordi's advice and all his research. And he was facing the Sunset pitcher who could best exploit his weakness.

So far the game's events had followed history faithfully. Was it even *possible* for Data to prevail when he came up to bat?

Denyabe led off the Icebreakers' half of the ninth. Castle's first pitch was a curveball out of the strike zone. The second baseman swung anyway and missed.

"Stee-rike one," called the umpire.

The second pitch to Denyabe was in the same place as the first. Again he went fishing for it. Again he failed to make contact.

It wasn't until the third pitch that he finally got some wood on the ball. But even then, it was only a foul tip that whizzed by the catcher.

As Data watched from the dugout, it seemed to him that none of these pitches were in the strike zone. Though they initially appeared as if they would get a piece of the plate, they consistently wound up wide to the right.

The android turned to Jackson, who was sitting beside him. "Is this the way Castle usually pitches? He has yet to throw an Uncle Charlie over the plate."

Jackson grunted. "It's called painting the corners, Bobo."

But Data was forced to differ; after all, Jackson didn't

have an android's visual acuity. Castle wasn't *painting* the corners—he was *missing* them.

And Denyabe couldn't seem to discern that any better than Jackson could. As Castle released the ball again, Denyabe swung—not as if to hit it somewhere, but merely to stay alive. He just got a piece of it.

The pitcher smiled as the catcher threw him a new ball. It appeared that he had Denyabe right where he wanted him.

Data didn't want his friend to be handled so ignominiously. It was one thing to make an out and quite another to be embarrassed in the process.

Nor could he help remembering Denyabe's words. Like everything else he'd ever heard, they were preserved perfectly in his memory: "Men can't depend on heaven, Bobo. They've got to depend on each other."

Suddenly the android knew what he had to do. He got up and walked over to the pitching coach—Terwilliger's replacement. "Coach," he said, "we must call time out."

The man looked at him. "What the hell for?"

"Because I have advice to give Denyabe."

The man's eyes narrowed. "Care to tell *me* about it?"

"I would prefer to tell him myself."

The coach thought about it, snorted. "Sure," he said finally. "Why not? Can't hurt, the way we're going." He climbed to the top step of the dugout and called time. Then, turning back to Data, he said, "He's all yours."

When Denyabe saw Bobo trotting out toward the plate, he smiled. "You know," he said, "it's a good thing Terwilliger's given up already. Otherwise, he'd have killed you for a stunt like this."

"Please listen," said Data. "You need not swing at the next curveball."

"I *need* not?" echoed Denyabe. "Why do you say that?"

"Because Castle has not yet thrown one for a strike."

The second baseman allowed himself a glance at the

pitcher. "You sure about that? They looked pretty good to me."

"I am as sure as I can be," said the android.

Denyabe pretended to inspect his bat. "Even if you're right," he said, "that's only what he's *been* doing. Who's to say what he's *going* to do?"

"He has been successful with the strategy thus far," insisted the android. "Why diverge? At least, until you give him *reason* to do so?"

Denyabe regarded him, looking not so much at him as into him.

"All right," he said finally. "I won't swing at a curveball unless it's right down Broadway. But you'd better be right."

"Trust me," said Data. He fashioned a smile. "Unless you would rather trust the goddess."

The second baseman chuckled. "No," he said, "never that." And as the android retreated to the dugout, Denyabe approached the plate with renewed purpose.

"Finished?" asked the pitching coach, once Data had returned.

"Finished."

"Think it'll help?"

The android shook his head. "I hope so."

A moment later Castle went into his windup. And a moment after that, the ball was on its way to the plate.

The pitch looked good. It appeared that it would find a piece of the strike zone. Denyabe tensed, as if every instinct was telling him to swing.

But he didn't.

"Ball," called the umpire.

Data felt gratified. However, Denyabe still had two strikes on him.

The next pitch was a ball as well. Again, Denyabe found the wherewithal to keep from swinging at it. Likewise, the pitch after that.

And finally, with the count full, Castle missed a fourth

time. Denyabe tossed his bat aside and trotted to first base.

"Looks like you knew what you were talking about," observed the pitching coach.

Data nodded. "It does look that way, does it not?" And removing his bat from the rack, he advanced to the top step of the dugout.

"What the hell did he tell him?" rasped Terwilliger. The android could hear his voice coming from the stairwell.

"Beats me," said the coach.

As Sakahara took his place at the plate, Data hoped he would benefit from Denyabe's example. As a veteran hitter, he would certainly have been watching the confrontation with great interest.

However, Castle crossed him up on the first pitch. Instead of serving up another curveball, he tried to sneak by a fastball.

Surprised, and therefore swinging a bit too late, Sakahara popped the ball up. The android watched as the ball landed in the shortstop's mitt.

And realized abruptly that it *had* to have been that way. After all, Denyabe had gotten on base. That meant that neither Sakahara nor the next batter could do so. Otherwise, Bobo would never have the opportunity to make the game's last out, as history demanded.

Simple mathematics. A formula worked out three hundred years before, on the field after which this holodeck simulation was modeled.

No doubt, even Denyabe's base on balls had been part of that pattern. As much as Data had wanted to believe it was *his* doing, he knew it must have been preordained.

At the end of the dugout, hardly bothering to conceal himself anymore, Terwilliger looked miserable. And why not? He was watching his last chance at success slowly slip away from him.

If he had been human, Data would have sighed.

The android came out to the on-deck circle just as Galanti's replacement—a squarish, stolid man named Houlihan—took his place at the plate. Castle started him off with a couple of curveballs, and he was patient enough to lay off them. But after working the count to two and one, he hit a high chopper to third base.

It was too late to throw to second—Denyabe had been running on the pitch—so the third baseman fired the ball to first. But the throw was low and the first baseman couldn't quite dig it out. What was more, as the ball dribbled away, Denyabe was able to scoot into third.

The crowd roared its approval. There were runners on the corners, with only one out.

And in the on-deck circle, Data stood as if rooted to the spot, rapidly trying to make sense of what had just transpired.

"Stop program," he called.

Everyone and everything ground to a halt. It was strangely quiet in the cavernous stadium.

"Computer," he said, "describe the historical performances of Icebreakers Denyabe, Sakahara, and Houlihan in their ninth-inning at-bats."

The computer didn't hesitate. "Noah Denyabe struck out swinging. Muri Sakahara popped up to the shortstop. Kevin Houlihan reached base on a throwing error by the third baseman."

Data considered the information. Apparently Sakahara and Houlihan had done exactly what history demanded of them.

But Denyabe had *not*.

Hundreds of years ago the second baseman had not had Data to advise him. He'd swung at Castle's last pitch and missed it as he'd missed the others.

Data shook his head. Without realizing it, he had *changed history*.

It was a refreshing thought. A *liberating* thought.

And what was even better, Denyabe was on third base. Now, when Data hit his long fly ball to center field, it would *mean* something. Denyabe would tag up on the play and tie the game, keeping the Icebreakers' hopes alive.

The notion was immensely satisfying.

"Resume program," said the android.

The computer complied. Everything started up again.

Data approached the plate. He took a few practice swings and dug in. The pitcher eyed him, perhaps a little shaken after the latest turn of events.

The first pitch to Data was a fastball, but it was in the dirt. No chance to hit it.

The next pitch was a curveball, but not one of those tantalizing Number Twos of the sort that Castle had thrown Denyabe. This one was right down the middle— right down Broadway, as Denyabe had said.

A mistake. And maybe Bobo's best opportunity to hit the ball deep.

He waited, as Geordi had advised. Concentrated on the flight of the ball, trying to anticipate when it might break. And then he swung.

As soon as he made contact, Data knew he had done his job. The ball fairly leapt off his bat. Making his way down the first base line, he watched it take to the air.

It seemed that there was a hush in the big stadium. As if everyone was too preoccupied with the flight of the baseball to remember to breathe.

Out of the corner of his eye, the android saw his teammates in the dugout. They were rising out of their seats. And Terwilliger was among them, his expression one of open-mouthed disbelief.

Out in center field, the Sunset player named Clemmons started to backpedal. Then, realizing that the ball had been hit harder than he thought, he turned his back on it and gave chase.

Data paid little attention to him. After all, history had decided that the ball would be caught. The real Clemmons had made the same mistake and corrected it the same way some three hundred years before.

But he had *changed* history, hadn't he? He had interrupted the sequence of events, opening up a world of new possibilities. . . .

As he approached first base, pursuing this line of reasoning, he saw the ball sail over Clemmons's head, unrelenting in its progress, and a moment later, clear the outfield wall with inches to spare.

Data couldn't believe it. He knew he had hit it hard—but not *that* hard. Directly in front of him, Houlihan was pumping his fist in the air, unable to contain his jubilation.

The android rounded the bases behind him, feeling more mechanical than he had ever felt before—as if his body were moving of its own volition.

All about him the stands were erupting with a mighty sound. People were throwing things in the air and hugging one another. The entire stadium seemed to be vibrating with the force of their exhilaration.

By the time he rounded third and was heading for home, the whole team had come out to meet him. Denyabe, who had scored the tying run just seconds before, was foremost among them. Sakahara and Jackson and Cordoban stood behind him, and Galanti had limped out as well.

Houlihan vanished into their midst, slapping hands and whooping for joy. And Data came next, absorbed into the artificial mass of humanity that was the Fairbanks Icebreakers. Arms were flung about his shoulders, words of praise and exultation shouted in his ears.

Abruptly, without warning, the android found himself being raised up off the ground—lifted onto the shoulders of his teammates. And only then was he able to discern the chant that the crowd had embraced: "Bo-bo! Bo-bo! Bo-bo!"

But one face was missing from the celebration. One very important face.

Data searched for it—and finally found it back at the dugout. Slipping down from his perch, slipping out of their midst entirely, he approached Terwilliger.

The man was just standing on the dugout's top step, tears welling in his eyes. He wasn't quite smiling. He just looked dumbfounded.

"Congratulations," said the android, once he was close enough to be heard over the din.

Terwilliger focused on him, as if seeing him for the first time. He nodded. "Thanks." And then he seemed to come to terms with what had happened, for Data could see the fire ignite again in his eyes. "Good shot," he said, "for a snot-nosed, loudmouthed wise ass of a rookie. Just don't let it go to yer head."

The android smiled. "I will do my best," he said.

Lyneea opened the door. Obviously she hadn't expected *him* to be the one behind it. But like a good retainer, she recovered quickly.

"Riker," she said. "And without your sling."

She looked different from the last time he'd seen her. For one thing, she was wearing a dress—a long green and white shift that accentuated the color of her eyes. For another, her hair was pulled back and braided with a thick silver chain.

"I got tired of wearing it."

"Good for you." She paused. "I thought you'd left."

"I thought *you* had, too," he told her. "Until I learned that you live here in Besidia."

She shrugged. "Someone has to. And I like it better than most of the other places Criathis has posted me."

"I see." He gestured past her. "Mind if I come in?"

Her eyes searched his. After all, he hadn't yet said what his visit was about. "Not at all," she told him.

Riker went inside. The quality of the furnishings surprised him.

"Criathis pays its employees well," he noted.

"Skilled undercover people are hard to find. Though I don't know how much good I'll be to the madraga now that I'm so well known."

"Sorry about that."

"It was unavoidable. And not every retainer needs to operate undercover."

He nodded. "I'd hate to think I cost you your job."

She regarded him. "So. Why *are* you here?"

Riker found the bar in the room. In a place this well appointed, there was *always* a bar.

"Korsch?" he asked.

"No. Dibdinagii brandy."

He looked at her. "*Off*world refreshments?"

"I'm *off* duty," she explained.

Riker filed away the distinction and located the brandy. He poured two glasses' worth, put the pride of Dibdina back in its place, and delivered the libations.

In the meantime she had found a seat on a chaise longue. He hadn't noticed the slit in her dress before; he noticed it now.

"Thank you," she said, as he handed her a glass. The amber liquid sparkled with the day's last light. "But you still haven't told me why you're here."

He knelt before her, clinked his glass softly against hers. "Because when you've saved someone's life, and that person has saved yours, you don't part company without saying good-bye."

Her eyes narrowed. "*When* did you save my life?"

"When we were at Larrak's house, remember? That guard was going to blast you, and I knocked your chair over."

She smiled skeptically. "Oh, come on, Riker. *You* knocked my chair over? I had already tipped it when you fell on me."

He felt the mood slipping away, and resolved not to let it happen. "I *didn't* fall on you," he said gently. "I knocked you over. There's a difference."

"There certainly is. And you *fell* on me, probably trying to save your own skin."

This was getting annoying. "Hell," he told her, "you even *thanked* me."

"Thanked you? I don't recall."

Riker shook his head. "Forget it. Forget I even mentioned it. That isn't the point anyway."

"Then what *is* the point?"

He sighed. "When we were lying there on the floor, all trussed up on those damned chairs . . . I looked into your eyes. Just as I'm doing now. And I thought I saw something there."

"Of course you did. I was *relieved*. Nobody likes to be shot at while she's all trussed up."

His hopes sank another notch. "And that's all there was to it?"

Lyneea seemed not to understand. "What did you expect?"

Riker turned wistful. "I was *hoping* you'd say that, in some small way, you were attracted to me. But I guess I was mistaken."

She just looked at him. Suddenly he felt very uncomfortable. After all, he didn't find himself in this position very often.

He got to his feet, put the brandy down on an end table. "Listen," he said, "I guess I jumped to the wrong conclusion. No harm done." He put out his hand. "It was nice working with you."

She continued to look at him. He was about to take his hand back when she finally reached out and grasped it. Her grip was just as firm as he remembered it.

270

"Nice working with you, too," she told him.

He gazed into those eyes one last time and shook his head. How could he have been so far off base? He'd never been wrong about this sort of thing before.

"Right. Well, then . . . see you around." He started for the door.

His hand was on the old-fashioned doorknob before he heard Lyneea's voice.

"Chits and whispers, Riker! Can't a girl have a little fun without you going all to pieces?"

He turned. She was standing now, the light from the window tracing a silhouette within the delicate shift.

"Don't just stand there," she told him. Her voice had softened to a purr, with just a hint of humor in it. "Tell me again how you looked into my eyes."

Riker smiled. "I'll tell you more than that," he said.

Epilogue

"HI. NAME'S TELLER CONLON. Guess I'll be your room-mate."

"Guess so. I'm Will Riker."

"Where you from, Will Riker?"

"Alaska—on Earth. A town called Valdez. Ever heard of it?"

"Can't say I have."

"Don't worry about it. Hardly anybody has."

"Nice there?"

"Real nice. But don't get me started. I'll get all mush-mouthed and teary-eyed."

A shrug, a laugh. "Okay, then, I won't."

"What about you? Where are you from?"

"Anywhere and everywhere. My dad was a career diplomat for the Federation—while he was alive, that is. We traveled around a lot when I was a kid—Beta Sargonus, Gamma Trilesias, half a dozen starbases. Like that."

"Wow. Must have been incredible."

"Sure, incredible. Hey, listen, Will, do me a favor? If I even think of going into the diplomatic corps—I mean, if I wake up one morning and mumble something about

273

wanting to be an ambassador—I want you to strangle me. Don't ask any questions. Just do it—okay?"

Now it was Will's turn to laugh. "Maybe after I know you a little better. I don't like to strangle people I hardly know. But tell me, just what is it about diplomacy that turns you off so much?"

Teller looked at him. "Ever meet an ambassador? One who's been at it for a while?"

"I don't believe so, no. We don't get too many of them in Valdez; the Federation pretty much overlooks Alaska when it comes to diplomatic envoys."

"Trust me—if you bumped into one, you wouldn't like him. They're chameleons, Will—faint imitations of whatever race they've been kowtowing to most recently. Empty beakers: you pour out one alien culture and pour in another. And whatever was them—the unique commingling of needs and desires that set out to be an ambassador in the first place—is gone somehow. Evaporated."

Silence. "Well, Teller, don't beat around the bush. If you don't want to be a diplomat, just say so."

"I'm saying so. And I'm not kidding about the strangling stuff."

"We'll see."

"So now you're wondering what I'm doing at the Academy. I mean, if I don't want to get involved with alien cultures, why Starfleet?"

"I hadn't gotten quite that far. But okay—why Starfleet?"

"Because we touch things when they're new—when they're bright and shiny and they've never been touched before. And then we leave them to the bureaucrats. That's what life is all about, Will—getting in and getting out. Stealing a taste and putting the rest back. Take too big a bite out of anything—person or place—and it ends up taking a bigger bite out of you."

"Hmm. Dorm-room philosophy."

"Get used to it, Will. I'm chock full of such stuff."

"Hey, speaking of bites—it's almost chow time."

"Right you are. Say, how's your sharash-di?"

"It could be better, I suppose. Why?"

"There's this redhead that I got friendly with on the way from Delta Ganymede. She's some sort of expert at sharash-di, and she wanted to know if I played—which I don't. But . . ."

"But if I play her—say, after dinner—it'll give you a chance to get to know her better."

"Something like that."

He chuckled. *"Fine—on one condition. Just don't laugh when she whips me."*

"Absolutely not, Will. Absolutely not. Well, maybe a little."

"Come in," said Riker.

As the doors parted with a *shussh,* Data entered the first officer's quarters. He found Riker sitting in the center of the room, elbows resting on his knees, leaning over the low wooden table he was reputed to have made with his own hands. In the center of the table's glossy amber-colored surface there was a simple stoppered vase made of some gray-blue ceramic material. Riker seemed to be studying the vase, as if it held some special significance for him.

"Commander?" The android spoke softly, not wishing to interrupt.

The human looked up at him. "Sorry, Data. I didn't mean to ignore you." He indicated the vase with a glance. "My friend's ashes. In his will, he requested that they be returned to Beta Sargonus Four. That's where he was born." Riker smiled to himself. "There's a mountain pool there—a place where young women like to go skinny-dipping. Sort of a tradition, I guess—no men allowed." He shook his head. "Teller asked that his ashes be scattered in the pool. That, apparently, was his idea of paradise."

The first officer stopped, noting Data's puzzlement. "You know what paradise is, don't you?"

The android nodded. "Paradise, yes. It is the term 'skinny-dipping' that I cannot seem to find a meaning for."

Riker explained.

"Ah," said Data. "I see." And he did, for the most part, though he did not quite understand why swimming naked should be such a thrill.

Riker picked up the vase, rose, and placed it on a shelf built into the bulkhead. It sat next to a book called *Baseball Compendium*. Smiling again, he considered the vase.

"It's not going to be easy to get near that pool," he said, "much less dump Teller's remains in it." His expression became positively mischievous. "But I'm going to give it my best shot. After all, what are friends for?"

"Indeed," said the android.

The first officer gestured to the chair that stood opposite his. "Care to sit down?"

"Thank you," said Data. He sat. So did Riker.

"Now," he said, "enough of my friend's bizarre wishes. Unless I miss my guess, you're here to talk about that baseball game."

"That is true," said the android.

The human leaned back in his chair. "So? What did you think?"

Data regarded him. "I found it most intriguing," he said.

Riker looked a little disappointed. "I sort of hoped you would say you'd *enjoyed* it."

The android thought about it. "I suppose I did," he concluded, "to the extent that I am capable of such a response." A particular thought intruded and he brightened. "Especially *one* part."

"What part was that?"

"The part where I won the game."

Riker's eyebrows shot up. "You *won* the *game?"*

The android nodded. "Yes."

"You're kidding."

"That is unlikely," Data reminded him.

"Yes. Of course it is." Riker looked at him askance. "But how did you do it?"

"I hit a home run," said the android. "In the bottom of the ninth inning."

The human stared at him with undisguised admiration. "Why, Data—that's *great!* That's the kind of thing little boys used to *dream* about!"

"Yes," said the android. "Wesley has informed me of that fact."

Riker grinned. "You're full of surprises—you know that?"

Data didn't quite know what to say. And he still hadn't asked the question that had been bothering him.

Fortunately Riker picked that up. "You're wondering about something, aren't you? What is it?"

The android paused to collect his thoughts. "It appeared from your choice of persona that you identified with the Icebreakers. And with Bobo in particular."

"That's true," said the first officer. "The Icebreakers were the only Alaskan team in major league baseball. In fact, one of the few Alaskan teams in *any* professional sport." He shrugged. "When they made their run for the American League pennant, they made a fan of every Alaskan alive." He paused. "Of course, I was born hundreds of years after the last of those men had died. But when I read about them as a youngster, they struck a chord in me. They were my heroes. Particularly Bobo—I don't know why, exactly. Maybe because he was still a kid when they disbanded the Icebreakers—and since I was a kid, too, he was the easiest for me to identify with."

277

"But given your affinity for the Icebreakers," said Data, "why would you wish to experience their most crushing defeat?"

Riker looked at him. "That's simple, Data. When they lost that playoff game by a single run, it cast a pall over the state for years to come. It always seemed to me that it was some kind of injustice, and I wished I could do something about it. Or at least *try*. I guess it was an exercise in"—he seemed to search for a phrase, and find it—"in the art of the possible. In short, a challenge. Humans thrive on them, you know."

"A challenge," repeated the android. He found yet another source of discomfort. "Then . . . did I ruin the program for you? By finding a way to beat the Sunsets?"

Riker shook his head. "Not at all. I'll just have to find a *different* way."

He would, too. Data could tell by the set of his jaw. Somehow Riker would give the Icebreakers a reason to celebrate again.

"If I may be present," said the android, "I would like to see that."

The first officer laughed. Reaching across the table, he clapped Data on the shoulder. "That's a promise, my friend. And from now on, Will Riker keeps *all* his promises."